SARAH HAWKSWOOD describes herself as a 'wordsmith' who is only really happy when writing. She read Modern History at Oxford and first published a non-fiction book on the Royal Marines in the First World War before moving on to mediaeval mysteries set in Worcestershire.

Servant of Death

A Bradecote
and Catchpoll Mystery

SARAH HAWKSWOOD

Allison & Busby Limited
12 Fitzroy Mews
London W1T 6DW
allisonandbusby.com

First published in 2014 as *The Lord Bishop's Clerk*.
This edition published by Allison & Busby in 2017.

A CIP catalogue record for this book is available from
the British Library.

10 9 8 7 6 5 4 3 2 1

ISBN 978-0-7490-2172-6

Typeset in 11/16 pt Adobe Garamond Pro by
Allison & Busby Ltd.

The paper used for this Allison & Busby publication
has been produced from trees that have been legally sourced
from well-managed and credibly certified forests.

Printed and bound by
CPI Group (UK) Ltd, Croydon, CR0 4YY

For H. J. B.

Map of Pershore Abbey

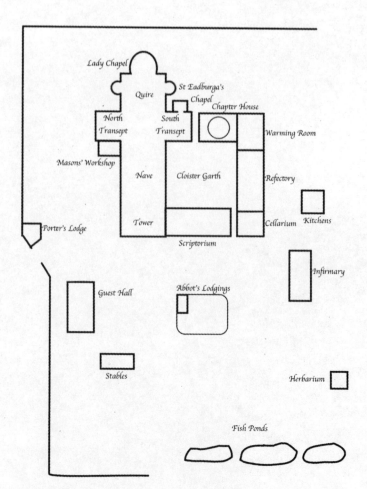

The First Day

June 1143

Chapter One

Elias of St Edmondsbury, master mason, stood with the heat of the midsummer sun on broad back and thinning pate, rivulets of sweat trickling down between his shoulder blades. The wooden scaffolding clasped the north transept of the abbey church, close as ivy. Where he stood, at the top, there was no shade from the glare when the noontide sun was so high, and today there was little hint of a breeze. The fresh-cut stonework reflected the light back at him, and his eyes narrowed against the brightness. He turned away, blinking, and then looked down to the eastern end of the abbey foregate, where the usual bustle of the little market town of Pershore was subdued. It was too hot for the children to play chase; many had already sought the cool of the river and its banks, although even the Avon flowed sluggishly, too heat-weary to rush. As many of their seniors as could afford to do so were resting indoors. The midsummer days were long, and the townsmen could conduct their trade well into the cooler evening, though the rhythmic 'clink, clink' from the smithy showed that some labour continued. The smith was used to infernal temperatures, thought Master Elias, and probably had not noticed the stultifying heat as he laboured at his craft.

One industrious woman was struggling with a heavy basket of washing she had brought up from the drying grounds to the rear of the burgage plots. She halted to ease her back and brush flies away from her face, then stooped to pick up her load once more. As she straightened she had to step back smartly to avoid being run into by a horseman who rounded the corner at a brisk trot, raising unwelcome earthy red dust as he did so. The man, who rode a showy chestnut, was followed by two retainers. The woman shouted shrill imprecations after the party as they passed from Master Elias's view, turning along the northern wall before entering Pershore Abbey's enclave, but he would vouch that they ignored her as they had her now dusty washing.

The scaffolding afforded a grand view of the comings and goings at Pershore, though Master Elias would have taken his hand to any of his men whom he saw gawping in idleness. As master mason, however, he could take the time to survey the scene if he wished. He never failed to be amazed at how much could be learnt of the world from the height of a jackdaw's roost, and he had an eye for detail, which was one of the reasons his skills were so valued. As the sun rose, heralding this hot day, and he had taken his first breath of morning air from his vantage point, he had watched as a troop of well-disciplined horsemen passed through the town, led by a thickset man who rode as if he owned the shire. Master Elias would have been prepared to bet that he did indeed own a good portion of it. Few lords had men with guidons, though he did not recognise the banner. They were also heavily armed, not just men in transit, and they rode with menacing purpose. The latest arrival, in contrast, was a young man in a hurry, for his horse was sweated up and he had not bothered to ease his pace in the heat of the day. His clothing, which proclaimed his lordly status, was dusty, and Elias did not relish the duties of his servants who would have to see to hot horses and grimy raiment before they could so much as contemplate slaking their own thirst.

The nobleman who had arrived earlier in the day had been much more relaxed. He had more men but had ridden in on a loose rein, one arm resting casually on his pommel. Everything about him had proclaimed a man who knew his own worth and had nothing to prove. Something about him was vaguely familiar to Elias, and the thought that he had seen him before was still niggling at his brain. It was a cause of some irritation, like a stone in a shoe. Elias liked everything in order, from his workmen's tools to his own mind. A question from one of his men dragged both thoughts and eyes away from the world below, and he turned back to the task in hand with a sigh.

Miles FitzHugh dismounted before the guest hall, head held proud. He rather ostentatiously removed his gauntlets and beat them against his leg to loosen the dust, but then ruined the effect by sneezing. Once the convulsion had passed, he issued terse commands to his long-suffering grooms, who led the horses away to the stables. The young man permitted himself a small smile, enjoying the chance to command others. In his home shire, and away from the entourage of the powerful Earl of Leicester, where he was only one of the young men serving as squires, he could flaunt his own noble birth and status. He had not the insight to realise that this pool, in which he saw himself as the biggest fish, was nothing greater than a stagnant puddle. He entered the cool gloom of the guest hall, his eyes unaccustomed to the low light, and collided with a tall, dark man who made no attempt to step aside. FitzHugh was about to make his feelings known, but his eyes had now made their adjustment, and before the hard glare and raised brows at which he had to look up, remonstration withered on his lips.

'You should be less hasty, my friend.' The voice was languid, almost bored, but the word 'friend' held a peculiar menace to it.

Taking stock of the man's clothing, Miles FitzHugh made a rapid alteration to his own manner. 'My apologies, my lord.' His voice was refined and precise, but with the deferential tone of one long used to service, and one also used to thinking up excuses swiftly. 'My eyes have been dazzled by the sun.'

'Then all the more reason to proceed with caution.'

The tall man was at least a dozen years FitzHugh's senior, and, by dress and bearing, far superior in rank to a squire, even one in the household of Robert de Beaumont, Earl of Leicester. FitzHugh mumbled an apology and drew aside, almost pressing himself into the hard, cold stone of the whitewashed wall. The older man inclined his head and gave a tight smile as he passed out into the sunlight. The squire would have been galled to have seen how much broader the smile grew once he was in the open.

'Jesu, was I ever that callow?' muttered Waleran de Grismont as he crossed the courtyard. His eyes were roving, sharp as a raven's, taking in everything going on around him. The usual routines within an abbey's walls were being carried out, as if the monastic world worked on a different level to the secular, aware of its existence but uninterested in its activities. The master of the children was leading his youngest charges to the precentor for singing practice. They followed him with eyes lowered, giving the casual observer the appearance of humility and obedience. De Grismont was amused to see that two lads towards the rear were elbowing each other surreptitiously, and another was picking up small stones and flicking them at a large, pudding-faced boy waddling along in front of him. The perpetrator sensed an adult gaze upon him, and he cast a swift glance in the direction of the tall, well-dressed lord. His eyes met those of de Grismont for an instant, and he grinned, correctly judging that the man would appreciate boldness. The nobleman gave an almost imperceptible nod, and the boy relaxed. The lord clearly remembered the misdeeds of his own youth.

In the shade of the infirmary, a woman was in conversation with the guestmaster. She had an air of competence and efficiency, and seemed perfectly at ease. She was dressed without ostentation, but the cloth of her gown was of fine quality. Her garb, thought de Grismont, was finer than her lineage. Her hands had seen work, and her face and figure were comely but lacking in delicacy. A few years hence and she would be commonplace and plump. He was a man who assessed women frequently and quickly, and he prided himself on his judgement. She held no further interest for him, and he turned the corner to the stables. Had anyone seen him within, they would have found that he looked not to his own fine animal, but to a neat dappled grey palfrey, a lady's mount. He patted the animal as one who knew it well, and smiled.

Mistress Margery Weaver knew the guestmaster from previous visits to the abbey, and each understood the manner of the other. In the comparative cool where the infirmary cast its short noontide shadow, she was arranging for payment for her lodging and that of her menservants, who acted as her security when she travelled far from home. In addition, she would leave money for Masses to be said for the soul of her husband. In some ways, she acknowledged to herself, this was a sop to her conscience, because although she had been a loyal and loving wife she was enjoying her widowhood. Her husband had been a man of authority within the weavers' guild in Winchester, but had died of the flux some three years past. Their son was then only seven years old and so it was Margery who took up the reins of the business, as was accepted by the guild. She came from a weaving family, and had no difficulty in assuming her late husband's role. What she lacked in bluff forcefulness she made up for in feminine ingenuity, and she had seen the business flourish. She had a natural aptitude for business, and she found it far more interesting than the homely duties of being a wife.

Each summer she headed west to the Welsh Marches, which was where Edric had gone for the best fleeces. She did as he had done, and the journey provided her with a welcome change of scene, almost a holiday. Both on the outward and return trips she broke her journey at Pershore, and the guestmaster regarded her visits as much a summer regularity as the arrival of the house martins in the eaves.

A habited figure emerged from the abbot's lodging and acknowledged her presence with a nod and the hint of a sly smile. She lifted her head and pointedly refused to return the gesture. The guestmaster was somewhat surprised, for Mistress Weaver was not a woman of aloof manner. He was also taken aback that the monk, who had no cause to acknowledge the woman's presence, had looked upon her. It was not, he thought, seemly that a Benedictine should do so, but the man was not a brother of Pershore, and there was no suitable place for him to raise the error. He would certainly not mention it at Chapter.

Margery Weaver's cheeks flew two patches of angry red colour and her bosom heaved in outrage. Her lips moved, and it was not in prayer. The guestmaster averted his own gaze for a moment, and compressed his lips. Women were definitely a wicked distraction. He wondered why she had reacted in such a way, but wisely refrained from asking for explanation.

Brother Eudo, clerk and emissary of Henri de Blois, Bishop of Winchester, permitted himself a silent laugh as he turned away. Mistress Weaver's refusal to acknowledge him did not distress him. In fact, her annoyance gave him a degree of pleasure completely at odds with his religious vocation. He was a man who gained untold delight in the discomfiture of others, almost as other men took it from the pleasures of the flesh. It was not an aspect of his character which endeared him to his fellows, and even the bishop had found it difficult to turn a blind episcopal eye to the fault, but Eudo was too useful, and the eye was therefore turned.

Way above the town, high on Bredon Hill, William de Beauchamp, sheriff of the shire, was making his dispositions as the day heated up. He had led his men into the southern part of his shrievalty, to the hill of Bredon, for the purpose of dealing with a lawless band that had been troubling the king's highway between Evesham and Pershore, and even southwards towards Tewkesbury. In a violent time when minor infringements were sometimes overlooked, their depredations on the merchants and pilgrims upon this route had become so heavy as to make the sheriff take action, if only to silence the vociferous complaints of the abbots of Evesham and Pershore, and even Tewkesbury, although the latter lived under the Sheriff of Gloucester's aegis. That de Beauchamp supported the Empress Maud, and not King Stephen, made no difference to the need to maintain the rule of law, the King's Peace. The office of sheriff was lucrative, since he was permitted to 'farm' some of the money he gathered in taxes for the king, and it made a man a power to be reckoned with within the shire. The day-to-day administration of justice he generally left to his serjeant and to his undersheriff, but this band had been big enough to cause him to lead retribution himself. Besides which, if they were upon the hill they were far too close to his own seat at Elmley, and he had no intention of being embarrassed by being told his own lands and tenants had suffered. In addition, his undersheriff, Fulk de Crespignac, had taken to his bed, sick.

His serjeant, old Catchpoll, was a sniffer of criminals, a man who could track and out-think the most cunning of law breakers by the simple expedient of understanding the way that they thought but being better at it. De Beauchamp had sent him to scout ahead, and he had returned with the news that the camp they sought was empty but not abandoned.

'They've gone a-hunting like a pack of wolves, my lord, and I'd vouch they'll be back as soon as they've brought down their prey. The camp was used last night. Their midden is fresh and there was fires still warm with ash.' Catchpoll mopped a sweat-beaded brow.

'Might they not move to another camp tonight?' said the lord Bradecote, a tall man, sweating in good mail and mounted on a fine steel-grey horse.

Catchpoll turned to him with a derisive sneer.

'They're coming back, my lord. They tethered a dog. Now they would not do that if they were on the move proper, but they might if the animal was like to ruin a good ambush.'

Hugh Bradecote nodded acceptance of this theory.

De Beauchamp sniffed. 'Then we ambush the ambushers upon their return. Which way did they go, Catchpoll?'

'Down onto the Tewkesbury road, about a dozen ponies, though from the hoof prints, even in this dust and dryness, I'd say as some beasts carried two, or else the living is far too good and we should take to thievery, for it would mean very heavy men in the band. Say up to twenty, all told.'

'If they intend to return then we want to push them. Bradecote, take your men and follow Catchpoll to the camp. He can show you where to lie concealed.'

'I think I can make my own judgement upon that, my lord.' The subordinate officer had his pride, and being treated like a wet-behind-the-ears lordling by the grizzled Serjeant Catchpoll did not appeal.

'As you wish, but if any escape this net, I'll be amercing you for every man. I shall take my men down a little off their track and await them starting back up the hill. We will drive them like beaters with game, on to your swords. They may be greater in number, but mailed men with lances are rarely matched by scoundrels with clubs, knives and swords they have stolen. They'll run for camp to make a stand where they know every bush. Be behind those bushes.'

The sheriff pulled his horse's head round and set spur to flank. 'Oh, and don't kill the lot. I want men to hang. Makes a good spectacle and folk remember it more than just seeing a foul-smelling corpse dragged in for display, and in this weather they will go off faster than offal at noon.'

A lull fell upon the abbey after Sext. Monks and guests alike ate dinner, and if the religious were meant to return to their allotted tasks, there were yet a few heads nodding over their copying in the heat. The obedientiaries of the abbey could not afford to be seen as lax, and went very obviously about their business, but mopped their brows covertly with their sleeves if they had cause to be out in the glare. Two or three of the most elderly brothers could be heard snoring softly, like baritone bees, in favoured quiet and shady corners, but their advanced age gave them immunity from censure. Many of the wealthier guests kept to the cool of their chambers, for they did not have to share the common dormitory, but a well-favoured and well-dressed lady promenaded decorously within the shade of the cloister, thereby raising the temperature of several lay brothers, already hot as they scythed the grass of the cloister garth. When their job was complete they were hurried away as lambs from a wolf by the prior, who cast the lady a look of displeasure. She smiled blithely back at him, but in her eyes lurked a twinkle of understanding, and when he had turned away her lips twitched in unholy amusement. Men, she thought, were all alike, regardless of their calling. The only difference with the tonsured was that they tried to blame women for attracting them. It was not, she thought mischievously, her fault if she could draw a man's gaze without even trying; her looks were natural, a gift from God, and it was only right to use them.

Isabelle d'Achelie was in her late twenties, with the maturity and poise to be expected of a woman with the better part of fifteen years of marriage behind her, but with the figure and complexion of a girl ten years her junior. It was a fascinating combination, and she knew just how to utilise it.

As a girl she had dreamt of marriage to a bold, brave and dashing lord, but reality had brought her the depressingly mundane Hamo d'Achelie. He was a man of wealth and power within the shire, a very good match for a maid whose family ranked among the lower echelons of landowners. Her father had been delighted, especially as he had three other daughters. None were as promising as his eldest, but one outstanding marriage would raise him in the estimation of his neighbours. Isabelle was a dutiful girl who knew that she had no real say in whom she wed, and besides, she was fond of her father. He would not have countenanced the match if d'Achelie had a bad reputation as man or seigneur. Hamo d'Achelie was in fact a decent overlord and pious man. He was, however, nigh on forty-five years old, had buried two wives over the years, and exhibited no attributes that could inspire a girl not yet fifteen. Isabelle had done as she was expected, but wept at her mother's knee.

Her mother had given her sound advice. A husband of Hamo's

years and apparent disposition, which was not tyrannical, would be likely to be an indulgent husband. She would be able to dress well, eat well and live in comfort. The duties of a wife might not be as pleasant, but, if she was fortunate, her lord's demands upon her should not be excessive.

So it had proved. Hamo had never sired children, within or outside of marriage, and had, somewhat unusually, accepted that this was not the fault of the women with whom he lay. It was a burden laid upon him from God, and he had learnt to live with it. His third marriage sprang, therefore, not from desperation for an heir but from his infatuation with a beautiful face. He adored his bride, and denied her nothing. Isabelle found that marriage was comfortable but unexciting. Her husband treated her as he would some precious object, and took delight in showing her off to his friends and neighbours. He decked her in fine clothes and watched his guests gaze at his wife in undisguised admiration. His pleasure lay in knowing how much they envied him.

Isabelle had learnt the rules of the game early on, and played it with skill for many years. She was a loyal wife, and would never be seen alone with another man, but when entertaining she had learnt how to flirt with men while remaining tantalisingly out of reach. She had become highly adept, and it both amused her and gave her a feeling of superiority over the opposite sex that she had never expected. What she lacked was passion; but then Waleran de Grismont had entered her life. Just thinking about him made her blood race as nothing else ever had.

De Grismont's lands lay chiefly around Defford, but he had inherited a manor adjacent to the caput of Hamo d'Achelie's honour some four years previously. His first visit had been one of courtesy, but he had found the lady d'Achelie fascinating, and had found excuses to visit his outlying manor more and more frequently. He had become good friends with Hamo, and never overstepped the line with Isabelle in word or deed, but she had seen the way he looked at her when her husband was not attending. She was used to admiration, but not blatant desire, and it oozed from every pore of the man. Three years since, Hamo had been struck down by a seizure, which left him without the use of one side of his body. He had been pathetically touched by her devotion and attention to the wreck he knew himself to be, and openly discussed his wife's future with his friend. She was deserving, he said, of a husband who could love and treasure her as he had become unable to do.

What neither Hamo nor his beautiful wife realised was that Waleran de Grismont liked things on his own terms, and was conscious of feeling his hand forced. He had resolved to distance himself from the d'Achelies for a while, and sought sanctuary in the ranks of King Stephen's army. He was not, in truth, very particular whose claim was most just, but since Stephen was the crowned king, it seemed a greater risk to ally oneself to the cause of an imperious and unforgiving woman, which the Empress Maud was known to be. The king's army was heading north to ward off the threat of the disaffected Ranulf, Earl of Chester, and it was not long after that de Grismont found himself fighting for his life in the battle of Lincoln. He was no coward, and fought hard, but, like his king, was captured, and held pending ransom.

In Worcestershire, as months passed, Isabelle d'Achelie had shed tears of grief and frustration, and even contemplated asking her ailing husband if there were any way of assisting in the raising of the required sum. Thankfully, such a desperate measure proved unnecessary, as she received news of de Grismont's release. He sent a message, full of soft words and aspirations, but did not return to see her. She had been hurt, then worried. Had he cooled towards her, found another? When next she had news, he was among those besieging the empress at Oxford. Only when Hamo d'Achelie was shrouded for burial did he come to her again.

Absence had certainly made the heart grow fonder, at least as far as the lady was concerned. Waleran looked thinner, and, thankfully, hungrier for her. His feral quality stirred her. For his own part, he was relieved to find that his absence had achieved its aim, for there had been low times when he had regretted his abandonment of the hunt. Now all that was necessary was to obtain the king's permission to wed the wealthy widow. It should not prove difficult to obtain, for had he not suffered imprisonment and financial hardship for Stephen, who, having been shackled in a cell in Bristow, well knew how harsh such confinement could be.

Isabelle was less sanguine. She had heard how variable the king's moods could be. He had allowed the defeated garrison of one town to march out under arms, and then proceeded to hang the defenders of another from their own battlements. He was known, however, to have a gallant and impressionable streak when it came to women. The fair widow believed she would have no difficulty in persuading her sovereign to permit her wedding de Grismont, and had set out for that purpose, delighted at having her future in her own hands for the first time in her existence.

She was surprised when Waleran de Grismont fell into step beside her. Her pulse raced, but a furrow of annoyance appeared briefly between her finely arched brows. She did not look at him, and spoke softly.

'I do not suppose you are here by chance, my lord.'

There was an edge to the tone, which he noted. He smiled. 'But how could I keep away, when I knew you to be so close, my sweet?'

The lady sniffed, unimpressed. 'It would have been better if you had mastered that desire.'

The smile broadened and his voice dropped. 'But, you see, you are so very . . . desirable, and I dream of "mastering" you.'

She shot him a sideways glance through long, lowered lashes. The wolfish smile excited her. Flirting with de Grismont still had an element of danger to it that was quite irresistible after Hamo's uninspiring veneration. Deep within there was a warning voice that urged caution. As a suitor he was bewitching, but as a husband? Would . . . could . . . such a man be bothered to even appear faithful once the prize was won? The voice of caution thought not, but in his presence caution could be ignored.

'Besides, in times like these it is not wise for a lady to travel unescorted.'

'You have not noticed the four horses in the stables, then, my lord, nor the d'Achelie men-at-arms?'

'Men-at-arms should be led.' His eyes glittered, both amused and irritated. 'Could you trust them else to stand firm in an emergency?'

'Would they risk their lives for me?' She turned to him with an arch look and knowing smile. 'Oh yes,' she purred. 'I rather think they would, my lord. Men so often "stand firm" for me.' Her eyes stared boldly; she need have no pretence of maidenly ignorance.

It occurred to de Grismont that his lady love was acquiring a dangerously independent turn of mind. That was something he would have to curb once they were wed.

'But without a leader their . . . self-sacrifice . . . might well prove in vain.'

'Nevertheless, I need no escort to the king, unless you fear that some other man should distract me from my purpose.'

There was a brittle edge to her voice, and de Grismont sought to smooth her ruffled feathers with flattering words. As they turned the corner of the cloisters by the monks' door into the church, he cast a swift glance around. Nobody was watching. He grasped her gently at the elbow, and, as the pair of them passed the chapter house door, he lifted the latch with a heavy click and whisked them both into the cool light within. As he had expected, there was nobody there, and there was room in one of the shallow embrasures, where an obedientiary sat during Chapter, for a man to hold a woman on his knee and whisper things which would have made the usual occupant blench and then blush.

He had hoped to distract her, and for a while was most successful, but her mind was tenacious, and eventually she returned to the point of their conversation, though a little breathlessly.

'This is all very well, Waleran, but you should, truly, not have come here. Your escort to the king may sound a good idea but might be harmful to our cause. King Stephen always likes to think ideas his own, and dislikes having his hand forced.' She grasped her suitor's hand and imprisoned it between her own. 'No. Stop that. You must attend to me. Return to your estates and let me do this alone. Be patient, my love, and all will be well.'

De Grismont's opinion of leaving such an important mission in the hands, however pretty they might be, of a woman, was not likely to please her. He chose therefore, the route of blandishment.

'You ask patience, sweet. How can I be patient any longer? How could I remain at Defford, knowing you were so close?' His voice was husky, and his lips close to her ear. 'You ask too much of me, Isabelle. We have waited, and the waiting is so nearly over.' His arm round her tightened, possessively.

'All the more reason to take care now.'

'You do not cool towards me, lady?' He did not fear her reply.

'I would not be here like this if I was, nor would my heart beat so fast.' She laid his hand over her breast once more, and sighed.

Waleran de Grismont laughed very softly. He was sure of her now. There was much to be said for a beautiful bride, with a passionate nature that had lain dormant all too long, and a dowry ample enough even for his expenses. As long as King Stephen did not refuse her request all would be well, as she said. He thought she had a point about the king, but a small niggling doubt remained, for Stephen did not always act as sense would dictate. But even if the worst happened, and Stephen refused the match, he had woken the sensuous side of her. He was confident that he could 'persuade' Isabelle d'Achelie to seek the ultimate solace for the disappointment in his arms, in his bed, and then, albeit reluctantly, he would seek a rich wife elsewhere.

Voices sounded outside the door, and he felt Isabelle tense within his hold. He laid a finger to her full lips, and sat very still, listening. He could hear and feel her breathing, which was a distraction, and he had to force himself to concentrate on what lay beyond the door. He judged that two men were in conversation, and though it was whispered and he could not make out words, it was heated. Once he heard a sharp intake of breath and muffled exclamation, followed by what he would have sworn was a chuckle. After some moments they passed on, and, after a short but pleasant interlude, de Grismont led his lady to the door. He opened it a fraction, listened, and then pushed her gently but firmly into the cloister. A short while later he sauntered out, much to the surprise of a soft-footed novice.

'Fine carvings you have in your chapter house, Brother,' exclaimed de Grismont cheerily, and strode off. The novice was left blinking in stupefaction.

Chapter Two

Brother Remigius was fairly new to Pershore, and was still finding his feet as sub-prior. His predecessor, a promotion from within the abbey, had succumbed to an inflammation of the lungs within only a few months of his appointment, and Pershore was not such a large house that it could provide a replacement with suitable experience. Henri de Blois, while still papal legate, had heard of the vacancy and offered the services of a brother from Winchester whom he considered worthy of advancement. Brother Remigius had leapt at the chance. In such a large house as Winchester, he was well aware that his modest talents were not so outstanding as to bring him to prominence, but in a smaller community he hoped to flourish. He was not a man of huge ambition, but the move suited him very well. It certainly cost him no pang to leave the abbey where he had spent over twenty years. The atmosphere, at least for him, had soured, and he was glad to shake the Hampshire dust from his sandals.

The brethren of Pershore had received him with open minds if not open arms, and after nearly two years he was truly beginning to feel at ease. He was engaged in serious but convivial conversation with the sacrist and cellarer, on their way to a regular meeting with Master Elias to assess the progress of the repair works. Lightning, so often the bane of Pershore, had damaged the north transept in the spring storms, though fortunately upon this occasion the ensuing heavy rain had kept the fire from spreading along the roof, and the damage was limited to a fissure and badly damaged masonry on the north and east faces. Brother Remigius took no notice of the cowled figure who walked past, head bowed, and could not see that the demeanour merely hid the veiled eyes and malicious smile of the Bishop of Winchester's clerk. The three obedientiaries passed out of sight as they rounded the west end of the church and made for the masons' workshop, a wooden structure put up against the west side of the north transept, where they were close to their work above and had access to the inside of the church via the little wooden door set into the transept wall.

Master Elias saw the black-garbed trio from above, and descended with surprising nimbleness from the wooden scaffolding to meet them. He exhibited the affable but deferential air of a hostel keeper. He might not hold them in high esteem, but he had learnt long ago how precious of their dignity minor officials could be. He also knew that he could provide answers to any question they might choose to put to him, even if he had to resort to baffling them with technicalities. He almost herded them into the welcome patch of coolness afforded by the north wall of the nave, for he doubted they had come to look at the work itself.

The sacrist was keen to know whether any additional, and thus, in his eyes, unnecessary, expenditure was foreseen. He pursed his lips and looked grave when the master mason explained that the stone had come at a premium.

'It is no fault of mine, Brother, that your church is built of a stone now in high demand. Abbot Reginald of Evesham has, as I am sure you have heard, commissioned a new wall for the enclave there. Indeed, it is because of the use of local masons upon it that I come this far west. This,' Elias patted the dressed stone of the great thick wall as a man might stroke a favoured horse, 'I can tell you, is fine stone, but your own quarry cannot meet our demand and we have gone further afield. Both we,' he used the inclusive pronoun, 'and Abbot Reginald have our eye upon the same commodity. The price has thus risen.' He spread his hands placatingly.

The sacrist was not appeased. 'Surely, you can make changes, cut corners . . .' His voice lost its authority and wavered as Elias's brow darkened.

'Cut corners,' he growled, his affability discarded. 'What would you have me build, Brother, an ornament to this House of God or a wall fit for you to piss against in the reredorter? And do not ask if I would cut corners with the pulleys and poles. I expect hard work from my men, but in return I try and ensure that as few as possible lose life or limb. Would you have me sacrifice them in the name of economy?'

The sacrist shook his head. 'No, no, Master Elias. I

would not, naturally . . . I mean . . .' His voice trailed off in embarrassment, and he looked helplessly at his companions. Although their feet had not moved, they somehow managed to distance themselves from him, indicating that they were not party to his error of judgement. The trouble, thought Brother Remigius, forgivingly, was that any sacrist ended up covetous for his house, always seeking to keep, whereas an almoner was always giving.

Master Elias did not let his expression soften. He would not have done so even if his emotion had been an act, but on the subject of workmanship he held genuinely strong beliefs. What the sacrist had said was as heresy to him. Brother Remigius sought to mollify the master mason with soothing words, and if Master Elias did not actually believe them, he was at least happy to see the situation eased without having to concede his position. The cellarer took the opportunity to tug surreptitiously at the sacrist's sleeve, and the pair of them withdrew. The sub-prior thought his brother obedientiary had been less than politic, and moved the conversation on to safer topics. He actually found the work of the masons very interesting, and had seen examples of carving at Winchester which he could describe to Master Elias. Mason and monk spent some time in amicable discourse.

It was then that Eudo the Clerk appeared, without advertising his approach, from the direction of the gatehouse. It was amazing how he could flit like a silent, black moth. He acknowledged the master mason with an irritatingly gracious nod, but turned his attention to Brother Remigius. Master Elias was about to excuse himself, when realisation dawned as to who this was. He had an excellent visual memory and had seen that unctuous, self-satisfied face before. Where? Ely, Abingdon, Oxford? That was it . . . in Oxford. He tried to recall the name. Eustace, was it? No. Well, he was certainly the lord Bishop of Winchester's man, and in Oxford rumour had been rife that he was always to be found where discord and deceit were hottest, and that he had an unfailing ability both to increase the temperature and to make sure that his master was on the side of the successful faction. Despite Henri de Blois, Bishop of Winchester, being the king's brother, he had been quite prepared promote the empress's claim while King Stephen had rotted in a Bristow dungeon, and then equally swift to return to his brother's side when the tables had been turned and Stephen was once more in command. Master Elias did not think much of such inconstancy.

He himself believed that the Empress Maud had full right to be Lady of the English, given that was her father's wish. He had thought well, in a distant and respectful way, of the late King Henry. He had even seen him once, while still a journeyman, when the king had viewed the building upon which he was working. It had been but a stolen glance before his superior clouted him about the ear for lack of attention, but it had left an impression. Pity it was that a king with such fruitful loins had sired but two legitimate offspring, and that the Prince William should have met an early death at sea. But the king had named his daughter, the widowed empress of the Holy Roman Empire, as his heir, and the baronage had sworn fealty. They had no cause, in Master Elias's opinion, to break that oath and accept King Henry's nephew as king. Some had come to regret their choice and raised an army for the empress. Elias was no warrior, nor of elevated class, but he had found that his work took him further afield than most in the realm, and that a man of quick eye and attentive ear could learn much. Master Elias was certainly not, in his own view, a spy. He did not plot or listen at windows; did not bribe or threaten to reveal his knowledge. He simply made note of interesting things and passed such information to men he knew to be both discreet and firmly on the side of the Empress Maud.

He was not paying attention to the cowled pair while he thought. Ecclesiastical business was usually far too parochial and small-minded to be of interest, but something in Brother Remigius's tone jarred. Having just been speaking with him, Master Elias could easily detect the new chill and dislike in his voice, and, surprisingly, a heavy overtone of fear. He stared at the sub-prior, frowning, and then suddenly realised that the lord bishop's clerk was watching him. He coloured, and, for an instant, the ghost of a smile flickered over the clerk's face. Brother Remigius looked distinctly uncomfortable. Master Elias was about to withdraw when the clerk addressed him.

'You have travelled a way west from your usual haunts, Master Mason. I last recall you in Oxford, at St Frideswide's.'

Eudo the Clerk had as good a memory for faces and voices as the master mason's, if not better. It had taken barely a moment to drag his image from the filing system of memory, and as he spoke, Eudo was contemplating what use could be made of the man. He recalled the master mason as a Maudist, but quietly so, and Eudo wondered if he had come into Worcestershire with the aim of discovering information in an area where the supporters of king and empress overlapped. It would be prudent to discover if the big man was as sharp as a chisel or as dull as a mallet.

Master Elias was wary. 'I came where the work was, Brother, and it is not so far from Oxford. As well work here as further north.'

Eudo inclined his head, with a suggestion of graciousness. 'Indeed, the north can be as . . . difficult . . . in terms of strife between the king and the countess.'

Master Elias blinked in surprise. The Empress Maud, now married to Geoffrey Plantagenet, Count of Anjou, still used her more exalted title and was not known as 'countess'. The only people who gave her the title were a few of those covertly seeking her elevation to the throne of England as 'Lady of the English'. He had heard it used as a signal among her supporters, but the lord Bishop of Winchester supported the king again, so what was his clerk up to?

'I would be interested to see the work you have undertaken here,' continued the clerk. 'Perhaps I might visit your workshop at some convenient time. We must arrange it.' He nodded a dismissal, and Master Elias, who would normally have bristled at such treatment, meekly withdrew, his mind whirling. Brother Eudo turned to the sub-prior. 'Now, Brother Remigius, we have, I think, much to discuss. Perhaps the cool of the cloister would be more pleasant.'

The sub-prior gave him a look that implied he would find standing in a snake pit infinitely more 'pleasant' than further conversation with Eudo the Clerk, but went with him nonetheless.

* * *

In the cool of the abbot's parlour, Abbot William of Pershore was conducting negotiations with two women, although one seemed merely there as silent support.

'It was not thought too great a thing to ask, Father Abbot, that a small relic of the blessed saint should return to the sorority in which her own sister lived.'

The speaker was a Benedictine nun, reverent in word, but with her own obvious authority. Her voice was low and controlled, as controlled as every other aspect of her, from her immaculate tidiness to her straight back as she sat, and the precise folding of her hands beneath her scapular.

Abbot William considered carefully. The Benedictine nuns of Romsey were offering both coin and a fine manuscript, copied and embellished by one of the finest illustrators of the Winchester school, in exchange for the bone of a finger of St Eadburga, who lay within the gilded reliquary in her chapel in the abbey church. That they were prepared to offer much for so little was proof of their eagerness to claim a part of the saint.

'I am perplexed, Sister, as to why Romsey makes this request when the blessed Eadburga has lain here so long. And why not approach the Nunnaminster, St Mary's, her own house in Winchester. Would not your Sisters in Christ part with a small bone? They retain several and must be glad of funds after the Great Burning.' He sounded cautious. 'Besides, Romsey has two saints of its own.'

'Indeed yes, Father Abbot. St Merewenna, and her successor as our Mother Superior, St Aelfleda, lie secure and venerated within our walls. We have been blessed by having two saints to exemplify the life we should lead, but only now has a benefactor enabled us to consider bringing a small part of the sainted Eadburga to our community, and Abbess Matilda has sent us to make the request.' The nun's voice showed no trace that she feared being rebuffed, nor yet arrogance.

Abbot William wavered. 'You claim earlier poverty, but yours is a house where royalty have sent daughters in the past, and surely not without bringing wealth with them?'

Sister Edeva permitted herself the smallest of wry smiles. 'Kings are wont to think the honour of housing their womenfolk generous in itself, and what has come to Romsey has been put to practical use upon the fabric of the abbey and in help for those about us.'

The Abbot of Pershore leant forward at his table, letting his chin rest against his steepled fingers. He was silent for some time. The younger nun's eyes darted between her sister and Abbot William nervously, but Sister Edeva kept her gaze fixed at a point somewhere on the wall behind the abbot's head. Eventually he spoke.

'I am minded to accede to the request of Abbess Matilda, but this matter must go before our chapter, as it concerns all in this house.' He was also mindful of the amount it was costing to repair the north transept. 'I will bring it to the attention of the brothers at Chapter tomorrow morning, and will give you a final answer thereafter. In the meantime I would welcome your presence at my table tonight. I appear to have many important guests and am set,' he sighed as if it was a burden, 'to entertain.'

He rose, and smiled his dismissal. The sisters made obeisance and retired, well content that their mission was proceeding well. They trod with becoming lack of haste and eyes slightly lowered, but both wore the hint of a smile. Their undertaking was important to their community, and though failure would have been accepted with outward calm, success would be greeted with delight. Sister Ursula had scarcely taken final vows and was too junior a member of the sorority to gain advancement from that success. She was content to have enjoyed a foray into the daunting but exciting secular world she had left but a few years before. Sister Edeva had withdrawn from the world over twenty years previously, and had rarely left the abbey enclave, certainly not for as long as this. She held the responsible position of sacrist, in charge of the abbey church fabric and the items within it. Her securing of a relic of St Eadburga would be remembered in years to come, when the sisters had need to select a new mother superior, and Sister Edeva knew she would be able to fulfil that role, if called upon.

She had not been concerned about leaving the confines of the abbey at Romsey, but she had not been prepared for how strange she would find the world without. The first day's journey had left her ears ringing and her head aching from the volume of activity about her, and the succeeding days had not proved any easier. For all the poverty and dirt that did not exist within the enclave of Romsey, there was a colourful vibrancy to the outside world that she had forgotten. Children laughed and played in the dusty streets and roadways; even the sound of argument in the marketplaces breathed life. When people, even lay people, entered the confines of the conventual world, their tones and actions were muted and respectful. Had she entombed herself all those years ago, not just to show the strength of her love for one lost to her, but to avoid the need to continue real life? Had she been afraid, deep down, that the day would come when she would look upon another man as she had looked upon him? Were such questions themselves proof of her faithlessness? For her peace of mind it would be good to go home as soon as possible.

As they crossed from the abbot's lodging to the guest hall, a brother passed by, and would have been ignored had he not spoken. Sister Ursula frowned, disconcerted by his action, for the brethren did not engage in unnecessary speech with women, even with pious women who had withdrawn from the world as they had. Sister Edeva slowly raised her eyes from contemplation of his sandals, and the smile was wiped from her face in an instant. The younger sister heard her draw in her breath with a distinct hiss.

'I give you good day, Sisters.' He smiled broadly. 'I hope your long journey has been crowned with success.' No reply was forthcoming, so he continued. 'It is strange that we, who hale from Hampshire, should find ourselves, at the same time, in this distant House of God.' He paused and shook his head. His tone was one of surprised delight. 'Who should have thought it, indeed.'

Sister Ursula had the peculiar feeling that the remark was addressed solely to Sister Edeva, but the older nun remained stony-faced and silent, and walked on as though nothing had been said. The brother turned away, and Sister Ursula was sure that she heard him laugh.

A birdlike lady, clearly aristocratic, who had halted to exchange a word with the almoner, half-turned at the laugh, revulsion and horror vying on her pale face. Her thin hands, which had been clasped modestly, were wrung in anguish, the knuckles showing white.

Mistress Weaver was returning from making purchases in the town, and was walking towards the guest hall. She had studiously ignored the habited figure with as much froideur as the sacrist of Romsey, but she took heed of the pale lady's distress, and hurried to her. The almoner stood by, somewhat at a loss, and beyond him a large, grizzled individual with the expression of a leashed mastiff, stiffened in readiness to lunge forward should his lady falter.

'You know him, my lady?' Mistress Weaver had little doubt, and it was more an assertion than a question. Her own eyes narrowed and she pursed her lips.

Lady Courtney nodded dumbly, and made no demur when the Winchester widow took her by the arm, and guided her towards the guest hall. The 'mastiff', watchful, followed at a respectful distance.

'I have my own knowledge of that snake, the lord Bishop of Winchester's clerk, and none of it is good,' Margery Weaver whispered, but with anger ripe in the tone.

Lady Courtney, who was regaining her calm, would have normally dissociated herself from such as Mistress Weaver, but this gave her pause. 'He is evil.' She too whispered, as if he could hear her words from the distance of the cloister.

The two women had reached the doorway of the guest hall, and would have entered but for Miles FitzHugh barring their path. He stood aside politely, though it was clear that he deferred only to the lady Courtney, but both women ignored him as they passed by, and he frowned.

'Not only is Brother Eudo a man who would seek to threaten honest folk with wicked lies, but,' Mistress Weaver's voice had risen with the bitterness in her tone, though she now dropped it confidingly, 'it is widely rumoured in Winchester that Eudo was deep in the lord bishop's confidence when he changed sides two years past and deserted his brother the king. The lord bishop was keen enough then to seek approval of the Empress Maud while she held the upper hand, and that conniving . . .' Mistress Weaver bit her lip lest she use a term unsuitable for a refined dame's ear and the religious surroundings. 'Well, anyway, he was the chief go-between. It's not for the likes of me to say how Henri de Blois should conduct himself, but suffice it to say that any member of the guild who reneged on a business deal as the leaders of Church and State do, would be cast out. That Eudo does not even hide behind the excuse of politics. He loves his work of intrigue so well he could not cross a street in a straight line.'

Lady Courtney was all attention, and Margery Weaver could not resist a dramatic pause before her final announcement. 'He is even said by some to be dealing with all sides now, the dirty spy.'

Emma Courtney's slightly protuberant eyes bulged further, and she made no complaint as the weaver's widow led her companionably into an inner chamber. Each was keen to know the tale that might be forthcoming from the other, and the social divide between them was temporarily bridged by a shared loathing. Lady Courtney's silent guardian stood impassively at the door.

Miles FitzHugh remained very still, the frown of offence at

the ladies' slight deepened by what he had overheard. He was a young man who wore his emotions upon his sleeve, and who regarded double dealing with a distaste that his liege lord had found naive and vaguely amusing until voiced in his presence. In changeable times, options were there to be kept open, and Robert de Beaumont, Earl of Leicester, was assuredly nobody's fool. Spies had their uses, and he had no objection to dealing with them. FitzHugh was young enough to hold to ideals that older and more powerful men could not afford. The squire had fallen foul of his lord for daring to express his distaste for treating with men of the opposite faction. That the man in question was the earl's own twin, Waleran de Meulan, Earl of Worcester, compounded the offence. After several weeks of demeaning tasks and being in his lord's bad books, Miles had taken swift advantage of his father's ill health to withdraw to his family's estates and hope that Robert de Beaumont's ire would fade. Life in the bosom of his family would be slow, and his mother would fuss like a hen with one chick over her surviving son, but he would lie low as long as possible.

Being the heir appealed to his sense of self-importance, but he was not so shallow as to think it worth the loss of his elder brother. Gilbert FitzHugh had been killed fighting for the king at Lincoln. Miles had always looked up to Gilbert, who had the natural assurance and easy manner that Miles sought in vain to acquire. Thinking about him, Miles wondered if de Grismont had come across him before the battle. Waleran de Grismont was certainly a man worthy of respect; there was one who had fought bravely and paid a heavy price, yet looked in no way discouraged by the experience. He had a reputation with women, but FitzHugh saw much in that to admire. His own conquests had been confined to impressionable rustics and serving wenches who feared to say him nay. He only wished he had one tenth of de Grismont's charm.

FitzHugh indulged in a pleasant daydream about future success with the opposite sex, but then his thoughts returned to what Mistress Weaver had said. So the Bishop of Winchester's clerk was a spy, was he? A man who listened at windows and spied at keyholes; one who set times for secret assignations with other dubious individuals? Well, Robert de Beaumont might see the use of such, but he believed it behoved a gentleman of honour to strike a blow against dissemblers and traitors.

Master Elias was addressed twice by one of his journeymen before making a reply to the man's question. He was trying desperately to work out whether Henri de Blois's clerk was hoping to find out some intelligence that he could take back to his master, a piece of the puzzle that was the politics of England during such times, or whether he was, beneath it all, a genuine Maudist supporter, who either had something important to impart or sought information. The stonemason was not inclined to trust the clerk, but was not sure that he dare ignore him. He eventually answered with only half his mind on the dressing of the stone, and with his eye focused on the enclave below. The journeyman shrugged and went to double-check his query with one of the older masons.

As a windhover scans the ground for signs of field mice in the grasses, Master Elias watched and waited. He saw Waleran de Grismont giving orders to one of his servants, and the bell of memory jangled in his head. This was how he had seen the man before, from above, and in close conversation. Something about that meeting had aroused his interest . . . his interest. Suddenly the master mason remembered why he had registered the meeting. He smiled, and for once it was nearly as knowing a smile as Eudo the Clerk's.

The lord of Defford disappeared within the guest hall, and his servant headed for the stables. A tirewoman nearly bumped into him as she emerged, looking comically furtive, probably, thought Master Elias, from some illicit assignation with a groom in the warm dimness of an empty stall. She was too far away for him to be able to discern whether she had tell-tale hay stalks clinging to her skirt. His smile this time was one of gentle amusement. A monk also appeared from the stables, cowl raised to protect his tonsure from the sun, though he paid the penalty of the added heat. He was carrying what had to be, from his lopsided stance, a heavy bucket. The lay brothers were never idle. *Laborare est orare* was the motto of the Benedictines: 'To work is to pray'. Master Elias thought, not for the first time, that the prayers of the unlettered and lowly lay brothers therefore exceeded those of their more erudite brethren, the choir monks.

The woman headed for the gate to the abbot's garden and soon passed from his sight. A short while later a lady emerged from the same gateway, head down, a rose bloom held delicately to her nostrils. As she crossed the yard she was intercepted by Eudo the Clerk, who must have been at the west end of the abbey church, where Master Elias could not see him. The wispy fair hair edging his narrow skull and the manner of walking were distinctive. Master Elias sighed and made his way swiftly

44

down to ground level. Here was the opportunity to arrange a meeting, before the bell called the brothers to Vespers.

He did not see, therefore, the agitation of the lady accosted by Eudo, neither the clasping of her hands in supplication, nor the flailing of those same hands in angry impotence. If she spoke, he did not hear her, and by the time he turned the corner of the west end, Eudo was standing alone.

Hearing the sound of purposeful footsteps, Eudo the Clerk turned to face Master Elias, though his face showed no recognition. He did not wait for him to draw close, but walked towards him while diverting to one side to pass him by.

'Workshop, sometime after supper', said the clerk, softly but unhurriedly, without so much as glancing at the master mason, and walked on. It was as much as the latter could do not to turn and gaze after him, both stunned by his composure and incensed by the sheer audacity of his cool assumption that he had but to command and he would be obeyed. Master Elias was certainly not used to such treatment. He coloured hotly and made a low, ursine growling noise in his throat. He would very much like to cuff that far-from-humble brother round the ear, as he would one of his lads. The violent thought brought him relief as he returned to the north transept, and it was a marginally less bad tempered master mason who climbed back to the level of the workmen.

Brother Remigius took his accustomed place in the file of cowled figures assembling for Vespers with a face clouded by worry, and began the chant of prayer without conscious thought. The action had long ago become instinctive, and sometimes he chastised himself for failing to concentrate on the service, dwelling instead on vague distractions. Today, however, his mind was such a swirling mass of confusion, fear and rising anger that to have given himself up to the spirituality of the office would have been beyond him, however much he tried. The words still came, as they always did, but he was clearly distracted, and Brother Simon, the most irreverent of the novices, later described him to his fellows as looking like a landed trout from the abbey fishponds.

Below the crossing, the lady Courtney stood apart from the citizens of Pershore who had come to hear Vespers. All the other secular guests were about their worldly business, but she came nearest to being at peace within the church, and her devotions occupied her so deeply that even had they been present, she would not have been aware of them. She made her responses in a thin voice made tremulous with religious fervour, and occasionally entirely suspended by emotion. Her bulky protector made no responses at all, but then he had no tongue.

The Sisters of Romsey stood side by side, incongruous among the laity. Sister Ursula felt awkward and out of place. Normally they would have been in the choir, but in this house of monks their sex meant that they were not part of that select number. The younger nun sensed her superior taut as a bowstring beside her, and wondered if Sister Edeva resented their exclusion.

Sister Edeva was staring blindly ahead of her, the Latin tripping from her lips without her needing to think. Unconsciously, her fingers closed upon the amber cross that lay upon her breast beneath the scapular. Her breath felt constricted in her chest, as if she had been winded. After all this time, when she had come to believe she had gained a form of peace, a single moment had brought everything welling up in her thoughts, as bright as if it was all yesterday; as bright as blood. There had been times recently when she had castigated herself for forgetting, for allowing his very face to become a hazy memory, something which could only be caught in the edge of vision. If looked upon fully it lost all form. Now she knew that she had not forgotten; would never forget. It was peace and acceptance which were illusory. A tremor ran through her, and Sister Ursula glanced at her companion, now pale and faltering in her responses, with obvious concern. At the conclusion of the service, the sacrist of Romsey remained long after it was needful, and eventually headed for the south door with Sister Ursula hovering solicitously at her side. The golden, afternoon sunlight flooded the eastern range of the cloister, and both women blinked in the unaccustomed brightness. The air was warm, yet another shiver ran through Sister Edeva. They had not got as far as the doorway from the cloister to the courtyard and guest range when the older woman halted.

'Sister Ursula, I confess that the thought of dining with Father Abbot is too much. My head is throbbing as if beaten with cudgels. I am no fit guest tonight.'

'Oh dear. I am sorry, Sister. I thought that you were unwell during the office. A headache is indeed a sore trial. Perhaps the journey has been overtiring.' The young religeuse regarded her companion, who must be nearly twice her age, with the unconscious pity of the young for the old. 'Would you have me fetch something from the herbalist, some lavender water for your temples perhaps, or some easing draught, and bring it to our chamber?'

Sister Edeva gave a wan smile, genuinely touched by Sister Ursula's concern. 'No, I thank you, though it is a most charitable offer, Sister. I think I will spend the time in St Eadburga's chapel. It is cool there, and prayer is always efficacious, for matters of the body as well as the soul.'

She turned and retraced her steps, her pace as ever measured and composed, betraying nothing of her troubled thoughts. Sister Ursula watched her until she re-entered the church, and sighed. She tried very hard to be pious, humble and dutiful, but she would have been weak and chosen rest upon her cot rather than the discipline of prayer. She admired Sister Edeva's devotion and obedience and reflected that it would be many years before she achieved such self-discipline. Had she been privy to the sacrist of Romsey's demeanour in the soft silence of St Eadburga's chapel, she would have been astounded. Sister Edeva sank to her knees and covered her face with her hands rather than linking them in the conventional pose of prayer, and her shoulders shook as she wept silently. When the tears no longer fell, she heaved a great sigh, straightened her back and began her orisons, commencing with a plea for forgiveness of a lie.

Brother Eudo knelt before the altar of the Lady chapel, head bowed and hands clasped, the very picture of tonsured piety. He knelt, however, because it was a position in which years of experience enabled him to relax, and because anyone entering the chapel would not wish to disturb his prayers and would probably withdraw; unless, of course, they were expecting to meet him there. Eudo had been engaged upon covert meetings for longer than he could recall, but the anticipation still gave him a surge of adrenalin. He was not the sort of man who had ever sought excitement from the clash of swords, but an engagement of wits was another matter. He made it his business to gather more information than he gave, and to put the other person, who was frequently nervous anyway, at a disadvantage. It was an added pleasure to leave them with the belief that he would disclose their identity and secret, without having to reveal his own, at the slightest provocation, or indeed, none at all. This evening he had two assignations, although it was the first that promised to be especially entertaining, and he had arrived early. He liked to feel master of the situation, and being already in possession of the ground, so to speak, gave him an edge. Besides, he was going through permutations of how the interview would progress.

After some time there came the sound of footsteps, not, he acknowledged with some surprise, furtive, but assured and purposeful without being heavy. He turned his head a little so that he could see who entered, and rose, a satisfied smile upon his lips.

'Ah, I did not think you would disappoint me.'

Chapter Three

The pace was slow as the weary horsemen descended to cross the Avon, and some of the men-at-arms slouched in their saddles. One who had suffered an injury groaned occasionally, while another whistled tunelessly through gapped teeth until Serjeant Catchpoll bid him shut up in the most colourful terms of his native English.

Hugh Bradecote smiled to himself. His own first language was the Norman French of the baronage, but he was also perfectly at home in English, and indeed had a good percentage of English blood in his veins. Its imprecations and expressive expletives had been one of his earliest discoveries. This had led to some painful interludes with Father Gerard, who had taught him his letters, but had been most useful in establishing his credentials with his father's English retainers.

Bradecote's manors were not large; all lay within an hour's ride of the most substantial, Bradecote itself, and neither he nor his father had ever seen Normandy. He held the majority of his lands from William de Beauchamp, Sheriff of Worcester, which accounted for his presence and that of his men on this punitive expedition.

It was not a very noble task, hunting down law-breakers, but he could see it as a larger-scale version of his duty to protect his manors, and a man with a cudgel was still a man armed, as his bruised shoulder-joint attested. He winced, as much at the thought of the fussing his wife would make over him returning black and blue as the discomfort. There was certainly nothing heroic in admitting that he had nearly been laid out by a lumbering oaf with a lump of ash, even if he had been tackling a man with a sword at the time.

The ambush had, however, been most successful, despite the fact that he had felt Catchpoll's beady eye upon every move he made in deploying his men. A dozen bound and bloodied prisoners staggered along, dragged behind mounted men-at-arms, and a further half dozen corpses were slung across pack animals. Only one body was that of a sheriff's man. There would be plenty to show the populace that the lord Sheriff of Worcester would not brook such lawlessness, even in a time of civil war. De Beauchamp had lost a man-at-arms, but the casualties among his own men comprised just two with serious injuries and a couple of others nursing fat lips and a few contusions.

William de Beauchamp, riding at the head of his small column, should have felt pleased, but if he was it did not show upon his heavy-set features. As the late afternoon drifted into evening, and the glare of the sun softened and ceased to pain the eyes, his body, after a long day that had begun with a hot ride and been followed by a brisk fight, began to ache, and his stomach rumbled. He wondered morosely if he would be in time to find good fare at the Abbot of Pershore's table.

Master Elias was not in good humour. The masons under him were not given free rein to go out and about within the town. He worked on the principle that any returning obviously inebriated to their temporary wooden lodgings in the enclave would bring heavy looks and harsh words from the clerics, and would thereby do his reputation no good. In addition, a man with a thick head in the morning might be careless with a chisel, and ruin a piece of carving, and he knew from bitter experience that, at best, several would be sluggish about their tasks and bemoaning aching heads. Even worse, there was the risk one would be clumsy with the winches and ladders, causing injury to himself or the death of others. Yet he had given his men unaccustomed permission to go into the town for an hour or so, to free him for his meeting with Eudo the Clerk.

When he arrived in the workshop his greying brows beetled in annoyance, for he found that even the anticipation of the evening had had a bad effect on the apprentice set to clean the workshop. Master Elias discovered a mallet left dusty and out of its allotted place in the rack, and his brows drew together in a heavy frown. Tools were valuable and could easily be mislaid; only by checking that everything was replaced carefully could losses be avoided. Neatness of workplace also went hand-in-hand with neatness of work, in his book. Arnulf the apprentice would feel the rough edge of his tongue, if not the back of his hand, upon his return.

The youth in question was not in danger of drowning in ale, though it was possible he might in the Avon. The youngest apprentices found the lure of the cool river more appealing than slaking their thirsts, and it had the advantage of being free. Arnulf, Godfrey and the youngest apprentice, Wulfstan, who thought he numbered fourteen summers, had discarded tunic and hose, and dabbled their toes in the sun-warmed shallows, seeing if the minnows would nibble at them among the green weed. After the initial cool pleasure, they were now goading each other in boyish bravado, to see who would be the first to immerse himself completely. There was much mutual splashing and high spirits, and the chance for lads, who spent their lives under the scrutiny of their elders and were expected to act like men, to let their natural adolescent exuberance bubble to the surface. None of the three could swim, but the river was low and sluggish in the midsummer drought, and they were able to play at swimming, bracing their arms with their palms in the mud while the water floated their bodies in a weightless sensation that was new to Godfrey and Wulfstan, who had grown up near trickling streams only.

While he waited for his furtive visitor, the master mason toyed with a design for a corbel to make use of a fault in one of the stone blocks; for a time his aggravations were forgotten in the contemplation of the stone, and he was happily occupied. Eventually, however, he pulled a face. His own internal clock told him that it was almost time for Compline, and the clerk had failed to make good the assignation. Master Elias opened the door into the north transept and headed towards the cloister. At least there he could give the man a look that would show just how little he liked having his time wasted. He turned to genuflect towards the high altar as he traversed the crossing, and was surprised to see the figure of a monk lying prone at the base of the altar steps, arms outstretched in the manner of a penitent.

Master Elias was a devout enough man, but some of the religious, he thought, took their calling to extremes. The figure was silent, lost no doubt in contemplation of his sins, perhaps rehearsing in his mind how he would make confession before his brethren at Chapter. It might even be that he planned to pre-empt another brother denouncing him, in all charity of course. The master mason sighed. The conventual life claimed many late converts, who saw how it could assist the passage of their souls, but having seen more of the monastic life than most, he felt that he was unlikely ever to take the cowl, even in extremis.

It was the buzzing of a fly about the penitent that made Master Elias halt. The annoying insect should have provoked some sort of reaction, but there was none. Intrigued, and with a dull feeling of unease, Elias approached the motionless form. A few paces short, he stopped with a sharp intake of breath. A small, dark pool of blood was spread over the flagged floor. It emanated from the back of the man's head, or rather what was left of it. The tonsure was indiscernible amidst the mess of blood and bone. Elias crossed himself, and swallowed hard. Even face down, and so battered, he was recognisable. Eudo the Clerk had not been able to meet him in the workshop, because he had a prior engagement . . . with his Maker.

After a moment of paralysis, Elias's brain began to work. Eudo had intended to visit him, so there might be documents in his scrip that would be of use, if not to the empress, then to

King Stephen. He dropped to his knees, careful to avoid the dark, sticky stain, and slid his hand beneath the corpse. Feeling around tentatively, he was relieved to find the cords of the monk's scrip, and followed them to the leather bag, which was still full. Whoever had killed him had not had time or inclination to investigate it. He drew out several sheets of vellum. One bore the king's seal, one that of his brother, Henri de Blois, Bishop of Winchester, and there were several scraps written in code. There was another, its seal broken, addressed 'Beloved'.

'So much for your vow of chastity, Brother,' muttered Elias, with a grim smile, but before he could read further the first bell tolled for Compline. He had to act quickly. He could not afford to take the documents with him, lest they be discovered on his person. Nor was there time to secrete them. The safest thing to do would be to burn everything. If the empress could not have information, well then, nor would Stephen. Taking the votive candle that burnt before the altar, he took the smallest fragment of vellum and held it to the flame, holding it long enough to catch light, and thereby also scorching his fingers. The inks gave fantastic colours to the flames, but Elias could not afford to watch them. The insistent tolling bell warned him of the imminent arrival of abbot and community.

Checking his slightly trembling hands for traces of blood, he rose and ran, surprisingly swiftly and lightly for one of his age and girth, to the south transept door and out into the cloister.

His pace and pallor halted those making their way to the last office of the day. The brothers were forming up in pairs behind the prior on the south side of the square, but despite that formality there was a gently relaxed atmosphere among those for whom Compline, simple and short, marked the end of a long day. A novice stifled a yawn. Abbot William approached from the direction of his lodging, and exchanged a quiet word with the Sisters of Romsey. He preceded them through the west door, and halted so quickly that the nuns nearly bumped into him. The abbot, startled by running in the cloister, was about to remonstrate with the master mason, but was forestalled by his blurting out his news.

'My lord abbot, there has been a terrible thing done in the church, before the altar itself . . . A foul murder. The lord Bishop of Winchester's clerk has been violently killed.'

There was a moment of stunned silence, when everyone seemed frozen in time, an echo of the gargoyles Elias so lovingly fashioned. The remorseless bell tolled and broke the spell. One of the ladies from the guest hall broke into hysterics, her voice caught in gasping sobs. The sacrist of Romsey Abbey sank slowly and very gracefully to her knees beside Abbot William, her lips moving in silent prayer. Her companion, as pale as her wimple, dithered momentarily and then knelt beside her. The abbot knew an overwhelming desire to follow suit; the appearance, at least, of prayer would grant him time to think. He overcame this inclination and made an effort to assert some control over the situation.

'Master Elias, are you sure of what you say? If the lord bishop's clerk is indeed dead, possibly it was some accident or . . .' His voice trailed off as he watched the mason shake his head. 'Nobody would break the sanctity of our church.' The tone was beseeching rather than confident.

Abbot William was not a pusillanimous man. He controlled

his abbey with authority, and was confident in his dealings with the secular world. Yet here was something beyond his experience, beyond his imagining, and all at once he was floundering. His mind worked slowly, as if clogged by the honey from the abbey hives, and raised problems rather than solutions.

He became aware of commotion behind him in the outer court; there came voices and the sound of horses' hooves. The abbot looked round and his jaw dropped. As if upon instant answer to his prayer, here was the embodiment of the law, with his minions about him.

Roused at last into movement, Abbot William side-stepped the kneeling nuns and walked into the cloister doorway with his hands outstretched. The lord Sheriff of Worcester looked highly bewildered. The Abbot of Pershore seemed about to greet him like a long-lost brother.

'My lord sheriff, you come just when we need you most. Scarce had I offered up a prayer for aid in this calamity, when you and your men appear.' The abbot took in the number of travel-worn men filling the courtyard beyond the cloister, and added weakly, 'Indeed, you come with so many.'

The sheriff took off his riding gauntlets, laid them wearily across his pommel, and stared frowning at Abbot William for some moments before answering.

'Father Abbot, I have no idea what you are talking about. I have come here to ask refreshment and a bed for the night before we take our prisoners from Bredon Hill to Worcester, and to leave a corpse to display here in Pershore as an example to those who might be tempted to break the law. I am weary and hungry and I care little what has occurred here as long as it does not interfere with your hospitality.' He had heard the Compline bell, and realised glumly that he was too late for whatever tempting delicacies the abbot had set before his more illustrious guests.

'Murder!' exclaimed the abbot, dramatically, waving an arm in the direction of the church. 'Murder within the sanctity of our church itself! You must help us. You must discover who has done this terrible thing.'

The sheriff closed his eyes for a moment, and gave a weary sigh. 'Father Abbot, this is not within my jurisdiction. The offence has taken place within your precincts, and I have no rights here.' He wanted none of this, just food for his belly and a bed for his bones.

'Yes, yes, my lord, but this is so serious an incident that I waive my rights and implore your assistance. The murdered man was clerk to the lord Bishop of Winchester and about his lordship's business.' That, hoped the abbot, would get the sheriff's attention.

It did. The sheriff's face clouded. He was torn between wanting nothing to do with this and the knowledge that the victim's identity meant that, assuredly, he should take an interest. 'I must return to Worcester tomorrow, and my undersheriff is sick of an ague. I cannot see that . . .' He stopped in mid-sentence, and a slow smile of relief mixed with malicious pleasure crossed his features. 'However, I am prepared to leave Serjeant Catchpoll, who is most experienced with criminals, and my lord Bradecote, who is no man's fool, to undertake this task.'

Hugh Bradecote's horse started under an incautious spur,

and its rider made a strangled noise in his throat. He had as little wish to remain in Pershore as the sheriff.

'But my lord, I am not a king's officer. I most certainly have no powers of jurisdiction.' He spoke in an urgent undervoice.

The sheriff was having none of it. 'You have as of now. I am appointing you as my undersheriff, in a purely temporary capacity. You can keep your men and a couple of my men-at-arms as well.' The sheriff dropped his voice. 'Catchpoll knows his business very well, but the witnesses here would appreciate neither his manners nor his methods. Keep 'em sweet and let Catchpoll ferret.'

Bradecote grimaced. He was to be a sop to sensibilities, was he? It grated that the sheriff, who had seen enough over the past week to judge him, should place him as a mere buffer. He rather thought he could do better than that. This was not a task he wanted, but if he was to be given command in name, he wanted to exercise it in fact.

He thought for a moment, and then urged his horse forward and dismounted before the abbot, handing the reins to one of his men. 'Father Abbot, I am at your service.' He made obeisance, surprisingly gracefully for a tall man who had been in the saddle all day. 'May I suggest that we begin after Compline. You must continue with the offices of the day, naturally.'

The abbot opened his mouth to agree and then halted. It was true that the office could not be abandoned, but there was the important matter of a fresh corpse lying before the high altar.

Bradecote smiled. He saw the abbot's dilemma, but he also knew how he wanted to proceed. 'The body must not, of course, be moved. Much can be learnt from studying the body as it was discovered.' He omitted to mention that it had occurred to him that much might also be learnt from studying the behaviour of the possible suspects, faced, as he hoped, with gazing at the crime throughout Compline. He hoped the body was not secreted in a side chapel.

The abbot still looked undecided. It was Serjeant Catchpoll who finally persuaded him, by coming forward and offering, in a most reverential tone, to cover the body decently with a blanket if it was in view, to spare the ladies. He nodded in the direction of the two nuns, visible, still on their knees behind the abbot. Bradecote shot him a surprised look. His knowledge of Catchpoll was limited to what he had seen of him over the last few days, and he would have considered the worthy serjeant neither tolerant of squeamishness nor particularly reverent. In fact, he thought him as hard as horse-nails. As a novice was sent running for a blanket, the man sidled up to Bradecote and gave him the benefit of a whispered, 'Don't want anybody making adjustments to their handiwork, do we, my lord.'

Bradecote should have been impressed by the serjeant's forethought, but it was obvious from his tone, which was that of one explaining to a dullard, that Catchpoll wanted to show who was really going to run the hunt for the murderer.

The sheriff watched Bradecote with a satisfied look. The younger man would make every effort to find the culprit, and would almost certainly put Catchpoll's nose out of joint in the process. It was a pity, in a way, that he could not stay to see the outcome. He gave a dismissive nod, which the abbot considered as much directed to himself as to Bradecote, climbed stiffly from the saddle, and headed for the guest hall. His stomach was more in need of sustenance than his soul, and he had no desire to attend Compline. Though supper was past, he had little doubt of being able to secure something to eat from the abbot's kitchen if he bellowed long and loud enough.

Hugh Bradecote gestured to the abbot to continue into the church. The younger nun was paying attention now, looking with doe-wide eyes at the sheriff's men. She placed a hand on the other sister's arm to rouse her from her prayers. The older nun looked up, blinking owlishly, and got to her feet a little unsteadily, leaning against her junior. The pair then stood back to let Abbot William and the two sheriff's officers pass. Within the cloister, Bradecote's glance took in the monks, their line now less than orderly, a large, pale-faced man, a hulking brute with what looked like a permanent frown of perplexity, and three secular dames who had gathered together, sheeplike, as if for mutual support. One of them was sobbing convulsively.

Two men came in behind Catchpoll. One was still almost a youth, a beardless squire or lordling, and the other Bradecote recognised as Waleran de Grismont, who held manors in the shire. De Grismont maintained his customary look of vague boredom, but the young man's eyes had widened in surprise at the tableau within the cloister walls.

The novice returned, breathless, with a blanket, and Catchpoll took it and went ahead into the church. Bradecote let the others enter before he went in to take his place. It gave him the opportunity to choose a vantage point from where he could best view what must now be 'his suspects'.

Within the abbey church it was cool, and motes of dust danced in the vaguely coloured evening light, streaming from the muted greenish yellow hues of a grisaille window. Hugh Bradecote positioned himself carefully by the crossing, at right angles to the nave and choir, although half the Pershore choir monks were facing in the same direction as he was, and all were largely hidden by the rood screen. Leastways, he could see the visitors. Then he groaned, for the great west door had creaked open, and townsfolk keen for the well-being of their souls came in. Bradecote's silent prayer that there should be few of them was answered, and none looked viable as murderers come to view the result of their misdeed. There was a bent and wizened old woman, leaning heavily on a stout blackthorn stick, and supported also by the arm of a skinny, sallow girl of no more than fourteen; grandmother and granddaughter had come to prayers. Behind them came a young woman with the waddling gait of the heavily pregnant, and a tattered, gap-toothed beggar with a crutch. A pompous-looking burgess, glancing round to make sure everyone noticed his rotund presence, entered and stood some distance apart from the others. He was accompanied by a wan and worried dame and three sulky youths, who clearly expected no spiritual benefit from appearing in church with their parents, and would have preferred to have been with their peers cooling themselves in the shallows of the Avon. All of the newcomers gazed with blatant incomprehension at the blanketed form before the altar. Relief flooded through Hugh Bradecote, and he raised his eyes heavenward in mute thanks.

Across in the north transept, Serjeant Catchpoll tried not to smirk. It did not take a reader of minds to see what the sheriff's freshly appointed acting undersheriff was thinking. Well, it mattered not what he thought, as long as he kept from interfering. Catchpoll had served the sheriff many years, and each had a healthy respect for the other's abilities and a knowledge of each other's shortcomings. He suspected the new appointment had been made from a mixture of social nicety and pure mischief, and certainly did not expect Bradecote to be more than a cypher.

Bradecote was mercifully unaware of his subordinate's insubordinate thoughts, and had turned his attention to those who had been present in the enclave when the sheriff's party had arrived. The two nuns, who had remained kneeling in the cloister during the exchange with the abbot, were easy to identify. The younger, who had seemed more poised in the cloister, was now obviously shaken. Her eyes had, if it was possible, widened even more, and were fixed upon the covered corpse, her cheeks ashen. It seemed that the enormity of what had taken place had now sunk in. By contrast, the taller and older sister was impassive. Bradecote was mildly surprised, for he would have expected her to be more disturbed. She had, however, given the blanket-hidden form a long, pensive stare as she took her place, and thereafter had ignored it. Indeed, she seemed to find the office particularly fulfilling, and at one point drew a breath and smiled unexpectedly, as if taking in the perfume of a sweet flower.

The lady behind her had none of her quiet poise. She was a woman about whom everything was pallid. Her pale, red-rimmed eyes swam with tears and her delicate, white hands fidgeted constantly. She was so thin and wraith-like that Bradecote wondered if she were in search of a miracle to cure some deadly illness. He recalled her as the female indulging in incontinent sobbing, though mercifully this had ceased. Her expression now was less of horror than of awe. A little behind her stood the perplexed brute, who he decided was her guard dog. Beside her stood a much younger lady dressed in fine fabrics of a sober hue, who did not concentrate upon the service. At first she looked at the dark heap before the altar, but appeared to tire of it and let her eye rove about the church, passing over Catchpoll and resting briefly upon Hugh himself. Seeing that he was himself regarding her, she gave a small, self-satisfied smile. Here was a woman well used to admiring glances. Her features were fine-drawn, her skin without fault, her figure slim but curvaceous. She was undoubtedly a feast for any man's eye. Her own dwelt longest on the tall form of Waleran de Grismont, lord of Defford. Bradecote knew enough of his reputation to know that the lady would do well to be wary of him. De Grismont did not return her interest, although Hugh had absolutely no doubt he was aware of it. Instead, he stood thoughtfully, black brows knit, as though he could not work out what lay before the altar or find any reason for its presence.

Isabelle d'Achelie watched de Grismont appreciatively and with a thrilling sense of illicit possessiveness. He was tall and dark, almost swarthy, with a mane of near black hair. His features were strong, with a wide mouth, aquiline nose and deep-set, storm-grey eyes beneath heavy black brows. There was a dangerous, lupine quality to the man, which had always attracted rather than repulsed her. After years wedded to Hamo, who had been very reliable, moderately kind and remarkably sickly, Isabelle found the idea of taming a wolf irresistible. Watching him made her throat tighten so much she could barely make the responses.

Standing behind the high-born widow, for Bradecote

assumed from her garb that that was her state, was the third lady who had been present in the cloister. She was partially concealed by the widow, but he could see enough to distinguish a woman who at least showed no shocked pallor at the event. Remarkably calm, thought the sheriff's new man, but that could easily be put down to her being the practical and phlegmatic type.

Mistress Weaver was indeed of such a disposition and sniffed disdainfully at what she took to be a display of aristocratic sensibilities when Isabelle d'Achelie kept her eyes from the body. A murder in such a place was a shock, but death was part of life, as the priest where she worshipped in Winchester so often reminded his flock. This particular death was certainly no loss to the world, though it would undoubtedly be so to the lord Bishop of Winchester himself. Margery Weaver concealed the pleasure at that thought behind her attitude of prayer.

The fair youth standing next to de Grismont was trying, none too successfully, to look worldly-wise. His chin was unshaven, but sprouted nothing that resembled a beard. He stared boldly before him, head held high, announcing to the world as clearly as if he had shouted it, that he was unmoved by the sight of a murdered man in the church. Unfortunately for him, with the exception of Bradecote, the other members of the congregation took no notice of him at all, and the acting undersheriff could barely repress a smile.

At the conclusion of the office the silent congregation trooped out the way they had entered, with the enclave's inhabitants moving into the soft evening light of the cloister, now casting long distorting shadows on its eastern wall. Bradecote and Catchpoll brought up the rear. The song of a blackbird, an everyday, innocent sound, sweetened the air, but was cut short by Bradecote's voice, raised so that all might hear him.

'None shall leave the enclave until the murderer has been taken. The clerk to the lord Bishop of Winchester lies dead, and be assured I mean to find out by whose hand. I will wish to speak to you all, individually, in the morning.'

A murmur of dissent rose, as he had expected, from his listeners. People had business to be done, the king's grace to supplicate. Above this there came the sound of hysterical giggling.

Catchpoll and Bradecote exchanged surprised glances. A reaction was to have been expected from the auditors, but they had looked to hear only complaint at such restraint put upon them. They gazed, stupefied, at the source of the laughter. It was the nervous lady with the pale face and fidgety hands. She was twisting them now in her cloak, but was definitely smiling.

'What is it that you find humorous, lady?' asked Bradecote severely, his dark brows drawn into a frown.

'"By whose hand", you said.' Her voice was brittle and unnaturally high. 'By none here, my lord. That evil little man was taken by the hand of God.'

There was a stunned, almost embarrassed, silence. The giggling became laughter, jarring, ragged and humourless. Some looked away, not wishing to be connected with what might seem a blasphemous statement. The abbot stood agape, like a landed fish, his mouth working silently as he tried to conjure up a reply. Nothing came. After a few moments of awkward silence, broken only by the unlikely laugh, the elder of the nuns went to the lady's side, and took her arm, firmly but gently.

She spoke to her barely above a whisper, but with obvious authority. The unnatural noise ceased with a whimper, and the nun, summoning the other sister with a small movement of her head, began to lead the lady to the guest quarters. The retainer followed in their wake. She made a nodded acknowledgement to the abbot and fixed Bradecote with a cool, almost challenging stare for a moment, as the little party passed him.

Their departure was an unspoken signal for everyone else to disperse. Only lady d'Achelie hung back. She approached the sheriff's men, hands clasped demurely before her, eyes downcast as chastely as any nun professed, but with a faintly provocative smile on her lips. When she did raise her glance, it was to look Bradecote full in the face. Catchpoll was eyeing her appreciatively.

'Of course you must do your duty, my lord.' Her voice was pitched low; artificially so, Bradecote thought, but it was soft and persuasive. 'But my business is with the king himself, and in such times it would be unwise of me to trail across the kingdom more than is needful. I have heard he means to depart to the north in the next sennight. I have nothing to do with such a deed as this, and,' her shapely hand fluttered in the direction of the church, indicative of her feminine fragility of body and will, 'I would ask you to take pity upon my situation.' She flashed him a stunning smile, which wavered in the face of his inscrutability.

'I am loth to inconvenience you, my lady, but there will be no exceptions.'

Bradecote thought he detected surprise in her eyes, before she veiled them with their lids. Men rarely refused Isabelle d'Achelie anything. Well, this time was different. She made a small pouting gesture, and shrugged.

'As you decree, my lord, but I protest it is harsh of you.'

She turned with a swish of her skirts, and walked away with a very conscious grace, knowing male eyes followed every swing of her hips. She would have been less than pleased to know that they belonged to Serjeant Catchpoll, and especially so had she seen the lascivious leer on his face.

'Mayhap the lady will try and persuade me next time.' He looked as if he would enjoy the experience.

Bradecote's face remained expressionless, and his tone unamused. 'I doubt it, Catchpoll. I doubt it very much indeed.' There was a pause. 'Come on then, let us view the body.'

Serjeant Catchpoll grunted, his momentary pleasure disappearing with the lady, replaced with his more usual grim cynicism. It had been a long day, and he was being held from getting back to the comforts of hearth and home. To cap it all, this lord, whom the sheriff had delegated to deal with the killing on a whim, had obviously decided to play law officer and take more than a nominal role in the proceedings. Catchpoll had noted the use of 'I' in Bradecote's announcement to the assembly. He heaved a heavy sigh. The serjeant had only known Bradecote by sight before the venture on Bredon Hill, as one of de Beauchamp's vassal lords who did his service, and although the last few days had left Catchpoll in no doubt of his ability as a soldier, he was clearly a novice when it came to delving into crime. He might be a man you would feel confident to have beside you in a scrap, for his sword arm was strong, and his actions decisive, but it did not mean he was welcome to interfere in serjeanting business. It was with deeply uncharitable thoughts that Catchpoll accompanied Hugh Bradecote back into the silence of the abbey church.

The body, a shapeless mass beneath the dark cloth that had hidden its horrors from the worshippers, lay incongruous in the tidy splendour of the choir; it was a thing of no worth, discarded in haste. Serjeant Catchpoll uncovered the corpse. It was both repellent and impersonal, lying as it did face down. There were no staring, accusing eyes, but the remains of the back of the head were a grim mess of splintered pale bone, blood and brain matter. The two sheriff's men stood gazing thoughtfully for some time at what had so recently been Henri de Blois's clerk, each drawing his own conclusions. Neither was squeamish. Bradecote squatted down on his haunches and disturbed the tatters of vellum with a finger.

'What do you make of these, Serjeant?'

'Charred vellum, my lord,' answered the older man, woodenly.

'Don't try my patience, Catchpoll. I am as tired as you are, and did not ask for this task. However, I will do my best, and expect no less from you.' He paused. 'Do I make myself clear, Serjeant?' The tone brooked no argument.

'Aye, my lord, very clear.' Unspoken animosity crackled between them.

'Well, then. What does the charred vellum tell us?'

'Either the clerk was killed in the process of burning some very private material, using the candle which I extinguished when I covered the body,' he pointed to the solitary candle on the altar steps, 'not wishing to burn both the blanket and

70

corpse together, or he was killed so that the material could be destroyed. The second reason is, of course, the answer.'

'Why?' Bradecote stood up, frowning, and Catchpoll, noticing the expression, smiled unpleasantly.

'Firstly, because the documents have been totally burnt, not removed. Secondly, because a man does not read or burn letters while lying face down on the floor, and thirdly,' Catchpoll paused for a moment for effect, 'because he did not die here.'

'Fair enough,' said Bradecote equably, thus successfully ruining Catchpoll's moment of triumph. 'The murderer may have read the documents and then decided to destroy them, rather than risk being found with them, but I agree that it seems unlikely that the clerk burnt them himself. It does tell us something about the murderer, of course.'

Catchpoll looked mildly interested, but said nothing.

'The murderer can read, Catchpoll.'

Serjeant Catchpoll sniffed. 'That may well be so, my lord, although they could have been sent to commit the murder and told to burn any documents, even if they could not tell what was in them. In some ways it is a cleverer thing to do, for if caught, the killer can reveal nothing of what was written. Very handy if it implicated someone in dark dealings.'

It was a fair point, and Bradecote acknowledged it. 'And I assume that you think the body was moved because of the stains on the scapular?'

Catchpoll regarded Bradecote with narrowed eyes. The man was quicker than he had expected. This fact did not necessarily please him.

'As you say, my lord.' Catchpoll knelt beside the corpse,

grunting as his ageing muscles complained, and lifted the back of the scapular, which was marked some way from the top by a large, dark and drying stain. He shook his head slowly, and spoke almost to himself.

'The blow which broke the skull could not have marked the cloth so far down the back like this, nor with little trace above.' Catchpoll outlined the limit of the stain upon the stone slabs with his finger. 'You can see the way the blood has gathered on the floor, and not as much as if it happened here, nor with the splashes you'd expect. No, this man was killed somewhere else and dragged here on his own scapular. The stain matches. I'd swear he was not long dead, though, because of the amount of blood soaked in the cloth.'

Bradecote nodded. He had seen enough violent death to know how much blood would come from so violent and fatal a blow. He formed a mental picture of the murderer pulling the back of the scapular up to the dead cleric's shoulders and rolling the body onto its back. Dragging it by the scapular would be easy enough over the stone floor, and would prevent an obvious trail of blood from the scene of the act to the altar.

'That raises two new questions. Where did the murder take place, and was the body left in the penitential pose as a disguise to casual observers, or for a reason?'

'The murder must surely have taken place within the church, my lord, but I couldn't make a judgement on the second point.'

'No matter. That might come to light later. Let's hunt around for signs of our victim's last journey.'

The pair split up, Catchpoll taking St Eadburga's chapel in the south transept, and Bradecote turning his attention to the north transept and then the Lady chapel. The serjeant met him there some time later.

'Nothing to be seen on my side, my lord, though I haven't searched the nave yet. It seemed an unlikely place, and the light is failing.'

'Mm,' replied Bradecote distractedly. 'What do you think about this?' He pointed to a darkened crack between two floor slabs. It, too, was losing definition in the deepening gloaming.

Catchpoll squatted down slowly, and pressed his finger along the crack. It came away with a dark, possibly brown, mark. He sniffed his finger tip, meditatively.

'I suppose it could be blood, but there's little enough of it. I'd be happier with flecks of blood and suchlike. Whoever killed the clerk smashed him good and hard with something heavy to do that sort of damage to the skull, perhaps more than once, and it was a blunt object, not something slicing. There would assuredly be signs, aye, and ones that a murderer in a hurry would not notice.'

He sat back on his heels and looked around him. Bradecote was put forcibly in mind of a dog on the scent, and forbore to say anything. Catchpoll certainly had plenty of experience of scenes of crime, and should pick up on things that he, as a complete novice, would miss. Bradecote took stock of the man. 'Grizzled' was the best description of him, in both mien and appearance. His hair was greying and straggling almost to shoulder length, and his stubble-beard showed even more white. The thin lips were merely a gash across the beard, and there were deeply etched lines running from his nose, which had been broken in the past, to his mouth. The eyes were deep set beneath sparse but beetling brows, and crows' feet creased their outer aspect. Everything about him proclaimed the hard bitten professional who knew just how he wanted to go about things, and was not about to change. Hugh Bradecote stroked his own chin meditatively, and realised that he must also present a rough appearance. There was two days' worth of dark stubble on his cheeks, dried blood from a minor head wound matting the lock of hair that fell forward over his frowning brow, and grime, from a long day in the saddle, all over him.

After a short while Serjeant Catchpoll grunted again and got up, easing his back as he did so.

'Well then, I'd say we have our place, my lord. If you look carefully at the stone you'll see a discolouration there.' He indicated a patch which, to Bradecote, looked no more than a change in the shade of the stone itself. 'That was noticed by our killer and wiped up. The edge is a smooth sort of line, not jagged from a splash. There's much smaller marks around and about, as I hoped, but in this light they're tricky to see.'

He stopped before the small altar, and his face performed a contortion that Bradecote interpreted as indicating deep thought. Catchpoll, he decided, could convey a remarkable amount without the need for speech.

'The clerk was hit from behind. We know that from the position of the wound. I would hazard a guess that he was here,' he edged a little closer to the altar, 'and fell forwards when the blow was struck.'

'How do you work that out?' Bradecote was intrigued.

'The altar cloth is slightly askew. The religious like everything just so, and would not have left it like this. I reckon our man fell forward, and though such a blow would be fatal almost instantly, his arm stretched out as if to prevent the fall, without him thinking. He just clutched at the cloth, but was no longer conscious to grasp it proper.'

Bradecote was genuinely impressed at the serjeant's powers of observation. He could not conceal his admiration for such deduction, and remarked as such.

Catchpoll gave an indulgent smile, which effectively doused the small spark of amity which had been kindled between them. Without so much as a word, the serjeant had asserted his place as the professional, forced by circumstance into partnership with an amateur. 'You can play at this as long as you like,' said the look, 'but just you let me get on with the real work.'

Bradecote tried to appear as though this had been lost upon him, but he knew Catchpoll was not fooled. He rubbed his eyes and yawned, suddenly weary beyond belief.

'We'll achieve no more tonight. Make sure that a man-at-arms is left on watch at the entrance to the guest hall. We don't want any sleep-walkers.'

'Indeed so, my lord. I'll set three of 'em to watch, the first up until Lauds. No one will get past.'

'Good. I am for my bed. We will begin again after Prime. Goodnight, Serjeant Catchpoll.'

'Goodnight, my lord.'

Bradecote strode off, determined not to let his shoulders droop with fatigue, though he had been up since the dewy summer dawn, and his stomach was reminding him, with unpleasant pangs, that he had not eaten since they had set off in the morning. Outside the church it still seemed warm, although the sun was very low and would soon be no more than a smudged, pink memory along the western horizon. The air was heavy with summer smells, and bats sped and dived and soared between the buildings, emitting barely audible squeaks. It was a time of day that Bradecote liked, though he was too tired and bruise-stiff tonight to appreciate it properly.

He was thinking of his bed and heading for the guest hall, but suddenly bethought himself of the abbot, who would desire to know what had been achieved thus far. 'Keep 'em sweet,' the lord sheriff had said. Heaving a sigh, he altered his course and went first to the abbot's lodgings, and only when over the threshold wondered if the Benedictine had sought his bed, with the night offices only a few hours distant. Fortunately, Abbot William was too overset to seek his couch, and Bradecote found him sitting in doleful silence. Their conversation was brief and largely one-sided. The abbot nodded frequently, but was only half attending. In the course of his briefing, Bradecote remembered to ask the murdered clerk's name. The sheriff's officer left after a short while, feeling his duty done.

He passed at last into the guest hall with a nod on the way to the man-at-arms by the stables beyond, who made every effort to look alert, and not as if he had been leaning sleepily against the wall. Once his eyes had adjusted, Bradecote sought out his bed without recourse to a rush-light. Ablutions could wait for the morning.

The Second Day

Chapter Four

Despite the weariness of his body, and perhaps because of its aching complaints, Hugh Bradecote awoke early, and lay for some time, gazing without seeing at the roof beams in the cobwebbed gloom above him. He was reviewing everything that had happened since his arrival, which seemed so much longer ago than only the previous evening. He had arrived simply a manorial lord giving service to his overlord, and now suddenly found himself an undersheriff. That, however temporarily, made him an officer of the crown as well as de Beauchamp. The sheriff had selected him from a mixture of weariness and mischief, as he well knew, but even in jest his overlord would not have picked a fool. So here he was, faced with a murder, and no clear indication of how to proceed, beyond letting Serjeant Catchpoll ferret around. That was not enough. He must think, clearly and logically, about exactly what they had discovered, and what linked together. If Catchpoll could do this, Bradecote told himself he was quite capable of doing it too. After all, it was surely not some form of necromancy.

He cleared his mind and began again, considering the victim, and how he was found. There was still a question in his mind about the positioning of the body. Had it been left in the Lady chapel it might not have been discovered until the next day, possibly after the murderer had left about their business. Was it that the murderer was making a point, something about the clerk owing penance? He could not see how the problem could be resolved without the motive of the killer. They did at least know where the murder had taken place, and how, although the exact nature of the weapon was unknown. There was also the matter of time. The man had been alive at Vespers and dead by Compline, only a couple of hours later, but they needed to find out if anyone had seen him during that period. Perhaps he had been in the refectory or at the abbot's table; he must check that. If he had been at neither, then what had been more important than filling his belly?

It was almost impossible that a stranger had walked into the church and committed the murder, and it was certainly none of the townsfolk who had attended Compline. He could not see the old lady's walking stick as a murder weapon. He smiled to himself. No, it had been someone within the enclave. How many of the brethren could be vouched for during the entire period? Bradecote groaned, and offered up a fervent prayer that the majority had chosen to be sociable, for the thought of interviewing upward of thirty choir monks, and Heaven knew how many lay brothers, and at length, left his brain reeling. There would also be the guests and their servants, not forgetting the masons. Once the list of suspects had been reduced to reasonable proportions, he supposed he had best start by interviewing the master mason who had discovered the body. Having made his plan of action he arose to break his fast, and found his presence had a very dampening effect upon the guest hall occupants. Hugh Bradecote was an open sort of man, quite serious, but not without humour, and to be greeted with cautious looks and a cessation of conversation as people looked cautiously at him over their bread, was a new experience for him. He consoled himself with the thought that he must look as if his new role suited him, and so it was a cheerful and apparently confident acting undersheriff who soon afterwards strode purposefully, but with a long-legged grace, across the abbey courtyard to where Serjeant Catchpoll was in quiet conversation with Gyrth, the man-at-arms, who was reporting a peaceful watch.

Catchpoll turned at the sound of the footsteps, and watched his unwelcome superior stride towards him. Bradecote was a tall man, fighting fit but inclined to the lean, and Catchpoll judged him to be but a few years over thirty, but the watchful expression that was natural to him made him appear older. Last night, the situation had kept his features serious, but this morning he was in good humour, and the vestige of a smile lengthened the line of his mouth. He looked younger, and far too keen for Catchpoll's liking.

'You'll be all right if there's any old crones to speak with,' ventured Gyrth, grinning.

'You keep your tongue still in your head, lest his lordship

hear you,' growled Serjeant Catchpoll, his thin lips scarcely moving.

Gyrth shut up, but the broad grin remained. It had been the one light moment during the hunt for the outlaws of Bredon Hill. Catchpoll, conscious of his position, and with the sheriff himself on hand, had made his enquiries en route with an unusual degree of high-handedness. It had been unfortunate that he had sought information from an old woman who had not responded in the manner he expected. She had looked upon him with a rheumy eye and a curled lip, as if he were of no more importance than a stray cur, and had turned away without even so much as a word in reply.

The lord Bradecote had been in the forefront, in conversation with the sheriff, and had urged his horse forward before Catchpoll could harangue the old harridan. He had leant forward, his arm nonchalantly across the bow of his saddle, and spoken to the woman in unaccented English, gently, and with a singularly charming smile. One moment there had been a cantankerous old witch keen only to see the back of them, and suddenly she was transformed into a beaming, grandmotherly figure, who bobbed a creaking curtsey, smiled up at Bradecote, almost blushing, and gave the desired information without demur. When Bradecote thanked her she simpered and darted back into her cottage, only to reappear a moment later with a couple of dubious-looking honey cakes in her gnarled grasp. She had pressed them upon him, much to his embarrassment, and to the sheriff's loud and obvious amusement. Catchpoll had not been as entertained, especially when the sheriff had suggested he try the lord Bradecote's methods on the next peasant woman they met, and see if she would feed him too.

The serjeant, recalling the incident as well as Gyrth, cast the memory aside and schooled his features into the semblance of a respectful greeting.

'Good morning, my lord.'

Catchpoll had, thought Bradecote, the self-satisfied look of a man who had been experiencing the joys of the day for some considerable time.

'Gyrth says that nobody left the guest hall after you went to bed.'

Gyrth nodded, confirming the pronouncement, with the slightly fatuous smile still fixed to his lips. Catchpoll continued, 'The lord sheriff is not yet about. Also, the lord abbot had the corpse removed to the mortuary chapel last night, my lord. I gave permission, because I did not think you would have further need of seeing the body as it lay, and it would disrupt the brothers at Lauds.' He made it sound as if the feelings of the brethren mattered to him, though Bradecote knew that they did not. 'I did not wish to disturb you after you had retired, my lord Bradecote.' Now he added equally insincere solicitude for his superior's rest.

The serjeant assumed the manner of the loyal subordinate who had no wish to burden his superior with unnecessary trifles, and Bradecote swore inwardly. Catchpoll was quite correct in his assumption that the removal of the body was in order, but he had shown the Abbot of Pershore that he was able to take important decisions alone, and had shown up Bradecote's failure to see that the problem would arise.

Serjeant Catchpoll coughed. 'I have taken the liberty of

finding out about the movements of the brothers during the time the murder must have taken place. Most of them, thankfully, seem to have been together and can vouch for each other. The infirmarer was with a dying man in the infirmary. The man died in the night, so I could not confirm his story, but the infirmarer has been a brother here since childhood, and the clerk was never here before. There seemed no reason to suspect him, so I let him return to his potions and patients.'

The cheerful mood in which Hugh Bradecote had crossed the courtyard had evaporated in moments. Catchpoll had everything under control, and was happy to show it. Gyrth was now studiously avoiding eye contact. The man-at-arms had known the serjeant some years, and did not give much for the chances of the sheriff's new man against the wily Serjeant Catchpoll.

There was nothing the acting undersheriff could do but commend Catchpoll's actions. 'Very good, Serjeant. Have we a final number, among the brethren, to whom we should speak formally?' He considered the use of 'we' a clever move.

'Aye, my lord. The lord abbot was alone after supper, until the Compline bell.'

Catchpoll noted, with pleasure, his superior's look of horror, and then continued, 'But there is but one door from his lodging and it is certain he did not leave the building. One of the novices wanted private word with him, but did not know if all his guests had left, and preferred to wait until the lord abbot himself emerged. This was only when the bell sounded.'

Bradecote was beginning to lose his temper, which gave Catchpoll secret amusement. 'I do not require a list of those we need not see. I asked for those with whom we should speak, Catchpoll.'

'Indeed, my lord. There remain only half a dozen monks to be seen; two novices, Brother Porter at the gatehouse, old Brother Jerome, who apparently slipped away to rejuvenate himself with sleep under a tree in the orchard, Brother Oswald the herbalist and the sub-prior, Brother Remigius.'

'That is to the good. We will see them in that order, but only after we have spoken to the man who discovered the body. The master mason, wasn't it?'

'As you say, my lord. Master Elias the mason, native of St Edmondsbury. He has been told to await your will. The masons, by the by, were all out ale drinking, and stuck together. Each and every one can vouch for the other, and judging by their fear of returning ale-sodden and being beaten by the master, none were so far gone as to be unreliable. Where shall I bring Master Elias?'

'The abbot's parlour. I had words with him before I sought my bed last night.' Bradecote gave a tight smile which as good as said, 'So I wasn't as cloth-brained as you supposed.'

Without waiting, he turned and headed for the abbot's lodging, but then halted and turned back.

'I take it that you will have no problem with the interviews if any of them are not in English? Your accent is appalling, Serjeant, but your words were perfectly clear to Abbot William.'

'It don't bother me if it's in fancy language, my lord. Most folk talk slow when they think their words important, like when there's a capital crime. The real undersheriff – and 'real' had just a hint of stress – 'my lord de Crespignac, well, his English is scarce beyond giving orders, and a few choice oaths, so it is well that I've picked up some Foreign. Not his fault, of course, because he was born abroad. It is fair enough for such as kings and earls to use it; men who have large land holdings across the water as well as here, but as for the rest . . . English should be all you need if your land is here, begging your pardon.'

'No offence taken.' Bradecote refused the bait. 'Did you find out if Eudo the Clerk was at supper, Serjeant Catchpoll?'

'He did not partake of food in the refectory, my lord, and those I've spoken to so far did not see him after Vespers. I should say whoever killed him did not do so having come upon him by accident. He went to the Lady chapel to meet someone, and that someone did for him.'

'Right.' There was little else Bradecote could say. 'Then let us get on with the task in hand.' He walked away, aware that Catchpoll had every right to think he was the master of the situation and the sheriff's new appointee was just a puppet. It was most galling.

The atmosphere at Chapter was a peculiar mixture of sombre reflection, unease and a vague, suppressed excitement, at least among the novices. Their elders looked more than usually thoughtful, but the optimism of youth meant that the novelty of the event had dispelled their initial horror. None of them knew the victim, nor saw themselves as being particularly at risk, and it certainly made a change to the regularity of their existence.

Abbot William was old enough and experienced enough to gauge their mood, however much he might deplore it. The whole thing was, in his view, a disaster. The very nature of the crime was abhorrent, but in addition he was going to have to write to the lord Bishop of Winchester both to give information and, hopefully, to exonerate his house. No doubt it was pure misfortune that had meant Eudo met his death in Pershore, but it was a stain on the community nonetheless and Henri de Blois was known to have a long and unforgiving memory. The abbot had spent several of the few hours in his bed in constructing suitable phrases in his mind, and it was a tired and somewhat tetchy abbot who presided in the chapter house.

'My brothers, whatever occurs we must continue in God's work. The routine of this house must be disrupted as little as the investigation will permit. I will not have,' and he let his eye fall upon the novices, who looked self-conscious, 'idle gossip about this wickedness, nor permit speculation and distrust to rear its evil head. Our duty is clear. We must pray for the soul of our brother in Christ, as we must also for the soul who faces damnation as the consequence of weakness. We are all sinners, my brothers, and if our sins are less heinous we should give thanks for God's aid and not set ourselves up in pride.'

He looked around him as he continued. 'Prayers for the deceased will be included in every office, but I would request that all of us keep him in our thoughts and prayers as we go about our tasks. We will now attend to Chapter business as usual. Brother Sacrist has news of a bequest of land at Throckmorton, I know, and I am desirous of your views upon the exchange of a bone from the finger of the sainted Eadburga in return for a fine Gospel of the Winchester school and a gift in coin from our sisters at Romsey. Representations have been made to me by the sacrist and another sister on behalf of Abbess Matilda. The blessed Eadburga's own sister was of that house of nuns, and they are most desirous of some relic. I am mindful to accede to this request, but it is a matter for the community to discuss.'

There followed some debate which dragged minds from the contemplation of murder, and Abbot William was conscious of a sense of gratitude towards the nuns of Romsey, however inadvertent their assistance in a time of trouble. When he drew the proceedings to a close, and with the agreement he sought, he thought he sensed a return to more normal concerns among the men within his charge who had stepped back from the world. It was, he mused sadly, typical of the strife-riven secular world that it had intruded so cruelly into their life. He would pray most assiduously for guidance and a swift conclusion to the investigation.

Master Elias had the air of confidence befitting a man who dealt on a daily basis with the upper echelons of society, both secular and religious. He looked suitably grave, but no longer exhibited the sickly pallor of the previous evening. He had not lost sleep over the events in the church. He nodded deferentially at Bradecote, took the offered seat, and planted his capable hands firmly on his knees. It declared him a simple, straightforward man, quite prepared to give simple and straightforward answers to the questions of the law, and secure in the knowledge of his innocence. Catchpoll wondered whether it was the way he dealt with authority out of habit, or whether it was a conscious act.

When his men had returned from the town, their master had been short with them, and had made his anger obvious to Arnulf, the thoughtless apprentice. While the masons were agog at the news of the murder, and keen to discover what they had missed, Master Elias had chivvied them to their beds and sought his own. Once he had decided upon how much to divulge about his own movements, he settled peaceably. Elias of St Edmondsbury had imagination, but only in his work.

The acting undersheriff began by asking about the events after Vespers.

Elias regarded Bradecote with a look of composure. 'Let us not creep towards what you seek. It was I who found the corpse, my lord, so it is what you want to know about. I admit that it fair took me aback for a moment or so, and then I came out into the cloister, where the lord abbot was leading the brothers to Compline, and told what I'd found.'

'What exactly were you doing in the workshop, Master Elias? Your men had gone into the town, yes?'

The master mason was quite prepared for the question, and answered promptly enough. 'Aye, my lord. I gave them an hour or so off, but it has always been my way to check the workshop. I am a good master, any will say that, but I demand high standards from my masons, in the craft and in how they leave the workshop each night. Good job I did look, too, because it wasn't left as I would want, not by a long way.'

'In what way did it fail?' Bradecote shot a quick glance at Catchpoll.

'Well, the floor hadn't been swept properly, nor the bench cleaned. I don't accept dust all about the workshop. Untidiness in the little things leads to untidiness with chisel and mallet, and that is both wasteful of time and stone, and dangerous to limb and eye. What was worse, there was even a mallet left out on the bench, not in the rack, and the men know how I expect all the tools accounted for. Mind you, I gave Arnulf the back of my hand when he returned. He was the apprentice given the tidying task last night, and his mind was on what was to come, not what was to be done. You can understand why I don't give them time off, regular.'

The sheriff's men tried not to appear too interested in this information, and Catchpoll said nonchalantly, 'I would not have thought you a master who was often disobeyed, Master Elias.'

The master mason puffed himself up importantly, and thrust his chin forward in an effort to emphasise his unassailable authority. 'No indeed. My men rarely act foolish.' He added fairly, 'Unless of course they've taken drink, and we all know that when the drink is in, the sense goes out.' His expression became very serious. 'I let them off of an occasional evening, because they are not permitted to drink ale when working, just small beer. Chisels are sharp, ladders are tall, and dying too easy. I have seen it often enough over the years, the waste of a good man through a moment of thoughtlessness.'

'So it was unusual for the apprentice to leave things out of place?' Bradecote interrupted what could become a list of the dangers facing masons. He could see what Catchpoll was trying to ascertain.

Master Elias furrowed his brow. 'Most unusual.'

Hugh Bradecote made a mental note to visit the masons' workshop, and cast about in a new direction.

'You are a craftsman of some note, Master Elias. Abbot

William told me you had come here with recommendations from Ely, Oxford and Abingdon. In your wide travels, had you come into contact with Eudo the Clerk before?'

The master mason shook his head. He had been expecting to be asked about the man, and it posed no problem, although he would be glad enough to set the conversation in another direction.

'I have worked in many places, but I have no cause to speak with the brethren, other than those obedientiaries concerned with the fabric of their buildings, and of course the head of the house.' He spoke no less than the truth, and he had not actually been asked if he had merely seen Eudo before.

'You have not been to Romsey? The two nuns are from there.'

'I have not. I prefer not to work in a house of women.' He grimaced. 'My father, who was a master mason before me, did so once, and complained ever after. Trouble, they are. They change their minds, see, enough to drive a sane man mad. You get half way through a design and then they think of something they want changing, as though you could add to stone as well as take away.'

Catchpoll nodded in fellow feeling.

Bradecote returned to more pertinent matters. 'How was it that you decided, yesterday evening, to give the men time in the town when you admit that you do so only rarely?'

'It had been a hot day, my lord, both in the confines of the workshop and up on the north transept. The heat takes it out of the men, and frays tempers, which leads to mistakes, and you cannot afford that up top, or with expensive stone.

That it happened to be the evening of a death is but chance, aye, and mischance for me if it leads to you suspecting me of wrong-doing.' The master mason sounded suitably aggrieved at the possible doubting of his honesty.

'Could you tell us exactly what happened, and what you found, as you did to the lord abbot.' It was an instruction rather than a question. Bradecote was not going to follow up the last answer by assuring the man that he was not suspected.

'Aye, my lord. It was simple enough. I was in the workshop, after supper, between Vespers and Compline, checking things over and considering a new design. There was a natural fault in the latest block and I would rather use it than discard the stone.' His voice warmed briefly with the enthusiasm of a man who loves his work. 'There's great satisfaction to be had, getting the best from a piece, especially when nature brings out a problem to be overcome.'

'Indeed. But to continue?'

'Well, eventually I came up with a solution and, since it had to be close to Compline, I left the workshop through the door into the north transept. I had thought to take my place early in the nave. As I reached the crossing I turned first to the altar, as you would, and saw the cowled penitent before it. I would have passed on without disturbing him if it had not been for the fly.'

'The fly?' Catchpoll looked puzzled.

'Aye, a fly was buzzing round his head, and even a man at prayer won't suffer a fly on his pate without a twitch. It was just odd, that's all, not natural. Then I got this feeling something wasn't right. I couldn't say what, just not right, so I drew closer, and that's when I saw his head had been stove in. Terrible it was, enough to turn a man's stomach.'

'But not yours,' Bradecote noted.

'Well, I'll not say I didn't feel my gorge rise, my lord, for I did, but . . . look, I've been a mason all my adult life, apprentice to master, and it is a craft with its dangers. I've seen what a man looks like after falling from eighty feet, or more, and often enough not to want to gawp. Still, this was nasty . . .'

The master mason shook his head, more in disapproval than shock, thought Catchpoll.

'What did you make of the burnt documents, Master Elias?' Bradecote had not finished. He made the question sound casual.

'Didn't make anything at all, my lord,' responded Elias, looking blankly at him. 'I was just concerned at having found a dead man in the church. Aye, and one who could not have taken his own life. The man who did it could have been close by, so I had no wish to linger. That would be a foolish thing, even though I would say I was a man who could take care of himself. I headed straight out as the Compline bell rang.'

'Did you see or hear anyone else in the church while you were there?'

This was easier. 'No, my lord. And it's not likely I would have heard anyone while I was in the workshop.' He paused. 'There now, I almost forgot. There was someone, someone in St Eadburga's chapel when I came in. I couldn't say who, but I could hear whispering, like one at prayer. Perhaps that was that clerk, before he was killed.' He smiled at Bradecote as if expecting recognition for his feat of memory.

The acting undersheriff did not smile, but nodded an

acknowledgement. 'Is there anything else you think might be useful?' Bradecote had no expectation of a reply and was surprised at the master mason's answer.

'Well, nothing directly so, my lord, but I was thinking that if you wanted to know more about the dead man you might try asking Brother Remigius, the sub-prior here. He used to be at Winchester, see, and yesterday, while I was speaking with him, the lord bishop's clerk approached and spoke to him. What he said was none of my concern, and I did not pry, but I tell you true, Brother Remigius looked about as happy as a man who's had a fox in his coop.'

'Thank you, Master Elias, for your help. You may return to your labours.'

The big man stood up from the chair, looked from Catchpoll to Bradecote and made for the door. As he reached it, Bradecote halted him with a final question, thrown as an afterthought.

'Your work must involve much calculation and planning. I take it you are a lettered man?'

Elias smiled proudly. 'That I am, my lord. Taught to read by the brothers in St Edmondsbury when I was a lad. My mother, God rest her, thought I would take the cowl,' he chuckled, 'but I was more interested in the building than the life of contemplation. Not for me, the tonsure.'

He left, looking cheerful.

'What do you think then, Catchpoll? Would a man like that seek to avoid a possible threat, or would he have been intrigued enough to see if any of the vellum was readable?'

Catchpoll sneered. 'He wasn't afraid of anyone else being present, not him. I don't see him being perturbed at the thought, just alert. Not the simple soul he would have us believe, is Master Elias, and observant too. His work means he looks carefully. If anything was still to be seen, he would have seen it.'

'Or been the one to set it aflame.'

'Oh, aye. The person who "discovers" the victim must be the killer, my lord?' Catchpoll shrugged. 'It is certainly common enough, but you have to watch what is common.'

'Perhaps, though, he could be one without the other.' Bradecote ignored the implied criticism.

Catchpoll was dismissive. 'If he read what was there, but was not the killer, it would be a strange coincidence if it turned out to be something he would wish to destroy.'

Bradecote agreed. He realised, with no little surprise, that he was suddenly becoming unnaturally suspicious, and, Heaven help him, like the serjeant.

'He could still be our man. We know of no motive, but he was in the right place, and is easily strong enough to have dragged the body.'

'So do we ferret around in the masons' workshop or work through the list of unaccounted for brethren, my lord?'

The younger man ran his long fingers through his dark hair and sighed. 'I have no doubt everything is now as it should be there, and nothing of significance will remain, but yes, we ferret, Catchpoll. And we pray for a sign.' He pulled a wry face.

'Not a sign,' muttered Catchpoll, under his breath. 'Priests wants signs. I wants evidence.'

Chapter Five

The lord Sheriff of Worcester saw his serjeant and newly appointed acting undersheriff emerge from the abbot's lodgings as he himself sought out Abbot William to take his leave. He noted the disgruntled expression of Serjeant Catchpoll, and the frown furrowing Bradecote's brow. Taking it seriously, was he? Well, all to the good.

Bradecote noticed the sheriff and abandoned his original intention of visiting the masons' workshop, heading instead to his superior. Catchpoll lengthened his stride to make sure he reached the sheriff at the same time.

'Good to see you both hard at work,' said the sheriff, cheerily. 'I hear de Grismont is one of the visitors in the guest hall. Seeing how he takes being left swinging his heels, while you get about the business, almost makes me wish I could stay.'

He shook his head in mock sorrow. In fact, what would

be entertaining was watching Serjeant Catchpoll and Hugh Bradecote establishing their positions. Catchpoll, de Beauchamp knew from long experience, did not think very much of his lords and masters, insubordinate and contrary bastard that he was. His undersheriff, de Crespignac, grumbled persistently and craved his removal in a half-hearted way, but the wily old fox was too good a man not to use to the full, and the sheriff had a sneaking respect for him, though he would not admit it out loud. How Bradecote would rub up against him would be very interesting; no fool was Hugh Bradecote.

'However, if I don't get the corpses back to Worcester today they'll be too far gone to string up properly, and besides, I don't like travelling with half the flies in the shire trailing in my wake like mourners.'

Bradecote and Catchpoll made vague noises indicating agreement.

'Right, then. I will make my farewells to the Father Abbot and be away. From experience, Bradecote, if you have got nowhere after a week, then you had best let everyone be about their business. I'd normally just leave the death unsolved. It happens that way sometimes. But in this case I would suggest you give out that it was a motiveless killing by a madman unknown in Pershore. It will give the Abbot of Pershore an answer to the Bishop of Winchester's questions, which is what he will need most. Otherwise I may end up returning to investigate the murder of my own men by those kept in the enclave, and de Grismont would be top of my list of suspects.' He laughed at his own joke, and nodded his dismissal. 'Good luck.'

De Beauchamp did not think Abbot William would like the

'unknown madman' to feature in his letter to Henri de Blois. It was so obvious as a cover for 'we could not find out who did it'. On the other hand, clerics were inclined to get very squeamish over hangings and retribution. Whichever the outcome, he was not going to be a happy man, but the lord Sheriff of Worcester was not there to make people happy.

As Bradecote and Catchpoll had feared, the wooden workshop was clean and tidy. Most of the men were up amongst the lashed poles of scaffolding, ropes and winches. A couple of the most senior carvers were working on blocks of stone, and Bradecote could see how Elias regarded the work as drawing out something from within. They worked deftly, though the muscles in their dust-covered forearms showed power as well as skill. They spared the two intruders barely a glance as they entered and began their search. It was a waste of time, thought Bradecote, merely a case of saying that they had checked. Serjeant Catchpoll, he noted with irritation, was hardly bothering to search at all, and was instead engrossed in the study of an angel's head emerging from the efforts of chisel and mallet.

'Ah, it's a mystery to me how you can create a thing of such life from a dead lump of stone.' Catchpoll sounded enthralled and admiring. 'A rare gift, indeed.'

His superior blinked. Catchpoll was not a man he would have seen as having a single fibre in his body that could appreciate the artistic.

'Aye, some has the gift and some hasn't, but each to his own, my friend.' The mason smiled slowly, keeping his eye on his work.

'The mallets vary in size according to the delicacy of the work?' The answer was obvious, but Catchpoll put the question nonetheless.

'Bless you, of course they do, and to match the chisels also.'

'I heard there was quite an outburst from Master Elias when one of them was out of place last night.' Catchpoll was fingering the smooth, hard surface of a mallet next to the craftsman, who chuckled, and then coughed as he took the pale dust into his lungs.

'Oh aye, the master likes everything in its place. Poor Arnulf swore blind he had left all as it should be, but it didn't save him from a hiding. No harm done, mind. If apprentices weren't shown their errors with a clout, occasional like, how would they learn? Now when I was first apprenticed in the craft . . .'

Bradecote had at last comprehended what Catchpoll was doing, and marvelled at the skill of it. He did not say a word, much as he wished to be involved, for fear of ruining the whole, but folded his arms and stood back, observing a master at work, as Catchpoll steered the mason from reminiscences of youth to the events of the previous evening.

'A mallet was left out and the bench was dirty, as was told.'

'That one there.' The mason jerked his head to one adjacent to the gap in the rack where the mallet in his hand would fit. 'And 'tis a mite odd, the dust, because nobody was actually working here yesterday afternoon. Edwin here was up top.' He nodded towards his neighbour.

'That I was, and have a hot red neck as a result of it.' Edwin set a finger gingerly to the back of his neck.

Catchpoll took the mallet from its place, handling it as if

it were a fragile item of great beauty, turning it in his hands and inspecting it carefully. His brow was furrowed with concentration, and Bradecote was conscious of a desire to hold his breath. After a short while Serjeant Catchpoll's brow cleared, and he inhaled slowly and contentedly. He looked across at Bradecote and nodded very slightly.

'I think we need not disturb you further in your work,' he announced brightly to the two stonemasons. 'Shall we continue, my lord?'

'Er, yes indeed, Serjeant Catchpoll.'

Bradecote did not need any encouragement. The pair stepped back into the peace of the church and headed for the cloister. There, where there were no echoes to betray soft words, Catchpoll confirmed what Bradecote knew he must have discovered.

'That mallet was what dashed the man's brains, no doubt of it. It was hefty enough and the right size. Besides which, there was a dark line where head met handle. Whoever returned the mallet tried to remove any sign of blood or brains, and probably used stone dust as a final disguise.' Catchpoll was jubilant.

'Which accounts for the dust on the bench.'

'Which accounts for the dust on the bench, yes. And for Arnulf getting a beating for laziness, which he did not deserve. We progress with the cwisker ruby.'

'The what?' Bradecote looked baffled.

'It's Latin, my lord.' Catchpoll beamed, clearly proud to show knowledge over ignorance. 'Something I have learnt from the lord sheriff himself. Always seek the answers to the cwisker ruby, oh, and the cweemodo. Who, why . . .'

'Where and how.' Realisation dawned on the sheriff's newest officer. He smiled. 'Of course. *Quis, cur, ubi et qui modo.*'

'As I said, my lord. We know the where and the how. We now proceed with the why and, most importantly, the who.'

Bradecote was silent for a moment, slotting the information about the mallet into place in his brain, and then spoke, almost to himself.

'This also means that the time during which the murder could have taken place is reduced, and that the murderer was afraid of discovery. He certainly did not think to return the mallet to its place. He could not have expected Master Elias, but when he did hear him in the transept he would have been trapped in the workshop.'

'You forget the door to the outside, my lord.' Catchpoll shook his head, and sighed, as a craftsman might at the cumbersome attempts of his apprentice. 'The murderer, who need not be "he", could have slipped out and returned through the main gate, innocent as you please.'

It was a blow, but Bradecote recovered himself. If the murderer had gone out by that route, Brother Porter would have seen them as they passed his gate, and it was quite possible that Master Elias, who was careful with his property, would have barred the door, and would have been certain to notice if it was unbarred when he entered.

'He was keen enough to tell us about the other things he found out of place. Had the door been unbarred, he would have added that to the list of reasons to clout his apprentice.'

Serjeant Catchpoll accepted Bradecote's theories calmly, and, if he was in any way impressed, he concealed it perfectly. Not wishing to recall the master mason too soon, which might be interpreted either as having failed to ask an important question in the first place, or holding him as chief suspect, Bradecote and Catchpoll divided the interviews of the monks between them. It was unlikely that any could be serious suspects, but they might have incidental information.

Brother Porter was adamant that he had not left his duties even for a moment between Vespers and Compline, and had admitted none but the sheriff and his party, excepting one of the lord de Grismont's men, who had taken his lordship's horse out for exercise in the cooler air. The horse had become cantankerous in the stable, had kicked a hole in a partition, and he certainly looked mettlesome and in need of a gallop to work off his ill humour, or so said the groom.

Hugh Bradecote found the novices as much in awe of the sheriff's representative as of their abbot, and singularly unhelpful. They lowered their eyes in humility, and were vague, as if they hoped to give him the answers he desired whether the truth or not. Their sub-prior, Remigius, could give no proof of what he had been doing after the end of the meal in the refectory, for he had sought solitude to consider a problem, an 'inner crisis' all of his own. Even had others seen him, he would not, he said, have noticed them. Only the Compline bell recalled him to his duties. Bradecote asked where he had gone for this contemplation, but other than denying being in the church, Remigius seemed unable (or was it just unwilling?) to say. There was certainly something still preying upon the monk's mind, but asking him bluntly what it was seemed unlikely to get a response.

'You came here from Winchester, Brother, so I hear. You must have known Brother Eudo then.'

'By sight of course, my lord, but he was oft times away upon the lord bishop's business, and . . .' Brother Remigius halted and studied the floor, and Bradecote groaned inwardly. He was going to have to drag anything useful from the man.

'And what, Brother Remigius?'

'It's not charitable to say so, my lord, but Brother Eudo was not well liked among the brethren. No doubt he was a conscientious worker for our bishop, but among those of us who do not venture much outside our walls he was considered lacking in humility and a sower of discord. In community we should live together in charity, but we are human, and fall into sin. We are guilty of not forgiving, of anger, of jealousy, and Brother Eudo was always glad to tell one man of the failings of another and then smile upon the consequences.' The sub-prior of Pershore shook his head, as if glad to rid himself of the memory.

The undersheriff hid his momentary delight. Here was one who had knowledge of the victim and disliked him. He tried to elicit more information in the subtle way Catchpoll had used with the mason in the workshop, but the man just looked more miserable and was as closed as an oyster. Bradecote did not see the man as a killer, however, and could see no motive. A Benedictine would surely not imperil his immortal soul because another brother did not match the pattern of rectitude expected, and 'told tales'.

He rejoined Catchpoll, who had passed an equally fruitless couple of hours, and looked as happy as a man with toothache. Bradecote decided it would be best not to unleash a morose

Catchpoll alone on the sensibilities of the ladies, especially the pallid fidgety one, whom he wanted to interview first in the afternoon. After the midday meal he waited in the abbot's parlour while the serjeant went to fetch her. He hoped more would be gained from the women than the monks, although he had his doubts. His own wife would, he thought, be totally useless at remembering anything that fell outside the scope of her daily round. Ela was almost pathetically keen to please, and fearful of failing her lord in any way, but faced with the sort of questions they were about to set these dames, she would be reduced to wide-eyed panic. He frowned, conscious that it was the first time he had thought of his wife since setting out with the sheriff, though she was advanced in pregnancy with their first child.

He had been told often enough that women in her condition had odd crotchets and fancies, but, rather to his surprise, Ela had become marginally less irritating and developed a measure of serenity as her pregnancy advanced. Theirs was the common sort of marriage for their station, based upon pragmatism and land, but on his side the best that could be said for his feelings was that he had some small affection for her, frequently offset by her fluttery and illogical behaviour. He tried to be a considerate husband, especially while she was carrying, but the strain of not showing frustration at her inherent stupidity was wearing, and he had regarded the sheriff's summons with no small degree of relief. He experienced a twinge of guilt, but set all thoughts of her aside as soon as the door opened, and he returned to the task in hand.

Serjeant Catchpoll ushered the birdlike lady, who had been

identified as the lady Courtney, into the abbot's parlour, and then stood by the door where his presence would be less intrusive. He made no mention of the difficulty he had encountered in keeping her 'mastiff' out of the chamber. Only the lady's soft command for him to stay on its far side had prevented him forcing his way in, and Catchpoll wondered if he might whine if his lady did not reappear within a short while. Bradecote recognised the usefulness of having an experienced watcher of people, especially guilty people, in the interview, and caught Catchpoll's eye for a moment before inviting lady Courtney to sit. That the serjeant was also watching his performance was best not dwelt upon. The nervous dame took her seat with a murmur that might have been thanks, her expression a mixture of anxiety and a peculiar childlike pleasure. She was not an old woman in years, and vestiges of an earlier ethereal beauty clung to her like wisps of mist in the Evesham Vale, but she appeared preternaturally aged by life. The stray hairs that had escaped her coif were white, and her face was gaunt, almost underfed. The skin was pale, and drawn taut over the fine bone structure of her face. She gazed at them with misty, pale blue eyes, whose rims were dully red, as if tears were a major part of her daily existence. Her hands, never still, worked agitatedly in her lap.

It had seemed an obvious move to question first the person who seemed only too pleased to talk to them, and appeared to have some direct knowledge of the deceased, but neither serjeant nor acting undersheriff held out any great hopes for the encounter.

'Well, my lady Courtney, why do you think that the lord Bishop of Winchester's clerk was murdered?' Bradecote began briskly, not wishing to give this strange woman the opportunity to let her tale wander.

'Not murdered, you must not say murdered.' She did not look at him, but stared into the middle distance. The voice was pale also, barely more than a whisper, echoing her appearance, but as insistent as a petulant child's.

'Killed, then,' Bradecote's tone was patient.

'Why? Because it was a Judgement of Heaven. God has punished him for his terrible sins. There is no crime.' She had an equally childlike simplicity to her approach.

'But, forgive me, his skull was smashed to a pulp with a mason's mallet. He did not fall dead without cause, nor was he struck by lightning.'

The pallid lady, surprisingly unmoved by the description of such a messy and violent death, smiled beatifically at the sheriff's men. She could see no problem, yet Catchpoll winced and his face performed a contortion that suggested he was suffering acute pain. Bradecote could not see why, for he was clearly not squeamish.

'God works in ways we are unable to understand, my lord.' Lady Courtney's response drew him back.

Serjeant Catchpoll now sighed meaningfully, and raised his eyes heavenward. Hugh Bradecote rubbed his chin thoughtfully. He was not getting anywhere on the reason for Eudo the Clerk's death, although the lady had obviously some deep seated reason for loathing the man, if one so insipid could achieve so strong an emotion as loathing.

'How do you know that his sins were any greater than yours or mine, my lady?'

Two spots of colour appeared on the woman's thin, white cheeks, and her brows drew together. When she spoke, her voice had dropped an octave, and held a vehemence at odds with her natural gentle mien.

'That man was a wicked, cruel thief,' she declared, her voice shaking with passion.

Catchpoll, who had apparently lost interest in the proceedings, and had been contemplating a woodlouse clambering, slowly and determinedly, across the rush-strewn floor, looked up suddenly, incredulous.

'Him, a thief!'

Bradecote shot him a quelling glance, and spoke to the lady, gently, as if eliciting information from a shy infant.

'Did he steal something from you, lady?'

Lady Courtney gazed at the floor and nodded, the action continuing as if she knew not how to stop it.

'What was it?' Bradecote was patient.

She swallowed hard and raised her face to meet him eye to eye, suddenly distraught.

'My husband.'

There was a momentary silence. Catchpoll now regarded her warily, as if her madness might make her dangerous. Bradecote strove to overcome his own surprise and puzzlement. 'I see,' he said slowly, although it was far from the truth, 'But how did he do that?'

'My husband is . . . was . . . is, a good man, a fine man.' Emma Courtney ceased to fidget. 'He went to Winchester, and there fell sick of a fever. He was terribly ill, cared for in the infirmary of the New Minster, he was, and Henri de Blois himself came and prayed for him. After a week he began to recover, but while he was still weak, that Eudo came to him. He said how important the lord bishop's intercessions had been, how little hope there had been before. He kept telling my poor husband how much he owed to God and to the Bishop of Winchester. He persuaded him to make over some land revenues to the abbey, but he also told him that God had spared his life and that he ought to show his gratitude by taking the cross and going on pilgrimage to Jerusalem. My lord returned home, and made instant preparations to leave. Goodness knows, I tried to prevent him, begged him to stay, but he said he had promised and that it was the will of God.' She snorted. 'The will of the lord bishop's clerk, more like!'

Suddenly the animation that had possessed her disappeared. She seemed to shrink before their eyes, and when she spoke, it was softly, to herself.

'He should have returned around Michaelmas this last year, for I heard that he was on his way, but there was no word thereafter. I managed, because that is what he wanted of me, but it has been so hard, so hard, and now I fear the worst. I have been to shrines; I have lit so many candles; but in my heart I feel that he will not return to me . . . and it was all that man's fault. God has punished him.'

She was rocking gently to and fro by this time, her arms folded round herself as if she were cold. Bradecote had no wish to push this sad, distressed dame further, but he had one more question that had to be asked.

'I am sorry, my lady, but I must ask you how you spent the time between Vespers and Compline.'

She did not respond.

'My lady Courtney?'

She looked up at him, blinking away tears, her brow creased as if she was surprised to see him.

'Me? I . . . I went to supper at the abbot's lodging, but I was not very hungry. I excused myself as early as possible and went to the church.'

'You were in the church.' Here at last was something useful, but Bradecote felt the need to be certain of what she said.

'Why, yes. I went to pray and light a candle. I left it before the high altar. When there is nobody else there I feel God may hear my poor supplications better.'

Bradecote and the serjeant exchanged glances. They had gained, at least, an explanation of where the candle used to light the documents had originated, and it meant that the death must have taken place during the latter period between Vespers and Compline.

'Did anyone see you . . . after supper, that is?'

'Sister Ursula of Romsey left with me, but we parted when she returned to the guest hall. I saw no one else. Ulf does not count, of course, and he remained in the cloister while I was at my prayers. He does not like me to be out of his view, but I find his presence . . . distracting to prayer.'

Ulf was presumably the name of her trusty follower. Bradecote focused on the nuns.

'Was the other Romsey sister not with her?'

'No. She did not come to supper.' The voice was listless. Lady Courtney had no interest in the whereabouts of her fellow guests.

110

Bradecote did not think there was more to be learnt from her, and had Catchpoll escort her back to the guest hall. When the serjeant returned he found Bradecote drawing on a scrap of vellum. Catchpoll sniffed and pulled a face. He did not see the need for writing, not that he could tell one letter from another. In fact, Bradecote was finishing a rough plan of the abbey enclave, and had marked the movements of the interviewees upon it. He did not raise his head from his work as Catchpoll entered.

'So, what do you think we have learnt, Serjeant?'

'That you've not done anything like this before, my lord,' Serjeant Catchpoll grumbled, and looked genuinely aggrieved.

'What do you mean, Catchpoll?' Bradecote spoke sharply, defensive but equally aggravated, for Catchpoll's tone was not in the least respectful.

'Well, you see, my lord,' the serjeant spoke patiently, but patronisingly. 'We are here to find out things, not tell suspects what we have discovered ourselves.' He paused, and added judiciously, 'unless of course it is intentional, or to draw out something, or a plain lie.'

'Yes.' Bradecote was keeping a hold on his temper. 'That is obvious.'

'Obvious, is it? My lord, you just sat there and merrily told the lady Courtney exactly what the murder weapon was, didn't you?' Catchpoll was exasperated.

'Ah.'

There was a pause as Bradecote digested this error and Catchpoll fought not to tell his superior just how much of an idiot he thought him. Eventually he spoke, very calmly and slowly.

'By keeping what we know to ourselves, we find out if folk have knowledge only the guilty could possess. If the lady had said, "But even a mallet can be an instrument of God", then we would have known that either she committed the murder or discovered the body with the mallet beside it and had some motive for concealing the crime. But now, the chances are that everyone will know the murder weapon within the hour, especially since you told a woman.'

'Perhaps she might not have taken much notice.' Bradecote was trying to sound positive, but only managed to sound as if clutching at straws.

Catchpoll looked gloomier than usual. 'Perhaps, but I would doubt it, my lord.'

There was another lengthy silence. Bradecote was angry with himself, both for what he had done, and for opening himself up to justified but insubordinate criticism. He was playing into the experienced man's hands. Would Serjeant Catchpoll be able to stand before William de Beauchamp if they failed, and say, in truth, that he had been hampered by being yoked to an incompetent novice? Well, there was no point in dwelling upon a mistake that could not be rectified.

'Let us consider what we have managed to discover from the lady Courtney, rather than what she has learnt from us. What have we got?'

'Several things, my lord. Firstly, we can discount her as our murderer, as if she was ever a realistic possibility.' Catchpoll did not look the least cheered.

'She had good reason to want him dead.'

'That's as maybe, but she's *wodlic*, that one, mind-twisted

112

for sure. Besides, she hasn't the strength to kill a man and move his body.'

Bradecote nodded absently. 'I know. But Ulf has, and with ease.'

'Oh aye, but you'll get nothing from him. He hasn't any brains to speak of, nor any tongue to speak with. If he had committed the murder there would have been blood still upon him, sure as night follows day. If he killed to protect his lady, or if he did so at her command, he would have no more idea of concealing the fact than a hound, and when we arrived she was having one of those mad laughing-crying fits of hers. It was not put on for our benefit, and in such a state she would not have been thinking.'

'*Wodlic*, perhaps, Catchpoll. Yet some of her information was worth having.'

'If she can be relied on,' scoffed Catchpoll, derisively.

'Oh, I think she can for simple fact of place and time. We now know where the dithering sister was during supper, and we know that her senior was absent. I wonder where?'

'That should be simple enough . . . the murmurer in St Eadburga's chapel, the one that the master of masons heard.' Catchpoll brightened at last.

'Probably, but if she was there so long, why has she not come to us with the tale? Surely she heard something.'

Catchpoll wrinkled his nose, meditatively. 'The murder might have taken place after she left, so it would not occur to her to come forward? She was certainly on her way towards the church when Master Elias made his announcement.'

'You said the murderer need not be a man, earlier, but surely while the act might as easily have been that of a woman, none here are burly enough to have dragged the dead weight.'

'Burly, no, my lord. But Eudo was not a heavy man. The senior Sister of Romsey is no sparrow, but a fine figure of a woman, and about strong enough, I would say.'

'But to place the body in such a position would be ... sacrilege.'

'Well, since whoever did so had just committed the sin of murder I do not think adding sacrilege to their list would worry the killer.'

'Which ought to discount the religious even more than the laity. How could any of them contemplate killing?'

Catchpoll laughed, and shook his head. 'Never you think that the cowl or wimple makes a saint. They are all of 'em as human as us, and prey to the same thoughts of fear and vengeance and greed, just they try and pretend to themselves they do not. I grant you that if it was one of them, their motive would be strong and deep, not a sudden moment of anger, but they could be our killer just the same.'

'So it does not reduce our number of suspects.' Bradecote sighed. 'Right.' He slapped his hands on the table and got up. 'We ought to see the Sisters of Romsey next. I think we will speak with the nervous one first.'

He turned as the door was knocked, and Gyrth poked his head diffidently round it. Catchpoll made a low growling sound, like a dog with its hackles raised.

'Wait until you're called, Gyrth. Don't knock like a battering ram and then peep round like a tirewoman.'

'Sorry, Serjeant.' Gyrth hung his head. 'Should I go out and . . . No. Right, then. Well, I'm sorry to interrupt, my lord, but there's something I think you should know. I have been in the stables, talking to the lay brothers from Romsey, like Serjeant Catchpoll told me.' Gyrth paused, uncertain, for the sheriff's new man had stiffened.

Hugh Bradecote looked sharply at the serjeant. He resented the fact that Catchpoll had not thought to tell him what he had set the men-at-arms to do. He also regretted having not thought of setting tasks for them himself. Gyrth looked at Bradecote and then Catchpoll, who nodded for him to continue.

'The lay brothers don't say much about the sisters, except the younger one is in awe of the older one, as you might expect. The sacrist has been at Romsey over twenty years. She is said to be competent and good at keeping her own counsel. She's not known for emotion at all, and they had no knowledge of the dead man visiting Romsey, though they would not be likely to have seen him if he had.' He spoke in a monotone, ending in a rush.

'And?' Bradecote could not see this as important, and resented the disruption of his train of thought.

'Well, my lord, we were next to the stall where the brother's mule was tethered. The murdered one. It is a good beast, but one of the lay brothers noticed it was very lame this morning. I took a look at it, since it was connected with the dead man, and the injury was never an accident in a stable, my lord. Someone has driven something real sharp into the frog of the animal's off hind. I've seen such wounds from caltrops, but there is nothing sharp among the straw. I dare swear it was done with a hammer and nail, but whoever did it was either quick or strong, because the mule would have kicked out hard when the blow struck home. She'll not be fit to ride for nigh on a week.'

'So somebody was determined that the lord Bishop of Winchester's envoy did not reach his destination in good time,' Bradecote mused. 'Thank you, Gyrth. You were right to bring this to my attention. I want you to speak with the servants of those in the guest hall and find out what background information you can.' That, he thought, should show who was in control.

Catchpoll coughed in a meaningful way. 'I took the liberty of talking with Messire FitzHugh's men this morning, my lord, when we broke our bread. Not the best of servants I would have said. Far too ready to talk about their master.'

'And was what they had to say of use to us?' Bradecote tried not to sound peevish, but failed. Catchpoll was already ahead of him.

'Not really. Had there been anything of importance I would have told you immediately, my lord.'

Bradecote raised a sceptical eyebrow at this, but Catchpoll continued, unabashed. 'The young man, Messire FitzHugh, seems to be a hot-headed youth given to acting without thinking of the consequences. It seems he has fallen foul of Robert de Beaumont's temper and has taken the excuse of visiting his ailing father to let his lord's displeasure fade. There is no indication, however, that he had ever set eyes on Eudo the Clerk before he saw him here, and whoever committed the murder did not do so without strong reason.'

'And what,' said Bradecote carefully, 'if the noble earl had set his squire to remove a dangerous tale bearer? Eudo made many journeys and must have had his eyes ever open, and his poisonous tongue ready to wag.'

Catchpoll gave the matter genuine consideration, his face working as Bradecote watched. It was not a thought that had occurred to the older man.

'If that were the case, FitzHugh must have had very accurate knowledge as to where and when he could find his quarry, or else he was mighty fortunate. It might be possible, my lord, but I would not say it was at all likely. And,' he added as a clincher, 'the Earl of Leicester is known as a clever man, and a clever man would not send a shaveling to do a man's job. I doubt the youth has ever killed anything bigger than a coney, though he would claim that was a boar.' Catchpoll snorted derisively. Messire FitzHugh did not impress him.

'No,' agreed Bradecote, 'I put it forward only as a possibility, not a probability. Yet until we have something better, we must bear it in mind. I wonder if it would be best to speak with the hot-headed squire now? No. We will continue as planned. Fetch the timid sister, and let us see if she can bring forth any gems of information.'

Catchpoll sniffed derisively. 'Likelier I'll see the Avon run dry first.'

Chapter Six

Sister Ursula was not as useless as the sheriff's officers had feared. True, she entered the room as if it were the den of some dangerous wild animal, and shrank in the chair placed for her, eyes downcast and hands visibly gripped together beneath the cover of her scapular. Her answers, though delivered in a high, almost musical voice, were quite clear. It was as if she were surprised at her own temerity in answering. She evidently had nothing to hide, and there were no considered hesitations in her speech.

'We are seeking to piece together the events of yesterday evening, Sister . . .' Bradecote left the question of her name hanging.

'Sister Ursula, my lord.' She looked him briefly in the eye and then lowered her gaze, lest it be thought immodest.

'Sister Ursula, we would like to know what everyone was

doing yesterday evening between Vespers and Compline so that we can get a full picture of what happened here.' Bradecote's tone was authoritative but calm, and designed to set her at ease. 'Can you tell us where you were?'

The young nun nodded, relief clear upon her face. She almost smiled, and raised her face again, confident. It was a simple question to answer, and not going to be the complicated interrogation she had feared.

'I was at supper at Father Abbot's table.'

'Not all the time, though.' Bradecote gave the ghost of a smile himself, and the youthful Benedictine dropped her gaze quickly again, her cheeks tinged pink.

'Oh, no. I came from Vespers with Sister Edeva, but I am afraid she was not well. She complained of a fearful headache and could not face supper with Father Abbot. I offered to visit the herbalist for her but she was very stoic. Then I went to eat, and at the end of the meal I returned to our chamber in the guest hall, and finished darning a tear in my travelling cloak.'

'So Sister Edeva did not accompany you to supper?' Bradecote already knew the answer but posed the question nevertheless.

'No. As I said, she had the headache and did not want food. It was a pity because there was a delicious partridge pudding.' Sister Ursula put her hand to her mouth. 'I should not be interested in such things. It is a weakness.'

'We will not inform upon you, Sister.' This time the acting undersheriff could not hold back a grin. 'But where did Sister Edeva go when you enjoyed this pudding?'

'She went to St Eadburga's chapel to pray in peace, and

then met me in the guest hall a short time before the bell for Compline. I think she was just a little better then.'

Serjeant Catchpoll spoke, without glancing at Bradecote. 'Did you actually see the sister go into the chapel?'

The nun flinched, for Catchpoll's voice, which he tried to make as smooth and calm as his superior's, sounded sinister in the extreme.

'No. No, of course not, because I did not follow her into the church. But I saw her enter the cloister and that was where she said she was going, so that is where she went.' A note of irritation entered the soft voice, like a child who cannot make an adult believe what it is saying. 'Sister Edeva would not tell me a lie.'

Bradecote tried a change of tack, to prevent the younger Benedictine from withdrawing and becoming defensive. 'Very well, then. Sister Edeva was at prayer. Who sat at table with you?'

'Well, there was Father Abbot, of course, and the lord de Grismont beside him. The sad lady, my lady Courtney, sat next to me, and then there were the widows; the one from Winchester and the beautiful one. The weaver's widow seemed very confident in company, though it did not appear seemly to me that she should take such an active part in conversation. The young man, Messire FitzHugh, was clearly not in good humour, and scowled a great deal. He arrived late to the meal, all in a rush, just before Grace was said. He had not even made himself presentable,' she flushed, 'for his boots were dusty and his nails dirty, and there was a straw stalk tucked in his jerkin.' She paused. 'I could not help but notice, because he was seated opposite to me, and . . . But the only woman not present was lady d'Achelie's maidservant and surely in so short a time . . .' her voice trailed away. She flushed, quite red this time, conscious of having admitted that she had studied a member of the opposite sex, which equated in her own mind with wickedness, and wondered if he had been engaged in carnal activities. She took a deep breath and continued. 'That was everyone.'

Hugh Bradecote repressed the urge to smile at her, and thereby discompose her further. It was, he thought, cheering to find that the confines of the cloister could not entirely repress the natural instincts of a young woman who could barely have left her teens. 'Did you depart alone?' he asked, gently.

'Oh no, the lady Courtney left the table as I did. She did not say much to me, but then I think she understood we should not engage in frivolous chatter. She is a very prayerful lady. We parted in the courtyard before the guest hall. She just said that she wanted to go back to the church alone, before Compline, but she did not wait there for the Compline bell, for Sister Edeva and I saw her walking in the cloister as we answered its call.'

Bradecote thanked the young woman gravely. 'Thank you, Sister. You have been of great help.'

The little nun looked relieved and rose to leave. Catchpoll held open the door of the chamber for her, but just as she was going Bradecote asked one further question.

'By the way, Sister, the dead man came from the minster at Winchester, not so far from Romsey. Had you ever seen him before?'

'No. He had not visited Romsey to my knowledge. But

then, I would have had no occasion to meet him, even if he had. I hold no office. Sister Edeva would be the better person to ask.' She frowned for a moment, a memory wakening in her brain. 'It is possible that they had met before. When we first met the brother after our interview with the abbot, I thought Sister Edeva stiffened a little, but it might as easily have been my imaginings. You should ask her.' She smiled sweetly, knowing her ordeal to be at an end. 'If that is all, my lord . . .'

Bradecote nodded. 'Indeed, Sister. Thank you.'

Catchpoll saw her out and returned, closing the door behind him. Bradecote raised his eyebrows interrogatively, but said nothing.

'Well, she's another off our list, if ever she was on it, my lord. Had nothing to hide and tried no tricks. Mind you, she's given us more than we could have expected.'

'She has that. It will be as well to speak to the sacrist of Romsey next. There are some interesting questions to put to her.'

'And then our young gentleman of the uncertain temper and dirty nails? I wonder if he had been tupping the lady's maid. Either he has attributes I fail to see, or she was very easy, if that is so.'

'Strikes me as desperate to prove he's a man, does Lack-beard, and not very good at it, especially if he would fumble anything with a gown and girdle without even knowing the wench's name, and I would swear he would not even ask.'

'Thinks all he has to do is flash his . . . rank,' sneered Catchpoll.

Bradecote smiled, but then grew serious. 'Indeed so. I doubt he was up to anything criminal, however sinful, unless he lamed that mule, and why do that if he was going to kill the man? Besides, he arrived late to supper, rather than left early, and we know now that the murder took place after the lady Courtney lit her candle.'

'Unless, and I grant it would be odd, he killed the clerk before supper and went back to move the body.'

'That won't hold water, Catchpoll, because there is no dust or straw in the Lady chapel.' Bradecote sighed. 'I think he is no higher on our list than Mistress Margery Weaver. A lady about to commit foul murder would surely not have been so talkative and bold in company.'

'Not unless she was very accomplished, no. Unless, mind you, it was nerves that made her talk so. There's some women I've come across who would act like that, and she does come from the same place, which provides a link. Even if she is innocent of the crime, she might have seen our murdered man in Winchester. The lord bishop's envoy would be no ordinary cleric.' The serjeant's face performed another of its contortions indicating thinking within, but nothing of note emerged, for he shook his head and departed to find the sacrist of Romsey Abbey.

Sub-prior Remigius was a troubled man. He sat upon his cot with his head buried in his hands, conscience and ambition vying in his brain. Part of him wanted to keep his own counsel, and trust that everything would be resolved speedily by the sheriff's men, but what if they dug into Eudo's past and discovered the extent of the connection between himself and Henri de Blois's man? Better to tell all now, risking the consequences, than be forced to do so later. Trust the weasel Eudo to threaten him even from beyond the grave. He had come to Pershore with such hopes, and basking in the knowledge that the powerful lord Bishop of Winchester himself had recommended him, and now this could ruin everything. He closed his eyes and took a deep, despondent breath.

He knew that the sheriff's officers were using the abbot's parlour. As he crossed from the dortoir he saw Abbot William in discussion with the precentor, and he made a decision. He hung back until the precentor turned away, and then approached his superior. He would rather that Father Abbot heard what was going to be said from his own lips.

The sun had progressed so far in its course that the western side of the cloister was now dim and cool, and abbot and sub-prior trod slowly up and down for some time, in low-voiced conversation. Eventually they emerged, blinking, into the sunlight, and walked calmly to the abbot's lodging.

Serjeant Catchpoll was just coming out of the chamber, and drew aside respectfully as Abbot William entered. It was, after all, the abbot's own residence. The sub-prior at his side looked distinctly uncomfortable, and instead of continuing on his way to seek out Sister Edeva, Catchpoll turned back and re-entered, closing the door quietly behind him. This was not going to be a situation where he would do anything but observe silently, but observe he would.

Bradecote was taken aback, and rose at Abbot William's entrance. The man's face was solemn and regretful.

'Brother Remigius has brought information to me,

information which he knows also to be of importance to the secular authorities. It grieves me that any of our order should be involved in this case, but as the victim wore the cowl, it has to be expected that others will have things to tell. I have only to add that Brother Remigius has my full support.'

The abbot took the vacant seat without thinking, thereby ensuring that Remigius stood. The sub-prior coloured, so that even his tonsure reddened. He moistened dry lips with the tip of his tongue. Bradecote wondered, for a brief moment, if there was to be a confession of the crime, the monk looked so upset. After giving a long look at his abbot, Brother Remigius turned to Bradecote.

'My lord,' he began, and had to clear his throat. 'I come forward reluctantly, but it is my duty to do so. You know that I was at Winchester, but it was barely two years ago that I came to this house.' His voice strengthened. 'The lord bishop himself did me the honour of recommending me for advancement, and I am most content here.'

He glanced at Abbot William, who nodded encouragement. 'I was in Winchester many years, and well, I did not tell you the truth about Eudo the Clerk, the full truth. I came in all too frequent contact with Eudo de Meon, Brother' – and he stressed the title with loathing – 'Eudo. He was, I am sure, always a good servant of his bishop, but in all other matters he was regarded with great suspicion. He always knew secrets, as though the walls themselves told him private thoughts. He also seemed to take malicious delight in denouncing the sins of others. On two occasions I myself had cause to make his errors known to Chapter, and he regarded me with dislike.'

Remigius's voice had gained in confidence, but now it faltered. 'It came as an unpleasant shock to see Brother Eudo here in Pershore. He recognised me instantly. I even thought he had planned to encounter me. At the earliest opportunity he sought me out in private conversation, and what he said, what he threatened, horrified me.'

The monk had Bradecote and Catchpoll hanging on his words, and, when he halted, Catchpoll had to bite his lip to prevent himself from showing his interest. 'He said that I was fortunate to be in a good position here, and that it would be such a shame if it were known why I had left Winchester. I was stunned, for I left in good grace with my superiors. Eudo hinted that as the lord Bishop of Winchester's trusted man, a word from him would be certain to carry weight. He wondered, he said, how long I would hold my position if it were known that I had been sent from Winchester to avoid scandal, and that I had been suspected of,' he took a deep breath, 'corrupting novices.'

His cheeks were scarlet with indignation and embarrassment. He looked at Abbot William and then at Bradecote. 'I swear on the Rood itself that I am innocent of such wickedness. It was all falsehood, invented by Eudo on the spur of the moment. I said that I would tell Father Abbot, who could check with Winchester and find no such accusation had ever been made, but Eudo just smiled and said that it would not matter. The accusation would be remembered long after my innocence was ascertained, and further advancement would elude me.'

'Did he give you a reason for wishing you so ill?' Bradecote thought it all sounded very melodramatic and unlikely.

'He said that it was never wise to cross him, and,' Remigius shuddered at the recollection, 'there was a great deal of satisfaction to be gained from the power to change lives.'

Abbot William's face was grim. 'My lord Bradecote, I never met the Bishop of Winchester's envoy before, but I have known Brother Remigius for the best part of two years. I can only say that he has been assiduous in his duties, helpful to his brothers and to me, and has never, in any way, caused me concern.'

'Thank you, Father Abbot, and you too, Brother Remigius. Your honesty, if a trifle belated, makes our work much easier.'

The confessional, for that was how it felt to Bradecote, was at an end. The monks withdrew, leaving Catchpoll and Bradecote to assimilate how this altered the situation.

'I don't see that the brother did the deed, howsoever he had reason.' Catchpoll pulled at his nose thoughtfully. 'He lacks the courage.'

'You are probably right, though even a weak man may be driven to bloody acts in desperation. We can at least forego any sympathy for the victim.'

Catchpoll frowned. Sympathy for the victim had not occurred to him, and very rarely did. He considered it a weakness.

'Sympathy, my lord, is not for the likes of us. It gets in the way. I leave that to others, and with respect, my lord, so should you.'

Bradecote stiffened. It was not Catchpoll's place to tell him how or what to think, and he deserved a sharp set-down. Honesty compelled him, however, to admit the validity of what the serjeant said. He held his tongue, but the reprimand, for that was what it felt like, rankled.

The older man watched him warily. He believed totally in what he had said, but realised it had not been wise to declare it. That Bradecote had not bitten his head off either showed good sense or weakness, and the serjeant had seen enough of him on Bredon Hill to know that whatever else, Bradecote was not weak.

Having failed to find Sister Edeva in the guest hall, Catchpoll eventually found her in the abbot's garden, only yards from his parlour and idly dead-heading blooms from the roses in the softened warmth of the late afternoon sun. She looked round at the sound of his approach, his boots crunching purposefully on the pathway, and sending a blackbird 'pinking' from the extraction of a worm from the flower bed, but there was nothing sudden in her movements, no suggestion of surprise. When the serjeant bade her come to speak with the sheriff's deputy, she assented with a gracious inclination of the head, and followed him without any increase in her pace to keep up with him. He therefore reached the abbot's door a few paces in advance and was able to turn and observe her as he held the door. Women religious had, he often thought, a greater otherworldliness than their male counterparts, but this dame was exceptional.

She entered the abbot's parlour, her garb the only similarity with Sister Ursula, who had occupied the same place earlier that afternoon. She glided rather than walked, and her posture was upright, confident and composed. When she sat, she folded her pale hands beneath her scapular and gazed at Bradecote unflinchingly. The Empress Maud herself could not have appeared more regal and remote. Without saying a word, the sacrist of Romsey had created the feeling that it was she who was granting an audience, not Bradecote instigating an interview. It was disturbing.

'You wished to speak to me concerning the death in the abbey church, my lord.' It was a statement, not an enquiry; her voice was low, calm and surprisingly melodic.

'The murder,' replied Bradecote carefully.

'I see.'

He wondered if she did. A shaft of sunlight from a narrow, unshuttered window lent colour to the nun's alabaster face. It was a visage that gave no clues to the woman beneath, her thoughts or even her physical state. With throat and hair covered, and a skin rarely exposed to the sun, she could be any age between thirty and nigh on fifty years. She was tall, a fact accentuated by her upright posture, straight as an arrow-shaft, and yet perfectly relaxed. Even the Benedictine habit could not totally conceal her shapely figure, though she clearly made no effort to use it. Catchpoll's words, 'a fine figure of a woman', returned to him. Bradecote had the unnerving sensation that she intended to conduct the interview on her own terms, regardless of his plans.

'You do not appear unduly distressed by this sacrilege, my . . .' he faltered, for without thinking he had been about to address her as 'my lady'. 'Sister.'

The nun permitted herself the merest hint of a smile. '"Sister" is perfectly correct, my lord, and no, I am not excessively "distressed", as you describe it. Death comes to us all.'

'Not violent death; not an unnecessary and senseless death, especially to a man in holy orders.' Bradecote sought to stress his point.

'Many better men have met death as violent and as apparently senseless,' her voice altered not at all, 'particularly in such troubled times as these.'

'Yet you were not so sanguine when the death was announced.'

'My lord?' The nun looked vaguely puzzled.

'Sister Edeva, when Elias the Mason entered the cloister and cried out that the lord bishop's man lay dead, as a result of violence, you went down on your knees, for you were at prayer when we arrived with the sheriff.'

Sister Edeva leant forward a little, her head to one side. 'You find it strange that a religious should behave in such a manner? That a nun should turn to prayer?'

Her voice was soft, though Bradecote felt he could detect mockery in its depths. The lady was providing no assistance at all.

He tried another approach. 'I am trying to ascertain the movements of all within the abbey between Vespers and Compline. You were absent from the abbot's table. Would you please tell me where you were.'

'I am sure Sister Ursula has already told you. I was at prayer in St Eadburga's chapel.'

'For the entire time?'

'Obviously not, since I was coming towards the church with my sister when the master mason emerged, and I am sure that Sister Ursula has told you that already.'

Her answers were clear, and yet . . . Bradecote felt that there was much to be said which was concealed, though he would have sworn she was telling no lie. They were engaged in a verbal combat, which the lady seemed to be enjoying, and in which she had the upper hand. He glanced at Catchpoll, who was eyeing the nun with both respect and suspicion.

'It seems an unusual time for prayer,' Bradecote tried again, 'immediately after the office and when a meal was to be served. What could lead you to spend the time thus?'

The grey eyes, which had appeared cool and vaguely mocking, hardened in an instant, and the voice had an icy, imperious edge. 'There is no such time as "an unusual time for prayer", for communing with the All Highest, and my prayers are a matter for none but myself and God, my lord.'

Bradecote could not conceal his amazement at the strength of her reaction, and without thinking, stammered an apology. Only as the words left his mouth did he wonder why she had reacted in such a way.

'Forgive me, I meant only . . .'

'To see if I killed Eudo the Clerk.' She stared at him, fixing him with the granite hard eyes. The voice was very deliberate. 'I did not kill that man.'

It was a bald statement, without explanation, without a reason but as though there ought to have been. Something important was being said, but Bradecote, inexperienced in such affairs, could not fathom what it was. As he watched her, the nun withdrew into herself again. It was as though she had emerged briefly into the secular world and then once more withdrawn. He wanted to ask her other questions, but they had become jumbled in his brain, halted by her stark announcement.

It was Serjeant Catchpoll who, clearing his throat respectfully, asked what Bradecote had intended. 'Since you were present in the chapel during the time when the murder was committed in the church,' he avoided mentioning exactly where, 'we have to ask if you heard anything, Sister.'

'I was at prayer, Serjeant, and my concentration was upon my orisons, nothing else. However, I can say that I heard no scream or cry, if that will help you.' It would not, but it was clear the Benedictine was not going to be more forthcoming.

The Sister of Romsey rose without either man saying anything to stop her. It was she who was bringing the interview to a close. She gazed calmly at Hugh Bradecote, and he thought she was assessing him. There was the briefest moment, perhaps even one of his own imagining, when her eyes narrowed in surprise, and then resumed their distant mockery.

'No doubt you will find me, should you have need to question me further, my lord.' She made him the slightest of obeisances, the spiritual deferring to the secular, and left.

There was silence. Catchpoll made no comment on his superior's handling of the interview, for he could not work out how it could have been different, although it was unlike any other he had conducted. Bradecote was besieged by a welter of conflicting emotions. He was annoyed with himself for having failed to control the conversation, admiring of the cool way in which this otherworldly woman had conducted the affair, and convinced that, deep down, there was so much more that he needed to know. Underlying the whole was a small icy feeling in the pit of his stomach that said Sister Edeva was cool enough and hard enough, strong enough too, to be the murderer. What was worse was the illogically desperate desire that he should be wrong. In this one, short, perplexing meeting, some spark had been kindled, both shameful and without any logical basis.

'What happened there, my lord?' Catchpoll's perplexity remained, and Bradecote was glad that it did not leave the older man opportunity to see his perturbation.

He shook his head. 'I truly cannot say. She interviewed us, didn't she?'

'I've been dealing with crimes and witnesses since long before the old king died,' Catchpoll avoided saying since the acting undersheriff had been but a gawky, pimpled youth, 'and never have I come across a lady quite like that. In general, they get nervous, women, whether they are innocent or guilty, which is why it can be a problem, but that one . . .' He shook his head. 'I don't say which she is, mind, my lord, but there was much more we were not made privy to than she revealed.'

Bradecote was trying to think. She had the opportunity, certainly, for she was in the church throughout supper and beyond. Even if it was true that she had been the person in St Eadburga's chapel when Elias passed by, it was always possible that she had already committed the murder, and then sought refuge to quieten her nerves. Only as an afterthought had she then moved the body, though it was an illogical and dangerous manoeuvre with the master mason liable to return at any time. It made little sense and besides, what could have been her motive? Without a very strong motive, Bradecote told himself, such a woman would not have killed a man.

Catchpoll watched his superior, unable to fathom his thoughts, but aware that he was in need of silence to put those thoughts into order. It was something he did himself, a mental filing and sorting of information, especially important to an unlettered man, and he kept quiet. Eventually Bradecote spoke, softly, as if emerging from a dream.

'If she is an innocent party, why should she be other than helpful to us? And yet, if she committed the crime, why not say she said a quick prayer but then needed fresh air and so went for a walk down by the fish ponds or the pease field, anywhere but within a hundred feet of the victim?'

'We do not actually know how long she did remain in the church though, do we? We only know she told Sister Ursula she was going there, and that is confirmed by the master mason, who heard someone in the chapel, which was doubtless her. But she chose not to tell us whether she went directly back to the guest hall shortly before Compline, or did go a-wandering.' Catchpoll shook his head. 'Makes no sense, that. Unless . . .' He stopped.

'Unless what, Serjeant?'

'There are those, and it's rare mind, that wants to be caught. They commit a crime but then get a fit of conscience. Some comes and admits it straight up, which makes my life easier, but once in a while you find they lead you to themselves slowly, by little steps, and at the end claim relief to have been taken. She's a nun, so maybe she committed the crime in a fit of passion . . . He paused as Bradecote's brows rose in disbelief. 'A fit of passion, as I say, and then it lies ill with her conscience and she half wants us to discover her guilty secret.'

'This is not a serious proposition, I take it, Catchpoll.'

'No, my lord, but it is always wise to consider even outside possibilities, otherwise you can look mighty foolish.'

Was there a hint that he meant 'You will look mighty foolish'? Bradecote ignored the possible barb.

'Well, we have considered it and dismissed it, so where next? I think, after supper, we will speak with the widow.'

Catchpoll's eyes brightened.

'Not that one, Catchpoll. The weaver's widow from Winchester. You'll have to wait before you can feast your lascivious eyes on the lady d'Achelie again.'

For once, the serjeant grinned. 'My eyes, lassivy whatever or not, can wait. I'm a patient man.' He turned and headed for the door, chuckling to himself.

Chapter Seven

Margery Weaver came to the abbot's parlour without any sign of perturbation. She had learnt how to cope in a man's world, and if she was not above using her femininity at times, she had acquired a masculine directness that Bradecote found disconcerting.

She acknowledged Serjeant Catchpoll with a nod, settled herself in the chair rather like a hen upon a clutch of eggs, and then gave Bradecote her full attention. 'You'll be wanting to know where I was when the killing took place, my lord.'

It was a statement, simply put. She placed her hands, capable, industrious hands that had seen labour enough in earlier years, palm down upon her knees. It was a peculiarly masculine gesture and exactly the same as Master Elias had done in the same chair that morning. Bradecote had moved the chair during Catchpoll's absence, so that it still caught the best light. The woman's face was serious but calm.

'Yes, Mistress Weaver.' If she wanted to be forthright, it would be foolish to prevent her.

'That is simple enough. I came from Vespers, behind lady d'Achelie as I remember. She was on her own, but it's not a state she'll have to get used to.' Her face broke into a smile, one woman acknowledging the prowess of another. 'Not her.'

Bradecote queried her with a look.

'Come now, my lord. It is clear enough. The lady is one best suited to the married state. I certainly do not see her taking the veil.' Mistress Weaver wondered for a brief moment if the sheriff's man was under the beauty's spell, but his face only exhibited slight shock at her frankness. She spoke more seriously. 'My husband, God rest his soul, was a good, hard-working man who built up his business and his status in Winchester. He was at the head of the Weavers' Guild the year before he died, and deserved longer to have enjoyed his success. But things are not as we would plan them, and he died while our son was too young to take over the business. He is still, though I have had him taught his letters by the monks, and he is learning now about the trade. I have stood in my husband's place these four years, and though I say it myself, I have failed neither husband nor son. Edward will inherit a flourishing concern.'

She spoke with head raised, and defiance in her voice. 'There's nothing for a lady like the lady d'Achelie to do except find a new husband, she having no craft beyond her womanliness, and nothing to sell except her dower and her own self. She knows her worth, and will not lie in a cold bed for long. Good luck to her, I say, even if it would not be my path.'

Serjeant Catchpoll was finding the Winchester widow refreshing. Simpering women turned his stomach, truth to tell, and here was one who could not have simpered if her life depended on it. Well, he conceded, perhaps then, but it would go against her nature. He found it amusing that she had Bradecote flustered. The man blinked like an owl, taken aback. High-class ladies must be less forthright.

'You followed the lady d'Achelie, and then?' It was Catchpoll who put the question.

'I went to the guest hall and tidied myself before supper. It was quite an honour to be invited to the lord abbot's table, and I would not do him the discourtesy of arriving late or dishevelled.' A frown creased her brow in annoyance. 'Not like some whose rank should give them manners, not be worn as a badge, entitling them to rudeness.'

'And this was?' Bradecote had found his voice, though he knew the answer he would receive.

'Messire FitzHugh.' The lady's lip curled in distaste. 'A shallow whelp, who could do with a lesson in manners. I care not what his station might be.' Margery Weaver spoke as one who would be happy enough to give the lesson. 'If my Edward ever behaved thus, I would take a birch bough to him, whatever his years. The youth arrived late, with barely a mumbled apology, and his person grubby and mired. You would have thought he had just ridden in after a wild chase. Disgraceful is what I call it.'

It was, thought Bradecote, interesting that the squire had offended the sensibilities of two such different women as Sister Ursula and Mistress Weaver.

'Did you linger at table, mistress?'

'Not beyond what was seemly.' The widow coloured slightly, on the defensive for the first time. Perhaps she had, in retrospect, regretted her involvement in so much of the conversation. In her work she dealt with men all the time, and it was hard to hold back in a social situation where higher-bred dames had learnt to appear meek and deferential. 'I was the last, no not quite . . .' She smiled. 'I left after Sister Ursula and my lady Courtney, but my lady d'Achelie lingered, just for a few moments, behind me. I believe she came out with Messire FitzHugh.' She could not repress a smirk. 'Without doubt he wished he had made an effort, then, not that she wanted more than to make the pup wag his tail for her.' She smirked, quite prepared, as a widow, to be less than coy.

There was a pause, and Bradecote looked a little uncomfortable. Mistress Weaver wondered if perhaps she had gone too far, and composed herself once more. 'Afterwards I returned to the guest hall. I could not say that anyone saw me, unless it was Sister Ursula. I heard her humming to herself in the chamber where the nuns have been placed. I came out when the bell rang for Compline and, well, from then on everyone was visible.'

She looked down at her hands, and then full at Hugh Bradecote. 'My lord, the man who was murdered was no loss to the world, excepting perhaps to the lord Bishop of Winchester. I did not kill him, that I swear, but if what I know of him was as he was with others, then it is not surprising to me that he should meet such an end.' Her eyes flashed for an instant. 'Not that I am one to gossip, but when I tell the guild of this in

Winchester, well there's many will want to know I saw the body, for they would think the weasel was just at his tricks again, and not really dead.' She sniffed. 'If you find anyone who tells you they liked the man, then I will show you a liar, my lord, and that's a fact. I doubt even the lord bishop's grace himself actually liked him.'

This was more than the sheriff's men could have anticipated. Bradecote looked noticeably cheered.

'Tell us, if you will, Mistress Weaver, everything that you know about the dead man.'

Margery Weaver settled herself more comfortably, reminding Catchpoll even more of the brooding fowl. She spoke calmly for the most part, though on occasion her bitterness showed through.

'I only came upon Eudo the Clerk after my husband's death – in person, that is. My Edric was a master of his trade. We . . . he . . . provided the finest woollen cloth for Henri de Blois himself. Cleric he may be, but the lord Bishop of Winchester is of royal blood, the Conqueror's grandson, and not one to be chafed by lowly garments. It was good business, and my husband was proud of the connection. When he died there was a roll of cloth in preparation. When it was delivered, Eudo the Clerk visited me to make payment.'

She halted for a moment before continuing. 'That nasty little man tried to threaten me with "do this or else". Yes, you could call it no less. He "suggested", and that was his term, the wyrm, that it would be unsuitable for his bishop to purchase cloth from a woman.' She snorted. 'As though I might be a contamination of his grace's holiness. However, if, after a period

141

of devout mourning, I were to go to the master goldsmith and commission a gold chalice and patten for the New Minster, in memory of my husband of course, it would be seen by all that I was a devout and righteous dame, and a few discreet purchases might be made by the lord bishop once again.'

She clamped her mouth suddenly shut, as if to prevent an unseemly utterance. 'I told him, Eudo the Clerk, that my husband's business had always been done openly, and on the quality of his cloth. Never had he engaged in anything underhand, and I would not betray his memory by doing so now, even if it meant the loss of a valued customer. That horrible little toad told me that it was only to be expected that others would follow his master's example. He threatened me. How dared he!'

The widow shook her head, still stunned at his temerity. 'Well, I sent him about his business, assuring him that quality of cloth would keep the business going, whatever he put about. And so it proved.' She sat more erect. 'If trade dropped briefly, it returned well enough, and our business was spared in the ruination of the Great Fire, and prospers.'

'Thank you, Mistress Wea—'

'That is not all, my lord.' She interrupted him without compunction. 'I had no more dealings with him direct, but Winchester, however great, is not so large that rumours do not spread like licking flame. The lord bishop has, shall we say, changed his tone according to whosoever held best grasp on the crown. In Winchester, I heard from differing sources, aye, and ones I'd trust, that it was his clerk that Henri de Blois used as his trusted man in dealings with both sides, and that he used information as a bargaining tool with each. Eudo the Clerk was, my lord, almost certainly, Eudo the Spy.' She finished on a note approaching triumph, knowing that she would surprise her auditors, and was not disappointed.

Catchpoll and Bradecote stared at the Winchester widow, not in disbelief, but astounded none the less. Catchpoll exhaled slowly, a whistling sound coming from between his teeth. Bradecote wiped his hand across his mouth, frowning. The serjeant recognised it as an habitual gesture.

'What you have told us, mistress, may be of great importance. But I must caution you to keep this knowledge within this room, for your own safety. Will you do that?'

Margery Weaver, her tale told, paled at his words, but nodded resolutely. 'As you direct, my lord, but . . .' she bit her lip, 'I cannot vouch for its not being known already. I was speaking with my lady Courtney, who has . . . had . . . her own reasons to dislike the dead man.'

'Did anyone else hear this confidence?' Bradecote tried to keep the urgency out of his voice.

'I cannot say for sure, my lord, though there was nobody close by that I noticed.' She paused. 'Is that all, my lord?'

'Thank you, yes. Escort Mistress Weaver back to the guest hall, Serjeant Catchpoll.'

Bradecote wanted time, and his piece of vellum. When the serjeant returned, he found the acting undersheriff had at least furnished himself with the latter.

'The more we find out about our victim, the more I see why he ended up dead. A nasty piece of work, Eudo the Clerk.' Bradecote sounded almost relieved.

'Indeed, my lord, but the more he got people's backs up the more complicated it is for us. For a start, nobody really wants the killer brought to justice when they think he, or she, was doing the rest of the world a favour.' Catchpoll shook his head sadly. 'Give me a nice simple killing, where the man does away with his wife so he can marry his neighbour's pretty niece.' He stifled a yawn.

The bell had tolled for Compline some time since. It was twenty-four hours since their arrival, and although he had learnt much, Bradecote felt that he was a long way from discovering the killer.

'Do we speak to anyone else tonight, my lord?'

'I think not, Catchpoll. The monks will have their silence undisturbed. We will speak to the other guests tomorrow. The retainers that haven't been examined can be seen by Gyrth or my man Wilfrid. We will only see them ourselves if anything important turns up. We can let everyone get their sleep, but first of all I want to address them all. We can catch most if not all after Compline and see the others individually.' He paused, and frowned as an unwelcome thought occurred to him.

'My lord?' Catchpoll's eyes had narrowed.

'What Mistress Weaver told us about Eudo being a spy makes a possible difference. If whoever killed him was engaged in the same business, they may be quicker and more dangerous than we think. It might be obvious to us, but the guests should be told, clearly, to bring information only to us.'

'Fair enough, my lord. I'll make sure the servants and workmen get the same message, if you give me leave.'

Bradecote's weary eyes narrowed. Catchpoll was being

remarkably correct for once, but it was too late in the day to question why, so Bradecote merely gave his assent.

Serjeant Catchpoll gave a nod that might just have been deference but was probably simple acknowledgement, and the pair parted.

Not all the guests had attended the final office. Lady Courtney and the nuns from Romsey were present, as was Mistress Weaver, but the lady d'Achelie and both de Grismont and FitzHugh were elsewhere. The thought occurred to Bradecote that two of that number might be found together, and it would not be lord and squire.

The scene in the cloister at the end of Compline was much the same as the previous evening, but the atmosphere was wary rather than shocked. The assembly were attentive when he cleared his throat to speak, but regarded him with, he decided, gloomy anticipation. I am become a harbinger of ill tidings, he thought to himself.

'It is only right that I should warn all of you that in the case of such a crime as this, it would be most unwise of any of you to confide any suspicions you might have to others. If something does occur to you, come only to me or Serjeant Catchpoll.'

'You are saying that one of us is the killer, my lord.' Mistress Weaver's voice was matter of fact.

'I am saying,' Bradecote replied with emphasis, 'that nobody who was not within the walls of this abbey is under suspicion.'

Sister Edeva gave him a cool, slightly mocking look. 'Much more circumspect, but the same thing underneath. Do you expect us to lie quaking in our beds, and screeching at shadows?

145

Are you perhaps going to confiscate Sister Ursula's darning needle?'

Sister Ursula looked horrified, but the sheriff's officer permitted himself a fleeting smile and his eyes, for all their weariness, flashed understanding. Sister Edeva was not one to be daunted by his words, and saw no benefit in spreading panic. She clearly thought his pronouncement over dramatic.

'I hardly think so, Sister Sacrist. Just be on your guard, all of you, and show sense. I do not desire you to "quake" but nor do I desire any further fatalities.'

'Heaven forfend.' Abbot William crossed himself and his cheeks paled. He had clearly not considered such an awful possibility.

'Then I will bid you all a safe goodnight. Father Abbot. Ladies.' Bradecote made a small obeisance that took in all present, and departed with a firm step. He was conscious of the gesture, and also that it would be understood and appreciated by the Benedictine sister. If he wished to be dramatic, he would be so, regardless of her opinion.

Isabelle d'Achelie was not cold, for the evening was warm, and so she had no excuse to request Waleran de Grismont's arms about her except perturbation. They stood in the long shadow of the wall to the abbot's garden as the heavy scent of herb and flower lay contained within its bounds, conversing in low voices.

'I am frightened, my lord.'

'Surely not here and now, my love.' His voice was honeyed, soothing.

'I might be murdered in my bed.'

'I have an answer to that, my lady. Share mine. I can promise to protect your body with my own.'

'My lord!' She blushed, outraged yet flattered. 'We are within the confines of the cloistered.'

'You do not ask me to let you go, though.' His hold tightened, and he lifted her chin. 'You would be safe with me.'

'I am not sure any woman is safe with you, my lord.'

'Let us say, safe from danger.' He kissed her, slowly, seductively. Why wait for a king's agreement if she would give herself now?

She fought the urge to relax into the seduction. Of all her animal instincts, self-preservation was still the most honed.

'Mmm, my lord, this is not the time for love.'

'When better? The night is warm, and I am hot for you.'

She pushed her hands against his chest.

'Waleran, this is not the time. There is a murderer in this place.'

'Why assume that anyone else must die? You and I both know the snivelling Eudo was the sort none love and many must have wanted silenced. I am not afraid. I just sleep with a dagger beneath my blanket, and I am not playing with words.' He was serious now. 'My offer stands, and if you will not accept it, keep your eating knife by your bed.'

'I could not kill a man, my lord.'

'If you feared enough, you could, my lady. I offer you the choice of sleeping with a warm body or cold steel, and I know which I would prefer you to select, but it is your choice.'

'I . . . I cannot . . . Not here. It would curse us to do so within the abbey walls.' She crossed herself.

He frowned. He did not think her an overly religious woman.

'And lies are sins also, my heart. You fear that if you say yes, I shall not bother with wedding you? You are the most beautiful woman I have ever encountered, but a wife is not just a woman, she is also a dowry, and the provision of sons. I would wed you, and delight in all three.'

His words took her aback. They were true enough, and yet vaguely shocking.

'I shall bed with the steel tonight, my lord, and hope to come to you with the second, and, God willing, provide you with the third.' She took his face between her hands, kissed him as if to seal the promise, and flitted away.

Waleran de Grismont leant against the wall and pondered long on the inconsistencies of the weaker sex.

Hugh Bradecote returned to the guest hall after personally checking the guards set to duty. He went first to Messire FitzHugh's chamber, which was nearest the entrance. He knocked, but there was no answer. He was about to pass on when a suspicion crossed his mind, and so he raised the latch and eased open the door. The room was scarcely bigger than a cell, and FitzHugh lay already beneath his blanket, a vague covered figure in the dimness. Bradecote began to withdraw softly, as the young man sat bolt upright, challenging whoever stood in the dark in a voice not quite steady.

'I am sorry, messire. I had not thought you would be asleep as yet. I have been warning the guests that if they discover anything, or have suspicions, they must reveal them only to myself or Serjeant Catchpoll.'

'You think the killer will strike again?'

'It cannot be ruled out. If they feel threatened, yes. Having killed once, killing again becomes easier.'

'Yet you incarcerate us here, expose us to the threat.'

'I keep you all here, messire, because one of you is a murderer. I give you good night. Sleep well.' His last words were delivered in a sepulchral tone.

Bradecote was not impressed by the squire's nervousness, and still surprised at his taking to his bed before it was even dusk. He next knocked at the door of the chamber occupied by the lady d'Achelie, but resolved not to enter if there was no response.

A soft voice bade him enter, and he opened the door to find the lady seated upon her bed, with her tirewoman combing out her long brown hair. A pair of best beeswax candles illuminated the scene and gave her hair a rich lustre. Ladies did not display their hair loose in public, it was not seemly, but she seemed unabashed at being found in such a state. Bradecote was embarrassed and dropped his gaze for a moment, flushing, but could not resist raising his eyes to observe her. She smiled, but there was a flicker of disappointment in her eyes. He felt that she had been anticipating the arrival of a different male visitor.

'I am sorry to disturb you, my lady.'

She gazed at him thoughtfully for a moment and feigned coyness. In truth, he was not altogether dissimilar from her lover; a little taller and leaner, younger certainly, but a paler version; not so dark of visage, without the lines of dissipation and with blue grey eyes that lacked the look of the calculating hunter that entranced her in de Grismont – there was a man who always stood out, attracting attention merely by his existence. This sheriff's officer had shown he could be commanding, but she felt that, if he chose, he could be perfectly anonymous despite his inches. Here, she decided, was an earnest man whose passions, if any, were too mild for her taste. Putting him out of countenance, however, would be enjoyable.

'Indeed, my lord, you choose your time and place for questions most oddly. I was shortly to retire to my bed.' She gave the word an almost imperceptible significance, patted the palliasse significantly, and opened her eyes more widely.

Bradecote reddened further, now both embarrassed and vaguely shocked. The lady was not to his liking, despite her very obvious attractions, but a man would be a liar if he said he was unaffected by her.

Isabelle d'Achelie regarded his discomfiture with amusement and a touch of triumph. So he had thought he could ignore her, or treat her like that sad ghost of a woman, Emma Courtney. Well, now he knew he could not. She laughed. It was a warm, sensuous sound, and she watched a muscle in his cheek twitch. It was so very, very easy. Then she took pity on him.

'My apologies, my lord. I should not have teased you so. Come, tell me why you have arrived on my threshold at this hour.'

Bradecote cleared his throat. 'It was my fault. I came because I wanted all the guests to know that their safety may depend on them keeping their own counsel if they think of anything which might assist us, and telling only Serjeant Catchpoll or myself.'

She stared at him, and then a crease appeared between her prettily arched brows. 'You think that whoever killed the clerk would kill one of us?' She concealed the thought that she had believed this for the better part of the last twenty-four hours.

'If it risked the killer's identity being discovered, yes. I should have thought of this before, but I am not experienced in such matters.'

'Thank you for the warning, my lord. I will be careful, though I am sure it will prove unnecessary, and,' she could not resist making him uncomfortable one more time, 'it does you credit that you admit your lack of experience. Men so very rarely do. They tend to prefer to boast of their prowess . . .' she paused just long enough '. . . in everything.' The accompanying smile, and lowered eyelids, spoke volumes.

Bradecote's jaw nearly dropped, and he coughed and looked away. When he spoke, there was a hesitancy. 'Right, er, well then.' He paused, and coughed again. 'I would wish to see you in the abbot's parlour when the monks go to Chapter in the morning, my lady, as part of my investigation.' Bradecote listened to himself, sounding official and officious.

'I will be ready, my lord, whenever you . . . want me. The sooner all this is over the better.' Her words were as formal but the tone teased him again. She inclined her head in gracious dismissal and Bradecote withdrew, almost stepping back into Waleran de Grismont, who viewed him with surprise tinged with mild amusement.

'Do your duties involve disturbing attractive women in their chambers? I confess I had never thought of the role of sheriff's man very appealing, but I see now that it has its advantages. Perhaps I should offer my services to de Beauchamp.'

Bradecote pulled a wry face. 'You could have the task

151

tomorrow, my lord, but I fear you would find the opportunities you envisage sadly lacking.'

'And I would have to work with that gallows-faced serjeant of yours. Hmm, you are probably right, Bradecote.' He paused, and resumed his natural air of vague boredom. 'Was there a reason for your visit?'

'I wanted to give the lady d'Achelie some advice.'

'Ah,' de Grismont dropped his voice conspiratorially. 'Women never take kindly to advice in my experience. They have a remarkable habit of doing just the opposite.' He cast the lady a very swift glance.

There was just a hint of the patronising man of the world in de Grismont's tone that set Bradecote on edge.

'And your experience is of course very wide.' The barb was obvious, but rather than take offence, de Grismont laughed openly.

'Naturally, or I would not have made mention of it. Come, Bradecote, it is too late of an evening to be at odds. Let us cry "*pax*".'

Bradecote smiled ruefully. 'You are right, my lord. I was, in fact, warning the lady to confide any suspicions she might have only to Catchpoll or myself.'

Waleran de Grismont grew serious. 'You do not think she is at risk?'

'I think everyone is at risk who remains within these walls.'

'Then the answer is simple. Let us go about our business.' He saw Bradecote's mouth open to expostulate, and raised a hand. 'Yes, I know that would mean losing your murderer, but I have seen many deaths, as I am sure you have. It comes to us all, and often unexpectedly, especially in times like these. It seems a waste of the many innocent lives cooped up here while the law, forgive me, scrabbles around to find out who sent a monk to the hereafter the tonsured anticipate with such hope.'

Bradecote shook his head. 'Murder is murder, and cannot be ignored.'

De Grismont stifled a yawn. 'Then I will see you on the morrow, no doubt. Sleep soundly. I certainly shall.' With that he passed on to his own chamber, and Bradecote sought his own bed.

Sleep, however sound, did not come quickly. Thoughts jumbled and tossed within his brain, weaving weird and illogical patterns. At one moment Bradecote thought he had made a fine deduction, only for an objection to rise up and pull it to shreds, and woven throughout was the disturbing presence of the Romsey sacrist. He had never come across a woman like her, with a sharp mind and willing to cross swords at every opportunity. In her own way she was far more bold than the lady d'Achelie. Beautiful women used their beauty; it was understood. But it was a rare woman who used her intelligence, treating men as her equal. His wife Ela, mild, loyal Ela, would not for a moment challenge any pronouncement he might make. In truth, she was not a clever woman, but even if he said something wildly impossible, she would merely blink and nod agreement with him. No, the Benedictine nun was something quite new and dangerously fascinating, and he should force her from his thoughts. Yet she was inextricably mixed up in them because she was part of the investigation . . . a more viable suspect than he would have wished.

Bradecote eventually fell asleep only to dream that Eudo the Clerk had been killed by his own mule, tired of travelling the length and breadth of the country, and egged on by Sister Edeva prodding it with a bone from St Eadburga.

Bradecote's night was further disturbed by an insistent knocking at his door, and the arrival of a man-at-arms, breathing heavily. The acting undersheriff fumbled to ignite the rushlight in the embrasure by his bed, and strove to focus both eyes and brain. The man was flustered, and sporting what looked very like the beginnings of a black eye.

'Could you come, my lord? Something's happened.'

For an awful moment Bradecote thought there had been another killing, but then why did the man-at-arms have a blossoming black eye?

'Right. I'm coming. What is it?' He tried to sound fully awake, which he was not, and his voice was thick with sleep.

As he rose and pulled on braies and boots, the man explained that he had been on guard duty by the stables and had heard a noise inside. Upon investigation, he said, he had found Messire FitzHugh saddling his horse and muffling its hooves with sacking. He had raised the alarm and went to detain the gentleman, who had hit him. The man-at-arms sounded affronted that anyone should have resisted. Despite this attack he had grappled FitzHugh to the floor and at that point another of the men on duty had arrived and the pair of them had restrained the squire.

Bradecote was assimilating the salient points of this information as they left the guest hall.

'How did you "restrain" him, Reynald, as a matter of interest?'

'Hit him on the head with a wooden shovel, my lord, that being the one they use for collecting the midden.'

'Is he unconscious?'

'Not any more, my lord. When I left he was dizzy, like, and not very happy.'

'You surprise me, Reynald. And could you explain how it was that you only discovered Messire FitzHugh inside the stable, not entering it?'

'Well, just for a moment, I wasn't concentrating, my lord.'

'You mean you dozed off.'

Reynald grimaced, expecting to be hauled over the coals, but Bradecote had more important things on his mind.

'All right, Reynald, I know it happens. At least you discovered him before he made an escape.'

The pair entered the stable and found Miles FitzHugh sat upon the straw, his head between his hands, complaining in a whining and aggrieved voice to Serjeant Catchpoll, who stood above him like a possessive dog of uncertain temper. He looked up as Bradecote entered.

'I protest, my lord. I have been treated like a common felon and . . .'

'Behaving like a "common felon" leads to such treatment, messire. You have attempted to leave the enclave in the middle of the night, although I had forbidden your departure, and you have attacked Reynald here, who is the sheriff's man.' Bradecote's voice was unsympathetic. He would rather be in his bed.

'But I am the Earl of Leicester's squire. My father holds four manors in this shire.'

'And I am sure neither would approve of your current position.' Bradecote spoke deceptively quietly.

'Indeed, it is disgraceful.' FitzHugh, misunderstanding him, was relieved that Bradecote realised the position at last, but Bradecote's next words brought home the truth.

'I am glad you are so contrite. Now you can tell me exactly why you were trying to leave.'

FitzHugh looked sulky. 'My father is sick. I have leave of absence from Earl Robert to visit him. I cannot stay here. I am not your murderer, my lord.'

'I have no proof of that, Messire FitzHugh. In fact, the information in my possession might even lead me to assume you had involvement in the crime. Additionally, I have not yet had the opportunity to question you about the death of Eudo the Clerk, and you might have important information. I had intended to speak with you in the comfort of the Abbot William's parlour in the morning, but since you have disturbed my rest, I might as well do so here and now.' He leant, with intentional nonchalance, against the end of a stall.

FitzHugh had ignored much of what the acting undersheriff had said beyond the fact that he considered he could be involved in the murder. He took on a sickly hue, and shook his head, as though trying to clear unpalatable thoughts from it by force. Bradecote's first question went unanswered until Catchpoll prodded him ungently in the ribs with his boot.

'You answer the lord Bradecote's questions or he will go away and I will ask them instead, messire. And I don't ask so politely.'

Miles FitzHugh rolled a panicky eye at Catchpoll and then Bradecote, and stammered a request for the question to be repeated. Bradecote wanted to know if the squire had ever come across Eudo before, perhaps in communication with Earl Robert. The young man not only denied any previous knowledge of Eudo the Clerk, but became quite agitated.

'I would have no truck with men like him. He was a spy, I heard it said so, and a man of honour has . . . should have . . . no dealings with him.'

Bradecote did not pursue this antipathy to spies, but sought rather to trace FitzHugh's movements since his arrival and elicit any information about the other guests and the lord Bishop of Winchester's man. There was not much to be gleaned, for the squire had only arrived late in the morning on the day of the murder. He had only seen Eudo the Clerk twice, once passing the two nuns from Romsey, and the second having speech with the widowed lady d'Achelie, which had struck him as a most unlikely encounter.

'Do you know what their meeting was about?' Catchpoll was keen to show he had a part to play in the interview, and that failure to answer questions could prove unpleasant.

FitzHugh attempted to look disdainful, but in his current position merely looked ridiculous. 'I am no eavesdropper, Serjeant.'

Catchpoll's eyes narrowed, and the squire continued in a rush.

'But for certes the lady was agitated, her face very mobile and her hands also. The clerk appeared,' he pondered a moment, 'well, to be pleased with himself.'

'Did they speak for long?' Bradecote sought to re-establish his control of the situation.

'I could not say, my lord, because I only saw them as I walked from the gatehouse to the guest hall.' FitzHugh felt happier talking to Bradecote. 'I do not believe so, because I heard the lady d'Achelie in her chamber only a few moments later, chastising her maid.'

'Chastising her?'

'Shouting a lot in a loud voice. I could not make out words but she was very angry.' FitHugh felt he was being helpful and cheered up.

'Very well, messire. Now can you tell us why you arrived late to supper at Abbot William's table and how it is that you were described to us as,' he paused, '"dishevelled", was it not Serjeant Catchpoll?'

'Indeed, my lord. "Dishevelled" and with dirty hands and boots.'

Bradecote raised his brows in mock surprise. 'I cannot believe Earl Robert permits his squires to show such discourtesy.'

Miles FitzHugh's brief improvement in spirits collapsed. He squirmed. Earl Robert would have more than just something to say if such information filtered back to him.

'I had forgotten the invitation.' He glanced nervously at Catchpoll, who was making a growling noise in his throat. 'Forgotten because I had been called here to the stables. My groom feared that my horse had strained a hock.'

'This horse? The one you were about to ride out upon tonight?' Bradecote pointed at the showy chestnut that was lisping at hay in a disinterested manner and had sacking tied inexpertly round three of its hooves. His voice was disbelieving.

'The groom was mistaken, as I told him myself when I saw the animal.'

'Mighty unhealthy, this stable,' commented Catchpoll, apparently to his superior. 'Messire FitzHugh's fine beast has a suspect hock and Eudo the Clerk's mule has something sharp and nasty driven into the frog of its off hind.' He shook his head. 'Both on the same evening, too. Strange, that.'

FitzHugh glanced from one law officer to the other. He was aware that they were toying with him now.

'All right, all right. It was me.' His voice was weary, sullen and dispirited, with no trace of the arrogant lordling. 'I came and lamed the mule. I wanted to do something to take the smile off that nasty little spy's face. He had upset the lady d'Achelie and the mere sight of him had upset old lady Courtney. I heard her with the Weaver woman, who said he was a spy. It was known in Winchester. Spies are underhand and dirty. I wanted to stop him going about his trade for a bit, that's all. I swear, my lord.'

The squire had had enough. His head hurt, he was cold, demoralised and disgraced, and the odour of ordure clung about him.

Acting undersheriff and serjeant exchanged glances. They needed no more tonight. Catchpoll instructed Reynald and another man-at-arms to escort Miles FitzHugh to the guest hall, and dragged him to his feet. He staggered, and Reynald took his elbow and led him away.

Bradecote called after him. 'I may choose to see you again, in the daylight, Messire FitzHugh, so do keep yourself in your chamber.'

The squire looked back over his shoulder, wincing, and threw him a look of dislike. Catchpoll grinned.

'That should keep him out of everyone's way, though I expect he'll be glad of the chance to nurse his head. You don't really think we will need him again, my lord?'

'No, I do not think so, Serjeant. I think we have discovered all we need about that puppy who wanted to run away with his tail between his legs.' He yawned. 'Now, I am for my bed again, and hopefully nothing else will disturb me till Prime. Goodnight.' He turned and headed back into the warm summer night, which was airless and oppressive. He hoped the weather would break soon.

The Third Day

Chapter Eight

The dawn brought glowering, slate-grey clouds massing like a besieging army on the western horizon, but the sun rose with a defiant and unabated glare in the east. There was a storm brewing, but there were some hours yet before release from the stultifying air would come. It was a tension that arose from nature rather than the misdeeds of man, but the two combined within the abbey walls. Hugh Bradecote awoke feeling jaded and sticky, his bruised upper arm aching, and with the seeds of a headache germinating in his brain. A wash in cool water lessened the former discomforts, but he wondered whether he should put a brave face on things and ignore the headache, or find the herbalist and take some easing draught before it took hold. He decided against it, fearing that if Catchpoll found out he would sink even further in his estimation. Pride overcame discomfort, and he headed out for the day's investigation.

The bags under Serjeant Catchpoll's eyes appeared heavier than usual, but otherwise he looked none the worse for a disturbed night. He acknowledged Bradecote with a nod and a report on FitzHugh, who was apparently still sleeping off the night's disruption.

'And Reynald has a stunning black eye, but is none the worse for it. In fact, I told him it suited him, and if ever I find him asleep upon his watch again I will give him one to match it.' He smiled, grimly. 'I take it we will finish speaking to the guests this morning, my lord. Do you wish to see the noble lord or the lovely lady first?'

Bradecote smiled. However disrupted his sleep, Catchpoll seemed in good spirits.

'Well, since our stable interview produced knowledge of a meeting between Eudo and the lady d'Achelie, perhaps we should start with her. But Catchpoll, restrain your natural inclinations to leer at the lady. We don't want to distract her from the events around the murder.'

Catchpoll's eyes twinkled as he turned to go. 'Might find me just too attractive, my lord? Wouldn't be the first.'

'Not quite what I meant,' Bradecote choked.

The only response was a sharp bark of laughter.

A short while later Isabelle d'Achelie preceded Serjeant Catchpoll into the abbot's parlour. She had graced the occasion with a different gown, neither grey nor blue, but somewhere in between. A lapis cross lay on her breast and her wimple was dazzlingly white. She presented a peculiar mixture of nun and siren. It was clearly the siren that Catchpoll appreciated.

Bradecote was less impressed. She had dressed with excessive care, and for a reason, which made him think. He wondered whether she was simply trying to captivate him on the premise that she liked all men to adore her, or whether it was to keep the investigators from finding out something she would prefer to keep hidden. If she thought to distract him then she was in for a bitter disappointment.

She seated herself with care on the chair provided, arranging the folds of her gown becomingly, and positioning herself so that Bradecote was treated to a beguiling mix of the profile of her curvaceous body and the full impact of her charming face. A provocative smile lurked in her limpid, violet eyes.

'I have come as you desired, my lord. I am sure there is nothing I can recall that will help you, but . . . She waved her hands in a vague gesture, and thereby wafted a rich and exotic perfume towards him. It was quite a performance.

'Thank you, my lady. It may be that there is something which appears quite insignificant to you, but will be meaningful to us. I would like to start by asking why it is that you are journeying to seek audience with the king? These are not safe times for a lady to travel needlessly.'

The merest flicker of annoyance pursed her full lips, then she smiled.

'I would prefer to keep my affairs in all forms private, my lord, naturally, but in the circumstances I suppose I have no choice. I am travelling to put forward my supplication to King Stephen. I am the widow of a loyal lord, not without wealth, and I may be able to persuade him that if I am to wed again, it should be to a younger and more,' she paused, 'able man than my first husband.'

She dabbed at the corner of her eye with a delicate forefinger, and explained how she had been a loyal and loving wife to the elderly, and latterly incapacitated, Hamo, dropping the heaviest of hints about finally having her 'needs' fulfilled. Bradecote could almost see Catchpoll imagining.

'I am hopeful that King Stephen will be swayed by my argument.'

Swayed by the swing of her hips and drooping of her lashes more like, thought Bradecote, but it seemed in keeping with the lady that she should seek to influence her future in this way. He remembered the Winchester widow's words.

'Have you anyone in mind to fill the vacancy left by your bereavement?'

'Are you putting yourself forward, my lord?' She blushed, but looked archly at him.

'No.' He ignored the lure.

The bald statement and uncompromising tone gave her pause for thought. Last night she had thought he would be easy to handle, but this morning he was as on the evening of the murder. She was perplexed, while Bradecote's temper frayed at the game of flirtation she was playing.

Catchpoll, while listening carefully, was letting his eyes feast on the prettiest thing to be seen within Pershore Abbey. He was a man many years married, and faithful enough of body, but he thought it a natural thing for a man to enjoy the visual temptations of a comely female. He might have a grizzled beard and crow's feet, but he considered that if his blood stirred at beauty then it proved, at least to himself, he was not yet old.

'Are you perhaps contemplating an alliance with Waleran de Grismont?'

'Why should you think so, my lord?'

'Because I have seen the way he looks at you, my lady d'Achelie, and I do not think he stopped at your door last night because of me.'

'That was mere chance, and you will find that the way he looked at me is the way most men look at me, if they have red blood in their veins.' She tossed her head, and there was a hint of sharpness in her tone. 'I am acquainted with the lord of Defford, it is true. He was a friend of my dear Hamo. He doubtless wished to see that I was safe.'

'And did Eudo the Clerk look at you in that way?'

Her eyes widened in genuine surprise. 'I doubt it very much, my lord, but then I had no contact with him to find out.'

Catchpoll reluctantly put his interest in the fall and rise of the cross upon the lady's bosom to the back of his mind, and concentrated on her words.

'No contact? Then why is it that you were noticed in agitated discussion with him before Vespers on the day of his death?'

Bradecote was pleased to see the effect of his question. The lady dropped her eyes and began to rub a fold of the skirt of her gown between finger and thumb. There was a short silence, and then she laughed, though it was false and mirthless.

'Oh, that. I had forgotten that. He had trodden on the hem of my gown as he passed behind me, and torn it a trifle. It is a good gown, and I was most displeased.'

'May we see it?'

She looked flustered. 'I . . . well . . . it was too badly damaged

167

and I had to give it to the almoner for some destitute.'

'You are not a very good liar, my lady. You just said that it "is" a good gown, not "was".'

Catchpoll nodded approvingly. This time the new man had grasped the important detail.

Isabelle d'Achelie was unsure what to do, so she did what women often do to gain time; she burst into tears.

Both Bradecote and Catchpoll were taken unawares, and stared at each other over the lady's bent, sobbing head. Bradecote mouthed, 'Now what?' and Catchpoll pulled a face which Bradecote interpreted as, 'Your guess is as good as mine.'

Neither man said anything for a few moments as the lady wept softly. When she raised her head, Bradecote noted that her eyes were not an unsightly red, but softly wet, with tears glistening on the ends of the lashes. So it was all part of the act, then. Whenever Ela wept, her eyes grew puffy and pink, and she sniffed a great deal, and also her nose ran. The lady d'Achelie sniffed, but it was a delicate affair, an affectation not a necessity, and her perfect little nose was dry.

'Let us have the truth, my lady. It will be known.'

She bit her lip and then took a deep breath, as if making a momentous decision. Catchpoll licked his lips; that was a sight to stir an old man on his deathbed.

'I am sorry, my lord. It is so distasteful to me, I had not wanted it known. The clerk approached me, and . . .' she faltered, 'and tried to threaten me.'

'Threaten you?' Catchpoll could not contain his surprise, and she turned to look at him as though she had forgotten his presence.

'Yes. He said he would send information to the king that I had already contracted an alliance, and was seeking to deceive him into sanctioning our secret union. He said that a Christian widow should be a generous benefactress of the Church, and that if, for instance, I were to offer up one of my manors to the New Minster in Winchester, his memory would prove remarkably adaptable.'

'An alliance with de Grismont?' It was a fair assumption, thought Bradecote.

She nodded.

'Is there any basis for the accusation?'

'Indeed not, my lord. No contract exists between us, before God or the law.' She dithered, just for a moment. 'It is true that I am hopeful that the king will permit Waleran to claim my hand. He has suffered imprisonment and ransom for King Stephen, and he will surely be rewarded for his loyalty. The clerk merely intercepted a note I was sending to Waleran, one I had instructed my maid to leave with his groom,' she scowled petulantly, 'but the silly wench could not find the groom and merely tucked it among Waleran's saddlery. It is quite distinctive. The clerk was sniffing about, and obviously saw her conceal it. The note was couched in,' she paused and looked coy, 'loving tones, and suggested that he, Waleran, leave all the persuading to me. That is all.' She hung her head.

'I see. What reply did you give him?'

'I tried to tell him it was not true, but he just smiled. Eventually, I told him to do his worst, but I would not give in to threats.' She pouted, as Bradecote was sure she had done in front of Eudo, trying to persuade him. 'He was a nasty little creep, and though I most certainly did not kill him, I cannot say I am sorry he is dead. In fact, I am quite glad.'

Catchpoll thought she very nearly folded her arms and added 'So there' at the end, like a defiant little girl. She blinked, and seemed to recollect herself, became again the siren.

'But of course you could not think that I would be capable of killing a man,' the voice was low and soft, and the damp, dark lashes fluttered, 'not a mere woman of my feeble frame.'

Catchpoll, whose appreciation of the 'feeble frame' was greater than his appreciation of the woman within it, pulled a face behind her back. She might, he conjectured, wear a man out, and there were worse deaths.

Bradecote was tired of the act, but kept back any retort. 'That will be all for the present, my lady.' His voice was deadpan. 'Thank you.'

Isabelle d'Achelie got up with less poise than she had when sitting, threw Bradecote a look of reproach and dislike, and withdrew.

'Best get hold of de Grismont before the lady has time to tell him what she has revealed, my lord.' Catchpoll was gazing after the lady's retreating form.

'I know, Catchpoll, I know. Fetch him now, but be polite. And at least I won't have your eyes on stalks, you old goat.'

Catchpoll gave his death's head grin. 'I'll have you know I am a good husband; no touching, but looking is something else. When a man can't get pleasure from the sight of a shapely female, well, he might as well be shrouded and dropped into the earth.'

'Thank you for that worldly wisdom, Catchpoll. Now fetch de Grismont.'

* * *

Bradecote was still considering the implications of what the lady d'Achelie had said when Waleran de Grismont arrived, supremely casual and at ease. He sat in the chair recently occupied by his inamorata, crossing his ankles and leaning back in the chair, lounging as much as it would permit.

'Well, Bradecote. I cannot see myself being much help, but try me with your questions and I'll see if I can give you useful answers.'

'Thank you, my lord. First, you arrived the day Eudo the Clerk was killed?'

'That very morning.'

'Had you ever met him before?'

De Grismont shook his head. 'Not to my knowledge, though it is possible we have been in the same place at the same time. He covered a lot of ground on behalf of Henri de Blois, so perhaps he was at Lincoln before the battle, or at the siege in Oxford, but I never took note of him.'

'What are your relations with the comely lady d'Achelie?'

This time the lazy look was replaced by a scowl. 'None of your business, by the Rood. It is one thing to ask about the victim, but not a lady.'

'I am sorry, but this is important, my lord. I have already spoken to the lady, and she does not deny that she entertains hopes, shall we say?'

'What woman doesn't.' He relaxed again. 'Well, if Isabelle has told you, I should not be so defensive. I would not have her honour impugned, you understand, Bradecote?'

'Your discretion does you honour, but in this case is unnecessary. You are hoping to take her as your bride?'

'I am. I knew her husband. Hamo was a decent man, but in his last years . . . well, it was his hope I could make her happy after he had gone.'

'Very friendly of him. Would you have been so keen to oblige if she had been ugly?'

Waleran de Grismont laughed. 'Of course not. What sort of fool do you take me for? Look, she is as pretty a piece as you could wish to find, and has lived a numbingly uninteresting life for many years, if you see what I mean. She's the sort of woman who needs a man in her life. Her manors march close to some of mine and, all in all, since it is certainly time I provided myself with heirs, who better could I pick?'

It was a pretty reasonable attitude, and Bradecote could not fault it.

'Did you know that she was going to the king, for his approval?'

'Not until after she had set off. I came here to recommend she go home.' He shook his head, and added, as a man like any other, perplexed by the female of the species, 'Why is it women cannot leave it all up to us, eh?'

'And you did not know that Eudo the Clerk threatened the lady d'Achelie that he would send to the king saying that your alliance was already sealed?'

'No, I did not,' he spluttered. 'If I had I would have taken a whip to him. How dare he upset her! It is not true either! Mind you, I cannot imagine how he reached that conclusion, because we have been mightily discreet.'

'I believe he intercepted a note written to you by the lady.'

De Grismont groaned and put his head in his hands. 'There

should be a law forbidding the teaching of either reading or writing to women. I had thought it an admirable, if rare, accomplishment, but now I see its dangers. It is bad enough that women simply have to tell someone if they have a secret. Now I find out they cannot resist writing about it too. Heaven protect us. If you sire daughters, Bradecote, keep them from ink and vellum, whatever happens.'

Catchpoll, who, Bradecote noted, had maintained the blank look of one who understood little of what was being said, was struggling to suppress a grin. Bradecote was aware of fellow feeling for de Grismont when it came to the constant mystery of the opposite sex. It was also mildly comforting that a man whose reputation with them was predatory, could still be amazed by their behaviour.

'My lady d'Achelie did not inform you of what had passed, then?'

'I told you, I knew nothing.' De Grismont's good humour faded. 'She probably did not want to tell me, because she would know it would displease me. At least she understood that much. What I cannot understand is why the clerk should want to meddle.'

'From what we have gathered, my lord, "meddling", or perhaps more accurately, "menacing with lies", was what he did most. It would certainly not be the first time he had tried to have women purchase either his silence or a good word. I believe this time he thought that lady d'Achelie might consider granting a manor to the New Minster.'

The frown that had been gathering on de Grismont's brow grew more pronounced, and he ground his teeth. He no longer sat at his ease, but upright and with fists clenched in his lap.

'Well, I don't care what the law says, I think someone did us all a service putting that cur where he deserved to be, firmly underground. Jesu, if I had known all that I would have been more than happy to do it myself. I cannot see why you are bothering to look for his killer, unless to thank them for a worthy deed.'

'Justice cannot be meted out by all and sundry, my lord, or else any murder could be claimed as justified. It must come through the law.' Bradecote was not unsympathetic, but was firm nonetheless.

The lord of Defford did not appear in any way mollified, but his temper was not Bradecote's concern.

'Could you tell me where you were between Vespers and Compline, my lord?'

'Look, Bradecote, do I have to prove where I was for the entire evening? This is getting ridiculous, and so I shall tell de Beauchamp when next I see him.'

'Nonetheless, I need to know.' Bradecote was losing patience. His headache, which had remained merely a background irritation for an hour or so, was now thumping behind his eyeballs, and his brows beetled with the pain.

'I went to supper with the abbot, as he and everyone else there can verify. When I left I cannot say whether anyone saw me or not. I was not trying to ensure that I was seen far from the crime, since I had no anticipation of a crime being committed. I went to my chamber, but I saw nobody as I arrived. I left some time before Compline and went to the stables to see that my groom had returned with my horse. He had taken it out for a gallop because it was misbehaving in the stalls. Neither my horse, nor I, enjoy confinement.' He pulled a wry face. 'I saw that all was well. Then the bell began to toll, and I headed for the cloister door. I met young FitzHugh crossing the courtyard and we entered at the same time. That will have to suffice, because I can provide no more detail.'

'Thank you, my lord. I appreciate your co-operation. I realise it must seem an intrusion, but we have to build a picture of what was going on that evening.'

De Grismont rose, and if he did not leave with the good humour in which he arrived, he was at least calm and polite. 'I take it this does not yet mean that I can depart, so I will await your further pleasure, Bradecote.'

Catchpoll held open the door for him and closed it carefully behind him. He heaved a big sigh.

'Not a man to cross, my lord, clearly. I thought at one point he was going to get up and leave, and I tell you straight, I did not fancy stopping him, not without playing dirty.' He sucked his teeth. 'You can see his point, mind.'

'But can you see him murdering the clerk?'

'He admitted he would have been happy to, but that was certainly no confession. A man like that, and that angry, surely he would have gone up to the clerk quite openly, pinned him against the wall, and then shaken him until his lying teeth rattled.'

'That's what you would have done, Catchpoll.'

'Yes, my lord, it is.'

'As would I, and it would not be murder.' Bradecote closed his eyes, and hoped his serjeant would only think he was concentrating.

'We have spoken to everyone now, my lord. What do you intend next?'

That was the difficult question. Did he start all over again, probing for cracks in everyone's answers? If so, then he had best spend a while with his vellum and consider whether any questions had been missed. He had no wish to ask Serjeant Catchpoll how he should proceed, and wondered if the man was angling for it to remind him of his novice position.

'I need to think first, Catchpoll, and to get some fresh air. Let us think independently and pool our thoughts after we have eaten.' He got up and walked out without waiting for Catchpoll's reply.

He had hoped to find a breath of breeze outside, and he had a desperate need to get away to the herbalist without Catchpoll knowing, but the air was oven-hot. His head was now throbbing as if bludgeoned by a blacksmith's hammer.

Chapter Nine

Isabelle d'Achelie was trying to look inconspicuous, which was difficult. She lingered within sight of the abbot's lodging, hoping to catch sight of Waleran de Grismont as he left. Since she had been asked about their relationship, and knew he had not yet been interviewed, it was reasonable to assume he would be next to occupy the seat in the abbot's parlour. She was almost pleased with herself for making this deduction when she saw the serjeant escorting the commanding figure to the lodging door. She wondered if his sense of honour would have him deny her, and hoped his nobility had not put her in the position of a liar. She waited, fiddled with her shoe, walked towards the guest hall only to think better of it and turn back as if she had forgotten something. Had anyone been observing her, she would have looked suspicious. However, the brother who did espy her was so overcome with thoughts that his calling should prevent that he did not actually think about her actions. At last de Grismont strode from the lodgings, his face marred by a scowl. Unthinkingly, Isabelle hurried to him and grasped his arm. He looked down at her, and the scowl did not lift.

'You did not deny me, my lord?'

'What good would it have done, since it seems you declared all? Would you have someone announce also from the bell tower to any who wish to be privy to our intentions? And what possessed you to write me a note, Isabelle? By the Rood, you have less sense than your own palfrey.'

He was clearly not in good humour.

'But they pressed me so, my lord.' She made it sound almost physical. 'And what harm is there, since all we admitted was our affection, and they will not be sending to the king about it?'

'I think private matters should stay private, that is all, my lady.' His mouth was set in a firm line. 'And I dislike kicking my heels in this dismal hole of chanting monks.'

She blinked away a crystal-clear tear, but saw it had no effect, and so tried to soothe him from ill humour.

'My poor Waleran. The heat is oppressive, and has put you out of sorts. Let me fetch you something from my . . .'

'Oh, by all the saints, woman, leave me alone.'

He flung away from her and strode to the guest hall, leaving her standing forlorn.

Hugh Bradecote was beginning to wonder whether his head would break before the weather. The hammering inside it made him feel physically ill, and he had decided to visit Brother Oswald, the abbey herbalist, rather than the infirmarer, because he might treat him more discreetly. It occurred to him, however, that he did not know where to find the brother. The easiest answer would be to ask Brother Porter, in a good official manner, as though it was part of his investigation. The black mass of cloud was looming ever closer from the west, gradually casting over the heavens like a leaden blanket. The storm would come, was coming, but overhead the sun ignored the threat. Bradecote did not stride directly across the court, but kept as much as he could to the shade cast by the walls of the abbey church, and was just passing the corner of the scaffolding-clad north transept when there was a clatter, and a swift cry of warning. He looked up, and jumped back as a chisel fell within five feet of him and embedded itself to the haft in the ground. He looked up, and saw Master Elias looking down upon him, his face livid.

'My lord, you are unharmed?' The master mason called down as he descended as fast as safety permitted.

'Since I still stand, that is clear. Had I been struck, I would not be living.' If his first thought had been self-preservation, his second was whether the act had been an accident, or intended, and his heart was pounding nearly as much as his head. He regarded Master Elias closely as he reached the ground. The man's face was a mask of anger.

'Thanks be to God! My lord, I cannot say as it never happens, but . . .' He shook his head. Behind him a young apprentice stepped from the bottom rung of the ladder, but came no closer, fearing retribution in hand and word. 'Foolish boy!' Master Elias had turned his head to glare at him.

'It wasn't me, Master,' grizzled Wulfstan the apprentice.

'Fool, and liar also! Come here.'

Wulfstan came, most reluctantly. Bradecote judged him on the verge of sprouting from boy to man, for his voice was not settled, but he was small and wiry, and his age could be anything from thirteen to eighteen if he had been used to mean fare. His eyes were full of fear.

'Now, you slack-handed whelp, apologise to the lord sheriff.' Master Elias elevated Bradecote without a thought, and to one as young and lowly as Wulfstan the difference was almost meaningless. He was addressing official power, greater than he had ever approached within three strides, and never would he have dared speak to such a personage. He trembled, and cowered.

'It was not—'

Elias's hand cuffed him smartly. 'Truth now, or I will have you sleep on the floor of the transept and have the brothers wake you for the night offices every night till Sunday.'

'I . . . I am sorry, my lord. It slipped, my lord. It just . . . slipped.' Wulfstan was not sure whether the lord would hit him, or get Master Elias to do it for him. 'My lord.' The apprentice bowed repeatedly.

'Carelessness, and disobedience. I have said, over and over, always to bring tools in there.' The master mason pointed at a leather pouch attached by two loops at the back of Wulfstan's belt, where it would not impede climbing.

'It was full and you said . . .'

'If it is full, you make two journeys. Nothing but bread and small beer for you this day, Wulfstan. Now go, before the lord sheriff has you taken up for assault upon his person.'

Wide-eyed and on the verge of tears the lad backed away, and then ran into the masons' workshop.

'It is sorry I am, my lord. I teach 'em, but sometimes lads forget.'

'No harm was done, Master Elias.' Bradecote's heartbeat was back to normal. He leant down and yanked the chisel from the earth, and handed it, haft first, to the mason, who regarded it balefully.

'No, my lord, but if . . .' He shook his head. 'And it will take a goodly time to get the edge back upon it now. The lad will have to do it, and you can be sure I will explain just what might have happened. If he fears enough, the lesson will not be forgotten.'

Bradecote said nothing. It was probably as had been said, an accident, but what if Wulfstan had been speaking truthfully, and taken blame for fear of greater punishment from his master? Master Elias looked grim, but was it an easy mask to wear?

'I had best get back up, my lord. The weather will not hold, and we must make use of every moment at height.'

'Yes, I understand.'

With a nod as obeisance, the master mason headed back up his ladders. Hugh Bradecote stifled a groan and crossed to the abbey gate, where Brother Porter gave him directions to the herbalist's little wooden hut. Bradecote was fighting nausea now, and took not the direct path but a more circuitous route out towards the fishponds, where he retched for some time.

There was, thankfully, no likelihood of his men observing his weakness, but when he finally raised his head, he was surprised to see the tall, habited figure of Sister Edeva walking alone beside the ponds. Her upright pose and measured gait made it clear it was her and not Sister Ursula, even at distance.

Disturbing her solitary cogitation felt an intrusion, and he would rather have had time to muster his thoughts, but he had to grab whatever chance he could to gain insight into this woman. He approached her from behind, but made no attempt to surprise her; rather he wanted her to be aware of his presence. At such a dangerous time it was not his intention to frighten anyone.

She turned at the sound of his footfall, and for a moment he thought her face brightened before she assumed her more distant expression. He wondered at it.

'Good morning.' He smiled hesitantly. The term 'sister' still stuck in his throat like a fish bone, and suddenly he was unsure how to begin. 'I think the weather will break before this evening. The ponds will not stay low.' He fell into step beside her, feeling suddenly as inadequate and tongue-tied as if he were a callow youth. She cast him a brief sideways glance.

'Indeed, my lord. Your concern for the fish does you credit.' She avoided his eye, and he would have sworn her lips twitched.

There was a silence between them, with which the nun seemed perfectly at ease, and Bradecote highly uncomfortable. He tried another gambit.

'Your name. It is a Saxon one.'

'Yes. We are not ashamed of our Saxon blood where I come from. It flows in the veins of most families to some degree, and is as red as any from Normandy. Indeed, it shows that our connection with the land goes back long before the sainted Confessor. My family has given daughters old names since the Conquest.'

'And where does your family have holdings? Near Romsey?'

There was a slight pause. 'Not close by, but further east, beyond Winchester.'

'I should have thought you would have entered the house of nuns there, then.'

'I chose not to go to Winchester. An aunt of mine had been at Romsey.' Sister Edeva halted and faced Bradecote. 'What is it you wish me to tell you, my lord?' Her voice was very calm.

Bradecote was taken aback. 'The truth would help.' He had not meant to say that, but it had risen to his lips before he could think.

'Nothing that I have told you is untrue.'

'And "nothing" is largely what you have told me . . . Sister.' The word games were annoying him now. His head hurt; he felt sick again.

'So? If there is nothing that I have to say that is relevant, I will say nothing.'

'It is up to me to decide what is or is not relevant,' he snapped, and winced as his eyeballs threatened to explode.

She made no answer, and her face, at which he risked only one swift glance, betrayed no emotion at all.

'How long before the Compline bell did you leave the church?' Bradecote specifically did not say 'the chapel' because he knew she would be exact, and if she had gone elsewhere in the church, would be unlikely to tell him.

'Not long before.' She paused a moment, sensing his irritation. 'I had time to go, directly, to the guest hall and wash my hands and face before the bell rang. Sister Ursula can confirm that.'

Yes, he thought, she had given him information that could be discovered elsewhere, but little else. She was most provoking.

'Why have you come here?' The question was put plainly.

'I thought it would be cooler, and . . .'

'No, Sister Edeva, not "here" but to Pershore.'

'Oh, I see.' The faint smile returned. 'I did not mean to be obtuse, my lord. Sister Ursula and I are here to offer Abbot William both coin and a fine illustrated manuscript in exchange for a finger bone of the blessed St Eadburga, whose sister was of our house. Abbot William told us yesterday that he and the brothers had agreed to our request. We will return to Romsey as soon as you, my lord, give your permission.'

'And you did not know that the lord Bishop of Winchester's clerk would be here?'

'Of course not. How could we?'

'Had you met the murdered man before? At Romsey, perhaps?'

'I never saw him there, no.' There was a long pause; an important pause.

'But?' Bradecote voiced the word which hung unspoken at the end of her sentence.

'But I knew him many, many years ago, before I took the veil.'

Bradecote said nothing, and waited. Sister Edeva's hands locked together beneath her scapular, and, for a moment, she closed her eyes. The acting undersheriff thought he could guess what she was about to say, though he could not see how Eudo the Clerk, even in his pre-tonsured youth, could have attracted a woman like her. Everything he had heard about the man showed him in a bad light. Had he deceived her and then shown his true colours? Had she taken the veil through disillusionment, or even shame?

'Tell me, was he the reason you became a nun?' His voice had lost its aggressive tone and was almost sympathetic.

'The reason? Not exactly. But without him my life would have taken a very different course.' Sister Edeva gazed past Bradecote, seeing not the enclave, but a life she had never had, a lost dream of love and contentment, of children about her skirts, of living in the fresh air of the Hampshire downland she knew as home, not within the cold, high walls of Romsey Abbey.

Bradecote frowned. It still seemed such an unlikely relationship. 'Did he mean much to you?' He put the question gently and was surprised at the vehemence of her reply.

'Him? Sweet Heaven, you could not think . . . Eudo?' She was outraged, and had stiffened, eyes flashing. He blinked at her vehemence.

The nun took a deep breath, and looked him straight in the eye. Her voice, very low and deliberate, held the trace of a tremor.

'Until I came here I had not seen Eudo de Meon since the day my betrothed was killed. Eudo was his brother . . . and Eudo killed him. He killed my Warin.'

Bradecote gaped at her. He had thought she might have knowledge of the man and concealed it, and then assumed she had been slighted by him, but never had he imagined such a declaration. Suddenly the woman with opportunity and ability had the strongest possible motive for murder, and one which even he could not deny sounded perfectly reasonable. Part of him cried out that he did not want to know, while the other claimed success in his task.

Sister Edeva continued, gazing through him as if he was not there. 'Our fathers fought alongside each other at Tinchebrai, and our families held manors in the same district. Fulk de Meon had three sons, and my father had only daughters. William de Meon was the eldest, and was a wild youth who followed in the entourage of Prince William. My father never looked to him, but wanted Warin to succeed him. He was steadier and had only a small manor to inherit from his mother. He would regard our manors as the caput of his honour.' Her voice softened. 'I accounted myself very fortunate to be betrothed to Warin. We knew, of course, what was intended for us from an early age. It just so happened that we fell in love. He was everything a girl could have wanted. We were going to be wed at Christmastide, shortly after my fifteenth birthday. He gave me an amber cross as a gift on my natal day.' Her fingers went unconsciously to the cross hidden beneath her scapular. 'I had special dispensation to keep it when I gave up worldly goods. Then news came that the White Ship, bearing the king's son and the heirs of so many noble families, had been lost en route back from Normandy. William was gone, and Warin suddenly stood heir to his father's lands and title. I would that it had never been so.'

Sister Edeva halted for a moment, collecting herself. 'Despite the family's mourning, it was decided that our wedding would take place as planned. A couple of weeks before Christmas Warin went hunting boar for the wedding feast. Fulk de Meon was lame as I recall, and did not hunt that day. Warin took his younger brother with him and my father also as one of the party.

It was unusual, because Eudo did not generally enjoy hunting. I remember seeing him, Warin, laughing with the hunters. The dogs were in full voice, keen to set off. He turned in the saddle and smiled at me. Then they all rode off, and I never saw him alive again.'

Silent tears were coursing down the Benedictine's cheeks, though she appeared unaware of them. Her voice dropped to a whisper.

'Eudo returned before the others, white-faced and sick. He said there had been a terrible accident. The quarry had broken away right in front of him and Warin, and he had thrown his spear, but Warin's horse had lunged forward at that moment and the spear caught Warin instead of the boar. The body was brought back shortly afterwards, slung over his horse and with the wound in his back. Everything was in uproar. Nobody had seen what had happened. It was only as the reality sank in that suspicions were raised. The hunters admitted their surprise that the boar had turned that way, for they had believed it had taken the opposite direction. Fulk de Meon said nothing, for it was a ghastly suspicion but nothing more. Besides, Eudo was his only remaining son, or so Eudo must have thought.'

A tight, mirthless smile appeared on Sister Edeva's face. 'It must have been such a nasty shock when William turned up alive. His favourite horse had gone down with colic before the prince's party even reached the coast, and then he himself had been stricken with an ague. So he arrived home nigh on a month late, to be greeted as a Lazarus. William was no fool. He had no desire to spend his life watching his own back. He and his father packed Eudo off to Winchester and into the novitiate before Epiphany. There was not enough proof for the sheriff, but they knew, as I knew, that Eudo had killed as Cain had.'

She paused for a moment. 'I begged my father to permit me to take the veil. He had other daughters, and could see I would be no willing bride to any other man. How could a woman who had been loved by Warin de Meon choose to wed another? So it was that I entered Romsey. I pray for Warin's soul as my last prayers at night and my first prayers in the morning, and shall do so until they lay me at last beneath the cloister garth. And I hope that his murdering brother burns eternally in Hell.' She said it as a curse, and her wet eyes flashed a challenge, daring Bradecote to accuse her of a lack of charity, but he said nothing.

She might be wrong, of course. Perhaps it had just been a cruel accident, but the family clearly had enough doubt and she had none at all. Evidence from other sources showed Eudo capable of evil. To have suddenly seen the man on whom she blamed the blighting of her life must have been a profound shock. In such a state she might well have reacted with violence, not thinking it murder, or even revenge, but justice.

'Did you kill Eudo de Meon?' He stared unblinking at her, and put the question firmly and without emphasis.

Her eyes did not waver as she gave her answer. 'Before God, I have told you and tell you again, I did not.'

Bradecote desperately wanted to believe her, but that very desperation urged him to caution.

'Then help me find out who did. You were in the church, probably throughout the time of the mur—the killing. If you heard or saw anything, you must reveal it.'

'So that whoever avenged Warin may hang?'

'If you did not commit the deed, then whoever did it had no knowledge of what may have happened between the brothers. This was not the act of an avenging angel, lady. This was murder, and in God's house.'

Sister Edeva frowned as if this interpretation of events was revelatory. Bradecote made no attempt to rush her response.

'I cannot tell you who did it, my lord. I was at prayer, as I said before, and saw nothing, nor heard any voices.'

Bradecote's heart sank, but then she continued.

'I heard footsteps while I was in the chapel. Several sets over the time that I was there, passing the south transept towards, or from, the crossing.' The nun spoke without hesitation, sure of what she recalled. They continued walking as they spoke, and Bradecote soon needed only to cut across the end of the pease field to reach the herbarium. He thanked her for her information, though he wished it had come earlier, and expected her to turn away, but she continued beside him, matching his pace.

It was she who spoke again.

'You did not seek this task, my lord, as I believe. Does it interest you, now you have become involved?' She cast him a swift sideways glance.

'It has given me an evil headache,' he replied grimly. 'I was actually on my way to seek relief from the herbalist. Unlike you, I do not find praying an efficacious remedy.'

'Me? I . . .' She halted. 'Oh, yes, of course. I hope he can cure it, though the weather must be making it worse.' Her voice sounded distant, as though she were thinking something else entirely. Bradecote stopped and turned towards her. She was gazing quite directly at him, and he could have sworn that a faint blush came to her cheek.

'I should return to Sister Ursula. She is nervous alone, and it will be time for Sext shortly. By your leave, my lord.'

She made the slightest of obeisances and turned on her heel, walking faster and with more purpose than before. Bradecote frowned, and went to the herbalist with greater worries than his headache.

A short time later, with no stomach for food, he returned to Abbot William's parlour to note the comings and goings and draw little arrows on a sketched plan of the abbey church. He found it hard to concentrate. Although the physical discomfort was beginning to abate at last, thanks to a foul-tasting preparation of Brother Oswald's own devising, the discomfort in his mind was increased. Sister Edeva seemed to have forgotten that she had said she went to St Eadburga's chapel to pray because of a headache. If the headache was imaginary, why else had she withdrawn from Abbot William's supper and gone instead to the church? One answer stood out, however much Hugh Bradecote tried to ignore it. She had motive, indeed reason, opportunity, ability, and had lied. He drew the patterns of movement on the plan, but they seemed a stupid diversion. He knew who had killed Eudo the Clerk.

Catchpoll did not return early from eating, and Bradecote eventually sent Gyrth in search of him. He arrived, trying to disguise the fact that he was wheezing from his haste. He had been thinking in the shade of a pear tree; with his eyes closed, his mouth open and snoring sounds emanating gently upon inhalation.

'You had need of me, my lord.' It was a statement, not a question, Bradecote noted.

'I would consider your views useful, Serjeant.' That ought to depress pretension, he thought. 'I have had speech with Sister Edeva once more, and learnt much, although whether it gets us much closer to the murderer, I haven't yet decided.' That was a lie, he thought, but I would rather he came to my conclusion on his own, or better still, not at all.

Bradecote recounted the nun's story about the death of Warin de Meon, and paused. Catchpoll's mobile features moved in a way that reminded his superior of a cow chewing cud. He concluded his deliberations with a sniff.

'As I see it, my lord, I would put nothing beyond the scope of our murdered man, so the story may well be true. Even if isn't, well, the sister has a remarkably strong motive. Now, it could be that she told the truth when she denied killing Eudo the Clerk. If so, then the information she gave is likely to be the most help we can expect to get. Mind you, if she is clever, and guilty, there would be no better way of throwing us off the track.'

'Thus far had I worked out for myself, Serjeant Catchpoll.'

'Well done, my lord.' The face and tone were impassive and respectful, but Bradecote knew he was being mocked. To rise to the bait would only please the man, so he held his tongue and pretended not to have noticed the undercurrent of disrespect.

'I have marked out the comings and goings, and I am sure there is something here we need to take heed of.' He pointed to his sketch and recited the movements for the serjeant's benefit.

'The first footfalls were light but firm, she said, and a sound

191

she knew without thinking. They were the sound night shoes make on stone flags. The monks change into their night shoes after supper, ready for the offices they attend from the dortoir.'

'Therefore the first person to enter was a monk, and quite possibly the victim, since we can account for certain for nearly every other brother.' Catchpoll was thinking aloud rather than commenting.

'Indeed. I am going to assume that was the case unless evidence turns up to the contrary. A short while afterwards, there came the sound of another person entering the church. The footsteps were light but came in short bursts, showing that whoever it was entered hesitantly. Sister Edeva said that she felt, though could not say for certain, that they were the footsteps of a woman.'

'That's better, my lord. That ties in with the lady Courtney coming to light her candle. She has that mousey, nervous way of going about, as though she would prefer to skirt about the edge of a room rather than cross it.'

'It could not possibly be the clerk, not in night shoes, and following someone who wore them?' Bradecote thought it unlikely, but wanted confirmation.

Catchpoll shook his head. 'I don't see him creeping about. He had too many years' experience to do that.' The serjeant grinned at Bradecote's incomprehension. 'If you don't want to attract attention, always go about as if what you was doing was perfectly normal, even if it isn't. Amazing the odd things you can do if you act normal. I know a'cos I have done plenty of them in my time. Creeping and peering is always noticed by someone.'

Bradecote smiled reluctantly. What Catchpoll said was very true. Eudo would have learnt that years since. Another cheerful thought struck him. 'If the footsteps were those of the lady Courtney, whom we know went to light a candle, does not that prove what Sister Edeva said is the truth, and therefore mean she is innocent?'

Catchpoll stared meditatively at the sheriff's new officer for a moment, but kept his thoughts to himself. A bumblebee buzzed somnolently beneath the parlour window; the sound was accentuated by the silence within.

'Not necessarily, my lord, though it is slightly in her favour. Concealing lies among facts is a clever way of proceeding, and that dame is nobody's fool. She might have heard lady Courtney from the Lady chapel, if she was guilty.'

Hugh Bradecote felt the invisible weight that had lifted briefly from his mind descend again with a thump. Resentment against his serjeant welled up inside him, all the greater for the realisation that he was perfectly correct. He wetted his lips and sighed.

'A fair point, Catchpoll. So the lady Courtney entered the church, went to light a candle and then, if,' and he stressed 'if' ironically, 'we can believe Sister Edeva, she left again by the same route before any other footfalls were heard. This means lady Courtney can shed no further light on the business.' He paused for a moment. 'It also means that whatever slight suspicion she may have been under is cleared, because if she had killed Eudo and then left, the next person to enter the church would have discovered the body.'

'Or been Ulf, ordered to drag the body, and he, of a certainty, would have trod so loud Sister Edeva would have heard him even if she was singing hallelujahs. It was never our nervous dame nor her man, my lord.' Personally, he had discounted the lady from the moment of her interview, but if the new man wanted to be painstaking in his process, so be it. No doubt he hoped to impress the sheriff with his thoroughness. Much good it would do him.

'The next footsteps,' continued Bradecote, 'were firm and hard, stout shoes or boots. The stride suggested a man.'

'Pity we don't use the nun of Romsey in all our investigations, my lord. She seems mighty adept at making deductions, for a woman who has renounced the world.'

Bradecote threw Catchpoll a look of acute dislike, and continued. 'That means this man was, if we discount servants, FitzHugh, de Grismont or Master Elias. We know that FitzHugh had been busy before supper, off to lame Eudo's mule. There would be no sense, unless you are going to suggest again a clever scheme to deceive us, in getting dishevelled in the stables to delay a man, if you are then going to murder him after supper, which "delays" him permanently. Correct?'

'Perfectly, my lord. Messire FitzHugh is out of the reckoning. There's no reason for the lord de Grismont to have been there either. He has no connection with the dead man; he never saw him before, and was unaware of Eudo's little discussion with the comely lady d'Achelie. We only have his word for that of course, but even so, such knowledge would be a reason to be mighty unpleasant but not commit murder. No, threatening the lady would not give him the motive for murder within a few hours of meeting, especially when everyone else seems to have had just cause to loathe the clerk.'

'Providing that the arrival of de Grismont was coincidental, and not a plot.' Bradecote raised a hand as Serjeant Catchpoll opened his mouth to expostulate. 'Yes, yes. That gives us the same problems as if FitzHugh had been sent by Earl Robert as an assassin. Mind you, I would have greater faith in de Grismont's abilities in that line than some wet-behind-the-ears squire, and I am sure de Grismont would be capable even of murder if circumstances demanded.'

'But those do not exist, my lord. Which leaves our master mason . . . the man who discovered the body and who admitted being in his workshop. And do not forget that Brother Porter saw nobody go in through the workshop door.'

'Motive?' Bradecote was conscious of wanting to be convinced. He did not mention the incident with the chisel, thinking that Catchpoll would think him too fanciful.

'Ah, there we have a problem at present. But I am sure we can discover one if we dig deep enough.' The serjeant smiled. Digging deep was, in his own opinion, his speciality, though his methods might not suit Bradecote, and his soporific cogitations had led more towards Master Elias as the culprit than anyone else. The pair parted once more. Catchpoll ambled over to the workshop, while Bradecote turned over all the evidence collated in his brain, and attempted, unsuccessfully, to make it point conclusively to the master mason.

Chapter Ten

In the early afternoon the gathering storm clouds drew together in menacing collusion, rolling over each other in their race to deluge Pershore, and the scribes found themselves unable to continue their labours in the gloom. Distant rumbles of thunder presaged what was to come, and the lay brothers who were completing the haystacks cast anxious eyes westward and worked the faster. The horses in the stable stamped and fidgeted, ears pricked, sensing the change in the air.

Around mid-afternoon the unnatural, heavy silence broke. A great fork of lightning crashed down into the brooding bulk of Bredon Hill, and the crack of thunder that came close on its heels made a mule buck and kick a hole in one of the side panels of the stable stalls. Monastic eyes were either closed in prayer or cast anxiously at the church. The thought of another lightning strike was terrible to consider, and for all those who believed, hopefully, that they had suffered all that nature would send them, there were others who believed that the presence of evil within the enclave would attract the bolt from the angry heavens. The prior was of the pessimistic faction, and jumped quite visibly at every flash. Sister Ursula, who had a mortal dread of thunderstorms, knelt, trembling, in the nuns' chamber, attempting the difficult manoeuvre of praying fervently while her hands were clamped over her ears. Sister Edeva knelt beside her, hands folded in the more traditional pose, but though her lips moved in the recital of prayer, her mind was otherwise engaged, and her face showed a pallor from an entirely different cause.

It was not long before the rain began, and describing what fell as raindrops was as accurate as saying His Holiness was a priest in Rome. Their sheer size and weight pitted the dusty ground, and swiftly created enormous puddles. It then progressed to a torrent that made it almost impossible to see from the guest hall to the gate house, no more than thirty paces away. A novice who had the misfortune to have irritated the almoner, and was therefore sent on an errand across the courtyard to Brother Porter, zigzagged across with habit raised almost to his knees, performing a peculiar frog-like dance, and trying not to yelp as he was pelted by the chilling rods of rain. His only consolation was that he was not in view of the boy scholars, who were gathered in the refectory and scrubbing the tables.

Eventually the thunder and lightning passed on towards Evesham, and the rain steadied. It beat an insistent tattoo upon the workshop roof that could be heard above the sounds of mallet on chisel and chisel on stone. The workshop was not designed for all the masons and apprentices to work in at one time. Usually the weather was fair enough for some to work outside, and Master Elias expected to have men up the scaffolding every day at this stage of the work. It was, in consequence, uncomfortable within. Elbows banged, tempers frayed, and the fine stone dust clogged noses and dried throats. Master Elias sent Wulfstan, the youngest apprentice and still under his own private cloud with his master, to the cellarer to request a pitcher of small beer to slake their thirst. The lad went off at a run, grumbling, for he had been sent by the outside route. The master mason had no wish to offend monastic sensibilities by having beer carried through the church, especially when he himself would not be the one getting wet, and it was another mild punishment upon the luckless youth.

When Wulfstan did not return quickly, Master Elias grew wrathful. No doubt the boy had lingered in shelter, hoping the rain would abate before he made his way, slowly, back to the workshop. Well, he would find his dilatoriness would cost him a clip round the ear.

Master Elias was remarkably patient with stone and impatient with men. He waited another few moments, made a garrumphing sound in his throat, and marched off, the drier way, to hasten his errant apprentice with a well-aimed kick to the backside. The cellarer looked surprised when asked about the lad, for he had given him permission for the drawing of beer some time ago. Master Elias returned to the workshop, frowning, but ready to find his men quaffing happily. Wulfstan, however, had still not appeared. The master mason swore and opened the workshop door. The rain made him blink, and he was about to withdraw his head into the dry when he noticed something out of the corner of his eye. He wiped a hand across his face and groaned. At the base of the nearest ladder up the scaffolding by the corner of the transept, a body lay prone, the head turned to one side, arms outflung carelessly. Master Elias's first thought was to rush to check the body, but a small voice of caution made itself heard in his reeling brain, and he called for his senior journeyman. If he was going to find another dead body, it would be as well to do it with another.

Wulfstan looked smaller, and even younger, a child in man's garb, when dead, and neither man had any doubt he was dead; the open, staring, surprised eyes and the unnatural attitude of the head proclaimed it. The journeyman shook his head in stunned disbelief.

'What cause had the lad to be climbing the ladder? It would be madness in this, an' he only went for beer. It makes no sense, no sense at all.' Rivulets of rain were already coursing down his cheeks as if he wept, and plastering his hair to his scalp.

'I know no more 'n you, Eddi, but for sure we had best fetch the sheriff's men before we lift the lad.' The master mason shook his head. 'You be off quick now, and bring that Serjeant Catchpoll or my lord Bradecote mind, not some minion.'

In the event both came running, with the prior not far behind, holding the hem of his habit from the worst of the puddles with the delicacy of a lady in her best gown. They halted by the body with grim faces. The serjeant knelt down, regardless of the wet, and pulled the back of the apprentice's cotte away from the neck. He felt the neck with an almost delicate touch, and then moved the head, gently. He spoke without looking up.

'Neck's broke.' He continued with a hands-on exploration of the limbs, and reported, 'No other bones seem damaged though, unless they're small.'

'Did you send him up the ladder, Master Elias? In this? What possessed you?' Bradecote asked, disapproval strong in his voice, and the germ of worry.

'Indeed I did not, my lord,' replied the master mason, outraged. 'I have always taken the safety of my workmen very seriously. You ask them. Ask the sacrist or the other obedientaries I have to deal with. No, to send anyone up top in this would be murd—' He halted, realisation of what he had just said dawning on him. He reddened, and his angry tone became merely sullen. 'I sent him for small beer for the masons, that's all. It's mighty dusty in the workshop with everyone inside today.' His voice trailed away, sounding like the excuse of a child caught in some minor misdemeanour.

''Tis true enough, my lord, but why did he go up?' Eddi the journeyman was not of quick mind, but he was as tenacious as a terrier.

Bradecote was frowning. 'Any damage to the face, Serjeant?'

'Not a scratch, my lord.' By now both men were thinking the same unpalatable thought. Bradecote was suddenly aware that the group around the body had grown. Despite the rain, several of the brothers had gathered by the prior, who was praying ostentatiously, two of his own men had turned up, and Waleran de Grismont was striding towards them. The acting undersheriff cursed inwardly. He did not want an audience to his deliberations.

'And where did the pitcher of beer go? That's what I would like to know,' Eddi announced loudly. He was like a dog worrying a bone, and Catchpoll and Bradecote exchanged irritated glances.

'What is going on? Has . . .' de Grismont stopped as the two men-at-arms drew respectfully out of the way, and he could see the pathetic, wet heap that had been Wulfstan. He frowned, and shook his head. 'You shouldn't send men up scaffolding in this rain, Master Mason.' His tone was reproachful.

Master Elias opened his mouth to expostulate, but was silenced by a gesture from Bradecote, who spoke instead.

'The lad was not sent up, de Grismont.'

'Is there anything I can do?'

Even wet to the skin and with a raindrop hanging from the end of his nose, de Grismont sounded a voice of calm authority.

Bradecote threw him a glance of irritation. He too was soaking wet, his fingers were losing sensation, rain was dripping from the end of his long nose, and he was facing the unpleasant fact that he was now investigating two murders.

'You can leave Serjeant Catchpoll and myself do deal with this, my lord. But thank you for the offer.' His tone held no thanks at all, and de Grismont smiled wryly.

'Quite right. I wouldn't want any interference either.' His eyes met Bradecote's, full of understanding and just a touch of dry amusement. 'I would suggest,' he raised his voice, 'that since we can do nothing of use, we all get back inside and get dry.'

He turned, and it said much about the man that, instinctively, the other onlookers made to follow him. Master Elias and Eddi remained.

'Can we take him in?' enquired the journeyman. 'It don't seem right to leave him here in the rain, not that he'll feel it now, poor lad.'

'Go and fetch something to place him on, and, you, Master Elias, had best seek out Abbot William and ask for the use of the mortuary chapel.' Bradecote's tone brooked no refusal.

Only for a moment did Master Elias look as if he would object to being ordered about, but he thought better of it.

Left alone, the two law officers could speak freely.

'He never climbed that ladder at all, my lord.'

'No, Catchpoll, I had worked that out. So we are left with someone breaking his neck. The first question that springs to mind is "why?"'

'Followed swiftly by "who?"' Catchpoll pulled one of his cogitating faces. 'Yet again our discoverer of the body was Master Elias, but this time he was not alone, so he could not, at first glance, have come out, done the deed, and then raised the alarm.' Catchpoll did not look totally convinced by his own argument, and Bradecote continued.

'I would prefer, however, to concentrate on "why" at present. Assuming we do not simply have a madman killing upon whim, there has to be a reason, and it has to do with the first murder. There are things I need to tell you.' He shivered, and blew on his cold hands, 'but let us do it in the dry, Catchpoll. We can learn no more here.'

'Except if we find the jug that Master Loudmouth so clearly wanted.'

'The jug?' Bradecote was thinking about something else, and looked puzzled.

'The pitcher of beer the lad was sent to fetch. He had permission to draw it, so it would be useful if we found someone who saw him do so, but then, as Eddi said, where is it now?'

It was a pertinent question, and Bradecote swore softly.

'I will go and find the cellarer. You begin hunting for the pitcher. I will not be long.'

Bradecote went in search of the obedientary, and he was not hard to find. Having seen the dead lad so soon before his demise, he was quite distressed.

'He came, my lord, and I gave permission for him to take the small beer. Polite he was, but . . . nervous. He asked if you were about, my lord.'

'He wanted to see me?'

The cellarer thought the lord Bradecote sounded surprised, although in reality there was more horror in his voice. Everyone had been told that anything they knew must be reported only to Catchpoll or himself. What if . . .

'To be honest, my lord, I could not say whether he wanted to see you, or was afraid of meeting you, if you understand. It could have been either. The master mason came looking for him, and I told him, as I tell you, the beer was taken.'

'When did Master Elias come, Brother?'

'A very little before the poor boy was found. He looked annoyed when he arrived. He said as how the lad had not come back and he thought him skulking in the dry.'

'Was he wet?'

'The lad? Oh yes, even as he arrived he was soaking.'

'I meant his master.'

'Oh, but a few drops that blew in the cloister garth, not nearly as wet as the lad. He complained at being wet at all, and said he had come through the church. He said as he was too old to skip about in puddles. To think, we laughed at that, and the poor boy was already lying out there, dead.'

This did not rid Bradecote of worry but perplexed him, and he went back out into the rain with a creased brow to join a miserable and sodden Catchpoll. He did not wish to discuss his findings until they had finished their hunt for the pitcher.

They made a good search, though there was no obvious place to conceal a jug. Catchpoll even wondered if it could have been lobbed over the perimeter wall. Before they had finished, Eddi and another mason returned with a blanket and a broad plank left over from the scaffolding. They rolled the corpse onto the plank, covered it with the blanket, and took it to the west door of the church, where they waited in the porch until told where to take it within.

The search revealed nothing, so wet, cold and disgruntled, Bradecote and Catchpoll headed for the warming room, where they hoped a brazier would have been lit to dry out any brethren forced by circumstance to be outdoors. They were out of luck, but a ruddy-faced brother made the appealing suggestion that they go to the kitchens, where Brother Boniface might take pity on them and provide hot ale spiced with herbs. The pair brightened, and took the advice with thanks.

Fortified by warm ale, smelling of wet wool, and steaming gently, Bradecote and Catchpoll resumed their ruminations.

'We can find out if the lad was with the other workmen, out in the town when the murder took place,' Catchpoll said, 'and if that is so, then perhaps he found something afterwards. If he did, then it must have been clear who it belonged to, else he would not have been able to approach our murderer with it, presumably thinking he would be paid for his silence. It could have been something dropped on the workshop floor. The apprentices are the ones who have to sweep up, remember, and it would not have had to be something very distinctive if it belonged to Master Elias. I expect they all know the things he wears or carries, but then there is the problem of "how". Master Elias went out with the journeyman, he said, and the journeyman agrees.' Catchpoll frowned, for Bradecote was clearly not concentrating on what he was saying.

'I seem to have half an answer,' Bradecote paused, 'but only half.' He relayed what he had been told by the cellarer. 'What I still cannot work out though, is if he killed Wulfstan before "seeking him" with the cellarer, how come he was not wet? The boy had to be dead by then or else he would have reached the workshop with the pitcher. Master Elias was out, and alone, but at that time could not have done the deed.' He shook his head in perplexity.

'There's ways to keep drier, my lord. What if he had a piece of sacking over his head when he went out? If the lad had lingered, as he was thinking, he might have met him coming back, and killed him upon the opportunity of a moment. There he was, alone, with a lad who might have hinted that he knew something that would send him to the noose.'

'It makes some sense, and yet . . . though if you add it to this morning . . .'

'You speak in riddles, my lord. What of this morning?'

'Because as I rounded the corner of the transept this morning, after we parted, a chisel "fell" from up top and embedded itself in the earth no more than a stride from me. Master Elias was very swiftly down the ladders, full of apologies and anger at Wulfstan for dropping it. The apprentice tried to deny it, and then gave up.'

'Likely he would try, with it landing so near someone, and someone far too important,' offered Catchpoll.

'But what if he was telling true, and it was not him? What if it was his master, and he accepted that he would get the blame for the "accident"? If Elias wanted uproar, what better way than kill me?' Bradecote managed to sound sanguine about his own potential mortality, but was increasingly worried that his own failure to take the incident more seriously had enabled the mason to get rid of Wulfstan.

Catchpoll scratched his nose. 'It has a sense to it, my lord, I will grant that, but does not mean the lad was not also privy to something that might incriminate. If you was done away with, then putting blame for the accident upon the lad Wulfstan would be easy and handy. Mind you, there could be no suggestion that he killed the clerk. I doubt not he was with the other lads that evening, or else they would have said.' Catchpoll tugged at his left ear. 'This would be as good a time as any to tell you what I found out about Master Elias of St Edmondsbury, my lord.'

Bradecote did not look pleased. 'Indeed, Serjeant.'

Catchpoll gazed at his superior innocently, but only partially concealing his pleasure. His methods for acquiring information were not all subtle, and usually involved a mixture of bullying, threatening, mild bribery, and, he preened himself, clever questions. The clever questions were what really pleased him, and, unknowingly, he felt much as Brother Eudo on the matter; discovering much without the other person being aware that they were even giving information was highly satisfying. He had gone earlier in the afternoon to the workshop armed with his wits and a tray of oatcakes. He managed to give the impression that he had persuaded the kitchen staff to part with them, rather than the truth, which was that he had fortuitously waylaid a brother bringing them as a gesture from the abbot. He was thus instantly regarded with favour, and invited to join the masons in their unexpected break. Master Elias was up the scaffolding, checking with his most senior man that the lashings would withstand the rough weather that was fast approaching, so they could afford to down tools, dust off hands and ease backs for a moment.

Serjeant Catchpoll might have a smile like a death's head, but he was able to ply them with a few choice tales at his own, and the lord Sheriff of Worcester's, expense. His own casual talk loosed tongues, and he was soon gleaning information about the places the team of masons had worked before, and when, without so much as a genteel enquiry.

Through all this, he had discovered that Master Elias's sympathies lay with the Empress Maud, and that, in his cups, he had been known to say that not only soldiers could be of service to her. The implication, to Catchpoll, was that he provided her with information. His work meant travelling about the country, and gave good opportunities to use both ears and eyes.

'One of the apprentices, not the one who was murdered, proudly listed all the places he had worked under Master Elias. These included Ely, Peterborough, Abingdon and Oxford, at the time of the siege.'

'I would not be surprised if Henri de Blois had sent a man to watch that situation, and a trusted man at that. Master Elias would have heard the gossip, if no more, about the lord Bishop of Winchester's clerk. We already know it has made its way round Winchester.' Bradecote spoke almost to himself.

'Exactly, my lord.'

'So the idea is that Master Elias meets Eudo the Clerk in the

Lady chapel, presumably by design, kills him with one of his own mallets, which he puts back in a haphazard way, because you would expect him to put it in the right place out of habit, and it is an obvious weapon. Then he goes back, drags the body to the position in front of the altar, and raises the alarm.'

'Having remembered to destroy any letters or information the man held. It fits, my lord.'

It certainly made sense, although it would be better with a clearer motive. Perhaps they had met to exchange information and argued. No, the mallet proved prior intent. Both law officers cudgelled their brains for reasons. Catchpoll was less worried than Bradecote about it, but came up with the most likely ideas. Either Eudo had discovered something about Master Elias, be it clandestine activity or shady dealings to do with the provision of materials, or he thought he could threaten him using unfounded allegations, as he had tried with Brother Remigius and the lady d'Achelie.

'So if the apprentice found something incriminating and thought to do a little "threatening" of his own, he paid for his stupidity. Having said which, it could likewise be that he knew Elias "dropped" the chisel and his master could not be sure that he would not come to us, quietly, and swear as much.' Bradecote was talking almost to himself, and Catchpoll thought he could detect perturbation in his voice.

'It might even be both, my lord. He might only have hinted about that to his master, after the chisel "accident", which might yet have been just that. If he found something in the workshop, he would have recognised whatever it was as his master's easily, and that would not be the case if it belonged to anyone else, and so perhaps, after being taken to task for his error with the chisel, he brought it up when closeted alone and feeling the edge of Master Elias's hand and tongue.'

Bradecote rubbed his hands together briskly. They were gradually regaining sensation, and had reached the painful stage.

'Either way it comes back to Master Elias, excepting that we cannot, without that sacking you mentioned, find how he managed to kill the apprentice. If there is enough suspicion do we corner Master Elias with our theory or simply arrest him and drag him off to the sheriff in Worcester? I have no knowledge of how these things proceed, Catchpoll.'

Serjeant Catchpoll gave him a 'Don't you worry, my lord, I have everything under control' smile, which irked his superior, as he knew, and intended that it would.

'I made sure Reynald stuck with him when he waited for the body to be laid in the chapel. The pitcher still niggles me, like the sacking. Wait! He wrapped the sacking about the pitcher and disposed of both at once, my lord.' Catchpoll sounded pleased.

'Then where, Catchpoll? I still cannot quite work out where he hid or threw it, because we searched thoroughly enough. It is the gap in our certainty.'

'Aye, but we have enough to begin, and many is the criminal who has confessed with but half the tale known by the law, and no great pressure brought upon them, neither.' Catchpoll sniffed. 'I expect we will find him still in the mortuary chapel at present, which would be a good place to confront him. We can place him in the cell reserved for erring brothers overnight, and remove him to Worcester in the morning.'

Serjeant and acting undersheriff headed purposefully for

the mortuary chapel. Bradecote was grim faced, for this was where the consequences of the law began to be felt. He was sending a man to trial and almost certainly a shameful death, and in cold blood. However justified, it was very different from striking a man down in the heat of combat. Catchpoll had no such qualms. This was his job, and the proof of his success.

Master Elias was kneeling in prayer before the body, now laid out before the little altar. Reynald stood impassive at the back of the chapel. Catchpoll indicated by means of a short jerk of the head that he should absent himself, and he slipped out silently.

'Murder is a foul thing, Master Elias,' announced Bradecote, 'and there have been two within the walls of this abbey in the last three days, undoubtedly connected. On both occasions you discovered the body.'

'I did, my lord, though it gives me nothing but sorrow.'

'Sorrow that you had discovered them, or sorrow at the thought that your soul stands damned for the crimes?' Bradecote's tone was harsh.

Master Elias rose swiftly, his face livid, though whether from terror or anger Bradecote could not tell.

'You are accusing me of killing my own apprentice, a mere lad?'

'Yes. And the lord Bishop of Winchester's clerk as well, of course.' Catchpoll, standing with arms folded, sounded quite matter of fact.

'It's a lie, a wicked lie!' roared the stonemason, the echo reverberating off the walls.

'We think it perfectly true, nonetheless.' Bradecote strove to be as impassive as the serjeant.

'I have no reason to kill anyone, my lord, believe me. No

fault has ever been found with my work or my actions, and I can call on abbots and bishops to attest my character.'

'Men of good character can be led astray, Master Mason, and once one crime is committed, others are easier, are they not, Serjeant?'

'Oh yes, my lord. In my experience, it is often the case.'

Master Elias was looking one to the other, horror and fear blending together in his cheeks. It was as if they were talking over him, not hearing his words. He blinked several times and then sat down suddenly upon the stone step before the altar, sagging like a dumped sack of grain, and dropped his head between his hands.

Bradecote expected him to admit his guilt, and waited patiently for him to pull himself together. Nothing happened, and Elias remained as motionless as the corpse behind him. Catchpoll was not as patient as his superior, and eventually broke the silence.

'You were in contact with Eudo the Clerk to pass or receive information of use to the Empress Maud. You arranged a meeting but did not trust him and came armed with one of your workmen's mallets. We do not know what was said, but he probably threatened you with disclosure and you had to silence him, so . . .'

'No, no, that was not what happened.'

'You did have a meeting arranged with him though, didn't you?' Bradecote kept his voice unemotional.

'Yes, my lord, but it was to be in the workshop, and he never came. He never came, I swear.'

Catchpoll ignored this interchange and continued, 'So you

hit him with the mallet, good and hard. You then left the chapel and replaced the mallet in the workshop.'

'If I had done so I would have put it back properly, so that it would not be discovered, not leave it out.'

'You probably did put it back, and only told us it was left out to distract us. Within the church there are few things that could have been used, and carrying a heavy implement into the church would have been too risky for our killer. It was highly likely that we would suspect a mallet of being the object used, so you might as well reveal it while covering your own tracks.'

'This is madness. Why would I then go back to . . . the Lady chapel you said . . . and move the body in front of the altar, then wait until the Compline bell to "discover" it?'

'Because it was good cover. If anyone entered after you had moved the body, well, you were in the workshop and could slip outside if you had to. You would have only to unbar the door and claim that your men had forgotten to put up the bar before leaving for the town. You see, you gave them leave of absence to help your plan.' Catchpoll was dogged.

'Yes, yes, I gave them the evening off. But it was just so that I could meet Eudo in the workshop, and he did not come. You must believe me.'

'Why the penitential pose?' Bradecote was keen to understand the minutiae of the murder. It could not have been the act of mere whim.

'I do not know. It was not me.' Desperation gave the mason's voice a strident quality. He was almost screaming.

'We now get to today's killing.' Catchpoll ignored him.

'Today,' sighed Bradecote, 'you were forced to kill again

because Wulfstan the apprentice found something of yours in the workshop yesterday that was out of place or,' he warmed to the theory, 'perhaps even had traces of blood on it. What did you actually use to clean the blood and brains from the mallet, by the way?' He did not mention the chisel.

There was only a stupefied silence, so he continued. 'You sent the lad for beer, and that was your chance. You guessed that he would not come back willingly across the courtyard, especially not slowly as he would have to with a full pitcher. He would hang about hoping for a lull. You then went to the cellarer and then nipped up behind Wulfstan on his return trip, broke his neck with those very capable hands of yours, and returned the way you had come.'

'But that couldn't be, my lord. I was only barely damp when I returned to the workshop, not soaking wet. What you say is impossible.'

'Not if you grabbed a piece of sacking and used that as protection and grabbed him as he passed the west porch.'

'I would have been seen.'

Catchpoll gave a mirthless laugh. 'Most unlikely. Once the thunder and lightning ceased everyone simply kept indoors, and the rain was so heavy at times that it would be difficult to distinguish anyone even if they were seen. No, it was not too great a risk. All you had to do then was find the body, and you made sure that you had someone with you this time, which was a clever move.'

Master Elias was at the end of his tether. Whatever he said, the sheriff's men had an answer. It was as if he could feel the noose tightening already round his neck. His breath choked within him, and he felt sick and faint.

'No,' he whispered. 'No, you have made a dreadful mistake.' He looked Bradecote full in the face. 'I have not killed anyone, I swear as a guildsman. I was going to meet Eudo the Clerk, yes, but it was at his instigation, and he told me where. It angered me, that, being told what to do like a journeyman. He must have recognised me when he came up while I was talking with Brother Remigius. He looked at me and said something, a phrase that only supporters of the Empress Maud use. He believed I was of her faction.'

'And are you her spy?' Bradecote's voice was chill.

He lifted his head then, and his voice was stronger. 'I am no spy, my lord, though I think she has the right of it and should have the crown upon her head. I have only ever given what I have learnt from my position, at meals, meetings and up high on the scaffolding. I recognised the clerk as having been in Oxford during the siege. There was rumour about him there, playing to both sides like, but I could not have said which was the true inclination of him or his master. I even remembered the lord de Grismont from when I was up at roof level on St Frideswide's.'

'He told us he was there, but we have no reason to think he ever met Eudo the Clerk.' Bradecote was unimpressed.

'I could not tell you that either, only that he met with the Sons of Abraham.'

'Met with? You mean he spoke to a Jew.' Bradecote shrugged. It was not important.

'I mean "met with", for he and the Jew of Oxford spoke at length and most privily, so as others would not see. Of course, they did not look up, no one ever does.'

215

'But you did not see him and Eudo together.' Catchpoll had had enough. The kitchen fire had warmed him but now the remaining damp had soaked through his cotte and he was starting to feel chilled in the cool of the chapel.

'No, I did not.'

'This gets us no further.' Bradecote, too, was cold. 'We will lodge you in the cell used for the punishment of monks for tonight. Tomorrow you will be taken to Worcester for the lord sheriff himself to decide whether you are to be arraigned or not.'

'But I protest . . .'

'Leave it for the lord sheriff,' Catchpoll sneered, and took the master mason gruffly by the arm. He stood up and went out without any further complaint or sign of struggle.

Bradecote was left alone with the body of Wulfstan the apprentice. He sighed, wearily.

'I failed you, lad. If I had understood things better to begin with, you might be living yet. God forgive me.' He crossed himself, and went upon his knees in prayer. After a short while he rose, and turned for the door.

He ought to report his success to Abbot William, but just at present it did not feel like success at all. He was here to discover a murderer, and beneath his very nose that person had killed again, the victim little more than a child, before he had been apprehended. He wanted dry clothes and a hot meal, and the chance to digest the events of the day in private. His stomach was reminding him he had not eaten since the previous day.

He went to the kitchen, and persuaded the cook to give him bread and a bowl of thick fish stew, which he wolfed down, with the half-truth of being too busy on the investigation of the latest death to eat with the abbot. He was, he reflected sadly, quickly adopting the subterfuge and craft of Catchpoll. There was, he realised, little to rejoice in with his unwanted job, but he was consoled as he remembered that this last fraught encounter had proved innocence as well as guilt. If Elias of St Edmondsbury was the murderer, then *she* was innocent. The dark fears that had grown to a sickening certainty by noon, had been dispelled as quickly as the oppressive heat by the cleansing storm. Tomorrow the nuns of Romsey could return home with their prize, and he could cast her image safely into the store of memory and dwell on it no longer.

He walked across the still puddled courtyard to the guest hall, making no diversions round the miniature lakes. The muddy water splashed unheeded upon his boots. The rain had ceased, and somewhere in the abbot's garden a wren's fluid treble song, sweet and fresh as the cleared air, poured out to all who would listen. Bradecote took in a deep breath and held it for a moment. It was then that the worm of doubt entered the certainty of his deliberations. He had said 'if' the master mason was guilty, not 'since' or 'because'. He told himself it was merely a phrase, but something niggled. He had not been convinced of Elias's guilt before Catchpoll had told him of his findings from the workshop, and was there anything revelatory there? Catchpoll was certainly convinced, but was that experience, intuition or just plain desperation? He had said he would dig up a motive, but had he truly done so? He, Hugh Bradecote, had been so relieved to find that Catchpoll did not share his own belief, that he had welcomed the serjeant's certainty with open arms. It did not fully explain events, and Master Elias, however shaken, had stuck to his claim of innocence. Could he be innocent?

Bradecote shook his head, trying to clear it. He had come to the stage where he was doubting himself for not having enough doubts. This was madness. It was not even his final decision. If de Beauchamp thought the case against Elias of St Edmondsbury was weak he would free him, castigate his temporary officer, but only mildly, and gratefully give the job back to his usual deputy. This did not prove as helpful a thought as he had hoped. Bradecote had certainly not wanted this task, but failure was not something he contemplated lightly. He was thoroughly confused.

His spare undershirt was dry, if stale, and would keep the lingering damp from his skin, at least for a while. He decided to escape from the pressures within the abbey and go into the town, but before he could leave the guest hall he heard his name called, in an urgent voice. It came from de Grismont's chamber. The lord of Defford stood at the entrance, frowning.

'Good. I am glad you are here, Bradecote. Look what my servant found when he turned back my blanket.' He pointed to the head end of the bed.

Bradecote noticed nothing at first, and then saw what had been left beneath the cot. Lying on its side, as if thrust under the concealing blanket in haste, was an empty jug.

'I am not one who avoids drink. I can take it as well as the next man, but I have never had recourse to keeping it under my own bed. I take it this has been put here to convince you of my guilt. Well, I tell you it is totally preposterous. Whoever did it wasn't thinking, because why would I put evidence in my own chamber? You might have demanded to search all our chambers. I shall leave one of my men here all the time from now on, until the killer is caught.' De Grismont spoke in a mixture of outrage and disbelief. He was clearly aggrieved.

'Your bringing this to my attention so quickly is of use to us, my lord. Thank you. With luck, your man should not be confined here much longer.'

What else could he say? 'We have someone in custody, but what you have shown me proves they are almost certainly innocent,' was not, however accurate, likely to engender confidence. He picked up the pitcher and took it to his own room, where he left the evidence beneath his cot, in a similar position to that in which it had been found. Then he sat for a while upon the bed, head in hands, thinking ever more depressing thoughts.

The finding of the pitcher only strengthened the case for the master mason's release. It must have been left in de Grismont's chamber while he came out to see the commotion round Wulfstan's body, and Master Elias was standing there, dripping, throughout. Waiting until later would have been risky and, as an afterthought, did not beat throwing it away in pease field or fish pond. No, it gave added weight to the circumstantial evidence against his other suspect, Sister Edeva, and the knowledge lay like a weight in his chest, constricting his breathing. By rights, he should get Catchpoll to release the master mason and save him a troubled night, but the concomitant to that was taking the nun into custody and leaving her in the cell instead. Well, it would do the master mason no harm, and he could surely afford to give the woman one last night of freedom. She was unlikely to go about the abbey committing acts of murder in the dark when there was a man in custody, nor to try and escape. The abbey walls were suddenly a prison to him, oppressive and forbidding. He needed fresh air.

He left the enclave and went out into the little town of Pershore itself. Walking through the gateway and back into the secular world, with shrill housewives calling children home to bed and ribald laughter emanating from the ale house, was balm to his troubled mind. Out here all the introverted, ritualised behaviour of the cloister took on a normal perspective. Bradecote wanted suddenly to go home to his manor and await the arrival of his child in peace, disturbed by no more than the rate of ripening in the wheat field, and the depredations of a roaming fox. Here was the everyday he understood, and it looked so deceptively simple. Only when Brother Porter closed the abbey gate with a deadening thump behind him did his disquiet return, and though Catchpoll snored contentedly in the sleep of the just, Bradecote spent another troubled night, his dreams a phantasmagoria of unknown hanging corpses, faces at windows, puddles so deep that they swallowed up those who trod in them, and a tall, alabaster-faced woman in Benedictine garb, who smiled at him with great, sad eyes as he approached her, and at the last moment withdrew her hand from beneath her scapular and, still smiling, stabbed him through the heart with a darning needle of impossible length.

The Fourth Day

The Fourth Way

Chapter Eleven

It was near dawn when Bradecote finally gave up hope of rest. He lay for a while with one hand behind his head, the other arm still too bruised to raise above his shoulder, revolving in his mind all the evidence and coming up each time with exactly the same unpalatable answer. His brain seemed to spin until he actually felt sick and dizzy.

Chinks of pale grey light pierced the edges of the shutter to the little window, and from without came the sound of the morning chorus, still in the preparatory stages with individual songs discernible. Bradecote rose, his limbs feeling leaden, pushed open the shutter, and thrust his head out into the new morning. The cold air made him catch his breath, but it was a deliciously sweet, fresh chill. Dew-bespangled spiders' webs glistened like silver and rock crystal in the growing light, as the eastern horizon turned from the soft grey of putative dawn to the gentle colours of the real thing. A wren, hidden deep amongst the ivy that clung to the wall of the abbot's garden, sang as if its tiny heart would burst. Bradecote wondered vaguely if it was the same bird he had heard the previous evening. A throstle's melodious song drifted up from the orchards running down to the river, and undertook a vocal duel with a rival from another bough. There was something pure and unsullied about the notes that made Bradecote forget, for a few moments, the unsavoury duty ahead of him. He emptied his mind of thought and concentrated only on the sound.

The grass had taken on its daylight green now, and from a muted world of shade and shadow the brightness of the day emerged, as bright as a butterfly from its chrysalis. There were no people in sight, and without them it was possible to hide from the ugliness of their deeds.

The birdsong became a crescendo, as though the latecomers feared being ignored. Bradecote could not see the sunrise itself, for the church and the abbot's garden wall and lodging blocked the horizon, but the change in the light was indicative enough. The long summer day lay ahead, and folk would be rising now to attend their tasks. Bradecote heard the first clumsy sounds of people, and then a yaffle calling in its distinctive dipping flight, somewhere among the beeches beyond the fishponds. It was well beyond Bradecote's view, but its mocking laugh, carrying in the still air, was an insult. It told him he was a fool to pretend, that life was a cruel joke and he had to get on with it. The brief respite from gloom that the other birdsong had given him was gone. He withdrew his head and set about his preparations for the day with a heavy head and heart.

The firm knock that preceded Catchpoll's cheerful arrival made Bradecote brace himself. The serjeant appeared far less lugubrious than usual, and rubbed his hands together as if in anticipation of some pleasant event.

'Good morning, my lord,' he announced airily. 'I thought we . . .' He halted as Bradecote slowly drew forth the pitcher from under the bed and held it up by the handle as if it was contaminated. He said nothing; words were unnecessary.

'Ah.' Catchpoll gazed at the jug, apparently in search of inspiration. 'I take it that is not a jug you have been keeping under your cot for emergencies, my lord.'

'No, Catchpoll, it is not. Nor was it put there by person or persons unknown. It was found by de Grismont's servant, under de Grismont's bed yesterday evening, and he called me to see it. He was less than pleased at having the finger of guilt pointed at him, you can be sure.'

'Ah,' said Catchpoll once more, 'pox on it.' His face worked for a moment as the full import of this information was considered. Then he sighed again. 'Oh well, I suppose we'll just have to let him go. No harm done, mind.'

'Yes, Serjeant,' Bradecote agreed, knowing who 'he' must be, 'I think we must, since he cannot have secreted the pitcher while standing beside us.'

Catchpoll brightened for a moment. 'How about he did so when we sent him off to the abbot?'

'And where do you think he was concealing the jug? No, don't bother to answer that one.'

'Well, he could have brought the thing to the cloister on the way back from the murder and picked it up again on the way to

225

the abbot.' Catchpoll sounded marginally more hopeful.

Bradecote gave this idea some consideration, but then shook his head. 'Too risky. There was no way he could have guaranteed the opportunity to go back to it before someone might notice it, and its position would point to him as the killer. Nor could he have put it in the workshop because it was crammed full of masons all keen to have a drink. They would certainly have noted the arrival of a pitcher, empty or otherwise. No. Whichever way you look at it, this puts Master Elias in the clear for the murder of Wulfstan. And if he was not guilty of that murder then neither was he guilty of the first. We therefore, reluctantly, return to the sacrist of Romsey as the killer.'

Serjeant Catchpoll looked most unhappy; not because, like Bradecote, he wanted her to be innocent, but because his 'gut feeling', his serjeant's instinct, told him that the second murder was not a woman's crime. It was he who now shook his head.

'I really do not see how, my lord. It simply does not fit. You are asking me, and in the end, the lord sheriff, to believe that a nun who has led an almost certainly blameless existence for years and years, commits not just a crime of passion, which I grant to be possible in the circumstances, but then kills an apprentice in cold blood. Aye, and breaks his neck at that. I'm not saying it would be impossible for a woman to do it, but I've never come across a case where a woman did so, not in all my years. The lad was not strangled; his neck was broke clean. It takes a deal of strength, and it isn't like killing a chicken. No, a woman would use a weapon, something heavy, or something sharp, and there was certainly no sign of marks from either on the body.'

Bradecote refused to be convinced, though Catchpoll's disbelief was welcome.

'And yet she did do it, Catchpoll. I am sure of it. If she is as cool and clever as we think, she may even have considered that an unwomanly method of killing would be an advantage. I accept it does not feel right, but there seems no alternative. Sister Ursula has no motive at all, and is probably not strong enough; the lady d'Achelie,' he pulled a face, 'would be too squeamish, and lady Courtney too fragile. Mistress Weaver, well, the only reason she could have for such violence upon the clerk would be if he was pressuring her more than she said, perhaps hinting that her husband's death was not from illness.'

'That thought had occurred to me too, my lord,' agreed Catchpoll. 'She might just have murdered him for that, whether the claim was true or false, but she has a lad only a couple of years younger than Wulfstan. Even given the strength, she would not have been able to kill him in cold blood.'

'No, she would not.' Bradecote sighed. 'We have discounted Messire FitzHugh, and de Grismont lacks motive. Master Elias is now out of our reckoning and Brother Remigius would have been off to confess before his abbot within the hour.'

'Don't you think the same applies to your nun?'

'She is not "my" nun, Catchpoll,' snapped Bradecote, 'and I'll thank you to remember it. She is a suspect and I think you will have to admit now, our likely killer.'

'But would she not have been driven to confess the second murder?' Catchpoll was dogged.

'I really do not know.' Bradecote grimaced, and ran his hand through his hair. 'As a religious, you would say almost certainly, but if her mind has warped with the recognition of Eudo, then we cannot assume anything any more. It is a tangle, Catchpoll, and Heaven knows I have struggled with it, but there is no other logical answer.'

Catchpoll rubbed his nose, and made one final attempt to dissuade his superior. 'How did she kill the apprentice in the pouring rain, and then change so that she didn't look like a drowned rat in a drain at supper?'

'We never asked Sister Ursula if she changed her habit, and however little they admit to worldly interests such as their appearance, I am sure they would each have brought a spare habit so that they would not meet with Abbot William in an untidy state after days upon the road or, indeed, in case they were caught in a storm. Being prepared to contract an inflammation of the lungs, just to avoid the sin of enjoying a dry habit, is not part of their final vows, I am sure. And you yourself said that the best way not to be noticed is to be bold and normal. All she had to do was return to the guest hall slowly, as if she ignored the weather. It would fit with her general demeanour and she could have come from stable or cloister for all the other nun knew.' Bradecote looked despondent, and closed his eyes wearily for a moment. 'I just want to get it over with now. We will confront her after breaking of fast, and see if she will confess.'

Catchpoll regarded his superior, not unsympathetically. It wasn't easy, the first time you sent someone to judicial death, even though you knew they deserved it, and it would be even worse if it were a woman, and one whom you, well, had taken a good look at, so to speak. Part of this he voiced.

'It comes with time, the standing back from it all, my lord.

The first time is never easy. Me, I had it better than most, for the first person I took for a hanging offence was a baker who had killed his neighbour because he wanted the man's wife, and thought she would take him if she were a widow. Nasty bit of work he was, full of his own worth and caring of nobody else's. But even then, I can tell you, it took some doing to actually take him in. He cringed like a whipped cur all the way, and mewled like an infant when they took him to dangle at the rope's end.' He shook his head, reminiscing. It had been said in an attempt to make things easier, but in fact it did not help at all.

Neither of them wished to eat with the woman they were about to arrest, and so they remained in the little room until the sounds from the main chamber, where the trestle tables had been set up, indicated that the brief meal was over. Bradecote took a deep breath, and got up from where he had been sitting on the bed.

'Right, there is no point in delaying this. Off we go.'

The pair left Bradecote's room and passed along the corridor to where the two nuns were accommodated. Catchpoll knocked firmly, and soft footsteps were heard. Sister Ursula opened the door cautiously, peering round the edge, her eyes pools of trepidation. The events of the last few days were totally beyond her comprehension, and had left her shocked, confused and very frightened. Death was not unknown to her, for everyone met it even early in their lives, but murder was something else entirely from accident and disease.

'My lord?' She looked past the serjeant and blinked at Bradecote in mild surprise, but sounded relieved. 'You wish to see me again?'

'No, Sister. It is Sister Edeva we wish to see.' Catchpoll's voice was colourless, and gave nothing away.

'But she is not here,' replied the young nun, opening the door wide. 'She went out after breaking bread and I saw Father Abbot talking to her, so I crept back here. I am too junior to be involved in their important discussions. Perhaps they are ensuring everything is in order, in case you let us go home today.' She frowned, as the sheriff's men exchanged anxious glances. 'There is nothing wrong, is there? I mean . . .'

They never found out what she meant, because at that moment there came a loud, anguished, female cry. Sister Ursula jumped, and put her hand to her mouth, but before she could exclaim, the two men were already running for the guest hall door.

The cry was not repeated, and they were not certain whence it came. Bradecote sent Catchpoll to the cloisters, and himself headed in the direction of the abbot's lodging and walled garden. The garden door was ajar, and a sixth sense made Bradecote's hackles rise, and his hand go to his sword hilt. He opened the door as cautiously as had Sister Ursula in her chamber only a few moments before. The first thing he saw in the narrow greensward that made the passage between lodging and garden wall was the large and crumpled figure of Ulf the Tongueless, who was making vague moaning noises. Bradecote advanced stealthily. At the rear of the lodging, the garden opened out in a pleasant arrangement of rose and lavender borders and green paths, where Abbot William could commune with his Maker amidst the wonders of nature and in grateful seclusion. Bradecote halted, feeling suddenly rather sick.

The sacrist of Romsey was on her knees beside a crumpled body. Bradecote approached, breathing unnaturally hard and moistening dry lips. The nun appeared not to notice him, even when he drew close enough to see who lay there.

'*Mea culpa, mea culpa, mea maxima culpa,*' she murmured, rocking slightly, her amber cross gripped tightly in her left hand and held before her face.

Bradecote's feeling of nausea increased. Lady Courtney lay on her back upon the wet grass, her mouth open, her eyes staring up at him, starting from their sockets. They were no longer vague and watery; they were hard, and full of reproach. The poor woman had been strangled, and he realised with horror that his own complaisance had been instrumental in her death. If he had acted earlier, if he had acted last night, she would not now be lying dead at his feet.

He knelt down and put his hand to the dead woman's cheek; it was as warm as if she still lived.

'It is my fault, all my fault . . .' Sister Edeva caught her breath. 'It was I who . . .'

She was going to confess, confess at this moment to him, and although he knew beyond all doubt that she was guilty, yet he still wanted above all things for it not to be her. Sacrist of Romsey though she was, she would pay the penalty for murder. The Church would cast her out to the secular authorities and she would burn, not hang as a man. Bradecote had seen such a death, long ago. He could not face being the agent of that fate. Let her confess to Catchpoll, not to him. He had to silence her, and, reacting purely on impulse, he grabbed her roughly by the shoulders and pulled her towards him. She let go of the cross in surprise. His mouth covered hers. She did not struggle, in fact he felt her warm and responsive, though perhaps for barely more than a heartbeat before she became entirely impassive, withdrawn within herself.

They stayed thus for a few moments, which seemed to Bradecote an eternity. Then a tremor ran though her. Realisation of what he had done hit him, and he drew back as sharply as if she had slapped him across the face.

She was still within his hold, her eyes not flashing anger as he expected, but full of an immense sorrow that added to their depth.

'I am sorry . . . I didn't mean . . .' Bradecote floundered. How could he excuse what he had done? Whatever else, she was a Benedictine nun, and he had kissed her. It was an appalling sin, even had he not been a married man. It was sacrilege. He was horrified and ashamed.

'It matters not, my lord. It was not intended. It just happened.' Her voice was suddenly flat and dead, as if her thoughts were elsewhere.

He tried to muster his own, for they were tangled.

'My lord?' It was Catchpoll's voice, urgent and questioning. Bradecote let go of the nun's shoulders. He wondered how much Catchpoll had seen.

'Lady Courtney is dead, Catchpoll, though the murder took place but a short while ago.' Bradecote stood up, hoping his face did not betray him, but the serjeant's gaze was fixed upon the face of the victim.

After a moment, Catchpoll looked from the corpse to Sister Edeva.

'Very upsetting for you, Sister, I'm sure, to find the body.' His voice was matter of fact.

She frowned at him, bringing her thoughts back to reality. 'I blame myself, Serjeant, for her death.' Sister Edeva kept her eyes on Catchpoll, and avoided glancing at Bradecote, who had himself under control again. He could not have put this off. It was utter madness to have tried. He attempted to listen, unemotionally, to what she now said.

'She had clearly remembered something important this morning, and would have spoken before all of us. But I bade her keep her own counsel and come straight to you.' She now transferred her gaze to Bradecote. 'If she had spoken, everyone would have known, and there would have been no need for the murderer to silence her.'

A wave of relief spread over the acting undersheriff, but it passed swiftly. What she said was true, but it could still be the nun who had done the silencing, if she was as cool and determined a dame as he imagined her. Had she even engineered the moment of his weakness?

'Could you tell us exactly what happened, Sister, in case that gives us a clue?' Catchpoll was focused on fact, not prey to Bradecote's wild imaginings or rampant guilt.

'Let me see.' She closed her eyes, and pursed her lips in concentration. She spoke without opening her eyes. 'Breaking of fast was nearly over in the guest hall. Lady d'Achelie was saying that she regretted not wearing a warmer gown, with the break in the weather making such a contrast in the early morning. Lady Courtney began to agree, and said that for her part, she always wore a warm cloak for church, where the summer warmth does not reach through the thick walls. Then suddenly she halted and said "Oh! But . . ." Her eyes grew very wide, and I thought she was about to say something important.'

Sister Edeva opened her eyes and looked to Bradecote, instinctively reaching out a hand towards him, but then pulling back. 'You said, my lord, that any information was to be given only to you or your serjeant here. I reminded her of that, and told her to seek you out after eating if she had thought of something. If I had said nothing, the others might have thought her mind was just wandering as it often did, or she would have told everyone. Either way, she would not have put herself into danger. This is my fault, all my fault.' She bit her lip.

Bradecote said nothing, but shook his head.

'Did you see her come this way?' Catchpoll was like a hound on the scent, disregarding her actions and his superior, and concentrating on the problem.

'No, for Father Abbot saw me as I was leaving the guest hall and detained me, wanting to be sure that the reliquary we brought with us had a good lining, and suggesting we pad it out for the journey home with wool. He even suggested Mistress Weaver might provide a small amount from the wool clip she is taking back to Winchester. So I did not see where everyone went, and then came to the garden simply to be alone with my thoughts. I did not expect to see anyone here, least of all the lady Courtney, for if she was seeking you out, why should she have imagined you would be here and not in the abbot's parlour? As soon as I saw her man lying upon the ground I feared . . .' The nun halted.

It was a perfectly sensible answer, and also appeared to be an excellent excuse, unless she had killed the woman only moments before raising the alarm, and if she had, then she had also laid out the massive ox that was Ulf. How? With what?

'Yes. Of course. I wonder why she came here?' Hugh Bradecote was thinking rapidly, and spoke almost to himself. An almost revolutionary thought was sinking into his brain. Sister Edeva really was innocent. He had become so convinced that she must be the killer, and that they only required evidence to confront her, that her own evidence had been cast aside. But if she was an honest witness, then everything else took on a new perspective, and the real murderer became clear.

He was about to ask Serjeant Catchpoll to escort the nun back to the guest hall, but caught sight of two brothers dithering by the garden archway, unwilling to enter but curious enough not to pass by. Bradecote called them into the garden. Both skirted the groaning Ulf, glanced briefly at the body, crossed themselves and took great care not to look again. The bulging eyes and livid marks upon the throat were not for the squeamish. He sent one to fetch prior or abbot, and instructed the other to escort Sister Edeva to her chamber. A command was certainly required, because the monk's eyes rolled in horrified surprise, as if he were being asked to escort a dangerous beast. Typical, thought Bradecote, that it should be one of those religious who were fearful of women. The man waved his arm in a general way, determinedly avoiding contact of body or eye. In more normal circumstances Sister Edeva would, thought Bradecote, have been amused, but she now departed with a frowning, pale countenance, although whether that was entirely because of the corpse at his feet, he could not judge.

The acting undersheriff let out a deep breath, and Catchpoll pulled a wry face. He was studying the face of Emma Courtney, and crouched down to draw the lids over the staring eyes.

'A pity.' He shook his head. 'The sister was quite right. If only she had come direct to us, we could have saved her from this. There could be no reason why she would think we would be here, unless . . .' His face, so capable of immobility and absence of expression before witness or suspect, was moving again, as he set his mind to the problem. He studied the ground in the vicinity of the body, and then nodded.

'Well, there's our answer, of course.'

'Which is?' Bradecote's voice was weary. He knew he was being shown up, but no longer cared.

'She was not strangled right here, for there is no sign of struggle. Even a weak woman like that would have struggled and there would be footmarks in the dewy grass. She was laid here, but was murdered elsewhere.'

'I can't see that it would have been in her chamber, otherwise the corpse would have to be carried, or dragged, in open view and there is Ulf to consider.'

'It was carried, my lord. And I would expect she was grabbed and pulled into the garden swiftly, quicker than her "mastiff" could react, and as soon as he did so he was felled. She would be easy to silence. Let's see.'

Catchpoll retraced his steps towards the side of the abbot's lodging, which was a blank wall. Bradecote followed dumbly.

'Yes, here we are. Definite scuffing marks in the ground

here.' Two paces from Ulf the ground was disturbed. He sighed. 'It means we know now who did it, of course.'

'But she didn't do it.' Bradecote could not help the urgency in his voice.

'She, my lord?' Catchpoll gazed at his superior in amazement. 'Of course she didn't. For a start how would she have dropped that ox?' He pointed at Ulf. 'I never thought your Romsey Sister was a likely killer . . .'

'She's not "my" sister at all, Serjeant, as I told you before,' interjected Bradecote.

'And,' Catchpoll continued, ignoring the comment, 'discounted her entirely when the apprentice was done away with. All that you said this morning, well you know it didn't sit well with me, but I couldn't counter it. I couldn't give you a real alternative. But now, of course . . .' He sighed, and then rose, slapping his knees in an action of decision.

'Right then, we had best be swift, my lord.'

Bradecote felt as if his brain belonged to someone else whom he was watching from a distance, but this brought him back to reality with a lurch.

'De Grismont must have realised we have found the body by now. I'll go to his chamber, you go to the stables, Catchpoll, and pray he hasn't bolted, because that horse of his would outstrip mine in a race six days out of seven.'

Bradecote was about to set off at a run, but suddenly thought of the body lying in the grass. 'But what about her?' He jerked his head towards Emma Courtney.

Catchpoll was already running, and didn't bother to stop, or even turn his head. 'The dead don't run away.'

As they crossed towards the guest buildings a great roar of distress was heard behind them. Ulf had come to his senses.

De Grismont's chamber was empty, though a cap was lying forlorn and abandoned on the floor, and there were signs of swift departure. Bradecote swore and turned on his heel. As he emerged from the guest hall there came the sound of a commotion from the direction of the stables, and a big bay horse slewed round the corner, wild-eyed and gathering speed as spur jabbed hard into flank. Bradecote lunged in a futile gesture to grab at the bridle, and went sprawling in the dirt.

He looked up and towards the gatehouse. A donkey pulling a small cart was coming in, and the gate, so often shut, was open wide.

'Bar the gate,' he yelled, as he picked himself up. 'Bar the gate!'

Brother Porter had been exchanging a friendly greeting with the carter and stood transfixed for a moment, mouth open. Then he roused himself to push the nearest door so that the entrance was completely filled by the donkey cart. The bay stallion was pulled up sharply, wheeling round at the insistence of the bit, and de Grismont vaulted from the saddle. If he could not escape mounted, he had no intention of being pulled down from his horse. He turned to assess his opposition. Bradecote was up now, and running to apprehend him. He was confident he could take Bradecote, but there was not only him to consider. Two men-at-arms had emerged from the direction of the stables, followed by the grim serjeant, who was holding his head and swaying a little. Jesu, the man must have a thick skull. He had had to leap aside to avoid being run down, and as he had made a grab for the mounted man, de Grismont had caught him in the head with a purposeful kick from his boot, which felled him instantly. The bulk of Ulf appeared from the garden, still bellowing, and assorted Benedictines had succumbed to the sin of secular curiosity. De Grismont thought fast.

Neither religious nor peasant had moved; the carter was standing by his cart in vacuous bewilderment. The fugitive took two long strides and made a grab for the gatekeeper. The monk was surprisingly strong for a man of his short stature, although he was hampered by his habit, but de Grismont, drawing his dagger, had no difficulty in grappling him so that he made an effective shield.

The monk noticed, out of the corner of his eye, and in a peculiarly detached way, that the dagger whose point was pricking his throbbing jugular was not a nobleman's pretty decoration, but rather a most serviceable weapon that had clearly seen good use. It was not heartening, and the little Benedictine attempted to ready himself to meet his Maker as calmly as circumstance permitted. It proved remarkably difficult to compose oneself to humble prayer and acceptance, the current world proving more immediately attractive than the world to come.

'Stand back, all of you!' De Grismont's voice was clear, calm, and commanding. 'Or more blood will be spilt on this very pious ground.'

Catchpoll, although dizzy, managed to grab Ulf's arm, and, ducking a swinging blow, twisted the arm up his back.

De Grismont edged towards the blocked gateway, where the

carter had at long last recognised the danger of his predicament, crawled under his cart, and beat a hasty retreat out into the road. His donkey, which was scrawny and moth-eaten in appearance, was of a particularly irritable and malevolent disposition. When de Grismont and his unwilling companion drew close, the donkey rolled a wild eye and brayed. Ignoring this warning signal, de Grismont reached out to yank on the animal's bridle, and the donkey promptly tried to bite him. The yellowing teeth only just caught his arm, but the unexpected attack caught him off guard, and Brother Porter, seizing this Heaven-sent opportunity, broke free and nipped smartly back into the gatehouse and barred the door. He then went on his knees and gave thanks, focusing on the fact that his Saviour had ridden upon a donkey, and that the humble beast had been placed there at Heaven's will.

De Grismont cried out in surprise and anger, and Bradecote took advantage of the distraction to close with him, drawing his sword with a scrape of steel.

'The only blood which will flow will be yours, if you do not yield, de Grismont.' There was a cold anger in his tone. This man, whom he still, in part, liked, had killed three people, and if he would be hard pressed to say he would like to see him hang for the clerk, he would have justice for the lad and lady Courtney.

De Grismont smiled, more lupine than ever. He felt his chances against the less experienced Bradecote were good, for he had never heard that the younger man had fought in a pitched battle as he had at Lincoln, or taken on a warrior of his own calibre.

Neither man had considered Ulf, who pulled away from Catchpoll so hard it must have nearly dislocated his shoulder, and blundered rather than ran at his mistress's killer. If de Grismont did nothing he would be run down. The lord blinked once in surprise, but that look was replaced by one that was dismissive. He still held his knife, and when Ulf was within five paces he threw it with all his force, and then drew his sword. The blade caught Ulf in the throat and he fell as if poleaxed, gurgling.

De Grismont did not even bother to look at him, but focused upon Bradecote. The pair circled each other warily, for they were not dressed for combat, and any stroke that made firm contact could cause irrecoverable harm. The only advantage that Bradecote possessed, and it was a small one, was that he wore a stiff leather jerkin, skirted almost to his knees, which might soften the impact of any deflected, glancing blow.

The courtyard was filling with a rapt audience. The novice sent running to the abbot was sped on his way less by dutiful obedience than a desire not to miss the excitement. The guests had emerged from the guest hall now, fired by the rumour that lady Courtney was dead. Miles FitzHugh stood frowning, arms folded, proclaiming to any that might attend him how he had come swiftly to the conclusion that de Grismont must have been the perpetrator because no woman would have been capable of such crimes. Mistress Weaver spared him one glance indicative of the fact that she, for one, would be happy to show him how capable a woman could be if goaded, and then ignored him. Isabelle d'Achelie was leaning against the guest house wall, shaking, and with her delicate hands spread over her face. She was prey to both the fervent wish that nothing might happen to Waleran de Grismont, and the sickening realisation that she had been about to wed a man calculating enough to murder not only an evil spy and truth-twister, which she could understand, but a youth and a helpless lady.

Serjeant Catchpoll was desperately trying to resolve two Bradecotes and two fugitives into one of each, but he saw, in however blurred a fashion, the opportunity to bring proceedings to a satisfactory conclusion. He grabbed Gyrth by the arm.

'Fetch your bow, swiftly now, and if you get a good clear shot, bring him down.' His voice was a little slurred, but Gyrth nodded and departed quickly.

While the two protagonists circled there was still a chance. Catchpoll had no qualms. This was not a trial by combat, proclaimed by a court and between two men only, merely the apprehension of a murderer. If Bradecote was prepared to risk life and limb, fired by some noble ideal, then more fool him. As long as the exits were barred, de Grismont was like a rat in a trap.

De Grismont was a man of limited patience, prepared to make a move as soon as half an opportunity presented itself, which was what Bradecote was anticipating. The donkey, now thoroughly upset, was bucking and kicking the little cart into taper splinters behind it, and scattering produce in all directions.

Bradecote's eyes were focused solely on de Grismont, and he trod on an errant cabbage, stumbling as he did so. Seeing his chance, de Grismont brought down his blade in a lunging slash, which Bradecote, off balance, parried as best he could. Steel juddered on steel as the last foot of de Grismont's sword, which would have sliced open Bradecote's face, was blocked by his weapon, and sent numbing reverberations down the arms of both men. The undersheriff's bruised left shoulder ached sickeningly, but the battle-blood coursing through his veins meant that he scarcely acknowledged it.

It was only at this point that the Sisters of Romsey emerged into the courtyard. Sister Ursula gave a muffled cry and shut her eyes in horror. Sister Edeva stood frozen, her lips moving silently, and her hands clasped together before her face, though it was only the whiteness of the knuckles that indicated more than prayer.

Gyrth returned breathless, bow in hand, only for Catchpoll to shake his head. Battle was now properly enjoined, and it would be more than his job was worth to explain to de Beauchamp how he had caused the shooting of the newly appointed acting undersheriff.

Bradecote, having survived the first murderous blow, rolled sideways to avoid a second slash and rose to his feet nimbly enough. He did not have the experience of the older man, but he was fit, agile, and hoped speed and his few extra inches of reach would make up for both that and power. The next attack was a more even match, and a flurry of stroke and counterstroke sent sparks from the glinting steel. De Grismont was the sort of man for whom attack was also defence, but Bradecote simply parried until a chance presented itself. Both men began to breathe heavily, their faces taut with concentration, the world beyond their opponent but a vague blur. De Grismont was still having the better of it, keeping Bradecote on the defensive, but the sheriff's man was biding his time, hoping for an error that would present the vital opening.

Lady d'Achelie was sobbing now, quietly, and without drawing any attention from the other guests, fixed as they were upon the fight to the death. She had shown the rare facility to be able to summon tears on a whim and remain beautiful, but these tears were no affectation, for beneath her parted fingers, the eyes daring to watch the fight were reddening rapidly.

De Grismont was breathing through his mouth, the lips drawn back in half-snarl, half-smile, and his onslaught was becoming disjointed. He made a poor single-handed parry, with arm and sword at an awkward angle, and Bradecote seized his chance. With a cry, he brought his blade across in a backhand stroke that should have taken sword arm and chest, but Waleran de Grismont foresaw the outcome and stepped back ready for instant riposte. Only as his stroke carried through, encountering nothing but air, did Bradecote realise his error. He made a futile attempt to avoid de Grismont's blade, but succeeded only in turning it from a fatal blow to a wound. The honed edge of the tip that would have eviscerated him struck higher than intended, cleaving the stout leather of Bradecote's jerkin like linen and bouncing from rib to rib. Bradecote felt the scrape of steel on bone and the sticky warmth of blood before the pain. The sound of a woman's scream made a vague impression on his brain, and his eyes saw the glitter of victory in those of Waleran de Grismont. He staggered.

'A pity,' gasped de Grismont, grinning wolfishly. 'You would have been a worthy adversary, given a few more years; years you won't live to enjoy.' The sweat ran into his eyes, and he blinked. Just once.

Bradecote lunged with all his remaining strength, off balance and more in hope and desperation than in anticipation of success. He almost expected the final, fatal wound, and braced himself for the icy, stabbing bite of the steel. But the blow did not come; the blade did not enter his flesh. His own sword, though more suited to slashing than stabbing, went onward, catching de Grismont below the sternum and meeting no solid opposition until it hit his spine, sickeningly. He wrenched it back.

Waleran de Grismont made a peculiar, hissing grunt, and sank to his knees, his eyes registering surprise, and his mouth opening as a last great exhalation left him. Then he pitched forward to leave a spreading scarlet stain upon the courtyard dirt.

Bradecote collapsed also, leaning on the pommel of his sword. His limbs, no longer forced to act, were as weak as straw stalks, and his chest protested at every laboured breath. He felt strong arms grab him from either side, and was aware of Catchpoll's voice, chiding like his old nursemaid had been wont to do.

'There now, you've been and killed him, so we won't know why he turned murderer. I was really looking forward to encouraging his explanation. It makes the job so much more worthwhile. Up you come now, my lord, and we'll see you don't leave any more nasty stains on the good lord abbot's domain.'

Bradecote did as he was bid, lacking the strength or will to remonstrate at being treated like an infant, and was assisted by Catchpoll and Gyrth towards the infirmary. He was dimly aware of the crowd now; of the lady d'Achelie being fanned by an agitated FitzHugh as she slumped against the guest hall wall; of Mistress Weaver nodding encouragement at him like a fond aunt, and Sister Edeva, her face as white as her wimple, her grey eyes moist, and her hands clasped, vice-like, before her.

He wanted to say something, but could neither find the right words nor the breath to issue them. He was half carried up the shallow steps into the infirmary and passed into the safe, ministering hands of the infirmarer.

Chapter Twelve

With his wound tended, and given the chance to rest for an hour or two, Bradecote began to feel that lying idle in the infirmary while the loose ends of the business were being tidied up by Catchpoll was not much to his taste. His chest still pained at every breath, certainly, his limbs felt stiff, and his shoulder had seized up entirely, but he told himself that as long as he took things at a steady pace, he could do all that was required of him. He sat up very gingerly, his left arm protectively positioned over his damaged ribs, still protesting at their ill usage. He permitted himself the luxury of a long groan, since there was nobody he knew within earshot. He had just swung his legs to the floor when he heard a female voice, tremulous but insistent, in heated conversation with a man, whom Bradecote thought must be the infirmarer. A moment later Isabelle d'Achelie erupted into the peace of the infirmary. The elderly monk who was the only

247

other current invalid pulled his blanket up to his chin with gnarled fingers, and rolled his eyes in a gesture of wild panic.

The events of the last few hours had not left Isabelle d'Achelie looking her best. Her flawless complexion was marred by the blotchy effects of prolonged and genuine weeping, her eyes were swollen and pink, and hair had escaped in abandoned wisps from within the confines of her coif.

'My lord,' she began, her voice throbbing histrionically, 'you must believe I did not know.' She threw herself at his feet, and he feared for one awful moment that she was going to fling her arms round his knees.

'My lady d'Achelie, I . . .'

'No, do not say it. You must blame me for concealing the identity of the murderer, but I swear I had no proof.'

Bradecote forbore to say he had not asked for proof, only suspicions, and the lady continued her rapid, exculpatory speech. She wanted to make clear that she was innocent of collusion in such crimes, while simultaneously admitting not having told the sheriff's men that she had told de Grismont of Eudo's threat, some time before Vespers, and that he had told her not to worry, because he would ensure Eudo kept quiet.

'I thought he would threaten him in turn, you see. I do not think the clerk was a brave man, not at all. Afterwards, well I obviously thought it might have been Waleran, defending my good name, but I had no proof.' An echo of the old Isabelle returned, and she smiled girlishly, the picture of naive frailty. 'I thought perhaps that Waleran would tell me if it was him, and if he said nothing, and I did not ask, well, it could have been someone else.' She paused for a moment, and added. 'Not that

I really minded if he had killed him, because he was a nasty, evil man and deserved all he got.'

'But the apprentice and lady Courtney?'

'No. Oh, no.' Her face registered revulsion. 'How he could have . . . I mean, lady Courtney was such an innocuous, devout lady, and that poor boy . . .' She shook her head. 'I did not know about the apprentice until supper, and then I was worried. I did not think I should give Waleran away without hearing what he had to say. He denied any connection, and said he thought it must have been a different thing entirely, because he had seen the master mason in the serjeant's charge. He said it was a matter amongst the masons, and I wasn't to worry. So I didn't.'

She paled again, and her voice dropped to a whisper. 'This morning, when I heard rumour of something horrible happening to lady Courtney, I sort of knew. And then I came outside and saw . . .' She covered her face with her hands, unconsciously mimicking her earlier action. She gave a couple of deep sobs, and then raised her head. 'I thought he would make me happy, and he has brought nothing but misery and shame.'

Bradecote sighed. He did not know the position of the law, but he did not think any ill intent could be proved against the woman, and even if it could, he, for one, had no stomach for it.

'Go home, my lady, and do not be over impressed with soft words and warm looks. You need have no fear of dwindling in lonely widowhood. A lady with your,' he paused, 'your charm and personality, will impress many a fine man. Do not be rushed into a new marriage.' He wondered at himself, sounding like a priest taking a confession. She would listen to what he had to say attentively, but he knew that deep down, here was a woman who broke hearts and whose own would always be vulnerable. He hoped, for the peace of her estates, that a good, reliable suitor would arrive in her bailey before she caused more mischief.

She rose from her knees, dusting her skirts in an habitual action, and swept him a deep curtsey. 'I will, my lord, and thank you.' She turned, and left, the faintest of swings to her lightened step.

A short while later Bradecote, having ignored the infirmarer's gentle remonstrations, was walking slowly and cautiously down the infirmary steps. He saw Serjeant Catchpoll coming towards him, holding some missive, and with the air of a man who would like to whistle but knows he is always out of tune.

'Ah, so we are feeling better are we, my lord?'

'I don't know about "we", Catchpoll, but I can say for certain that I am not feeling as bad as I was earlier, but I have frequently felt better.'

'Well, you might feel much better when you see this.' He proffered the document. 'It has just arrived from Worcester. According to the messenger who brought it, there has been a major discovery of treachery involving a Worcestershire lord who bought his ransom, not with gold, but with the promise of adherence to the empress, but has "forgotten" to do so. Now I wonder who that might be?'

'I wonder why de Beauchamp bothers with written instructions at all, if the messenger can tell you that much. Let us see if he has it aright.' Bradecote broke the seal and opened out the vellum. He winced, and Catchpoll solicitously enquired whether he would like to be seated. 'No, thank you. Getting up and down is worse than standing.' He leant against the infirmary wall, which provided shade and comfort, and read the contents. The messenger was not far wrong.

'The lord sheriff hopes we are close to solving the murder of the lord Bishop of Winchester's clerk, and bids me take into custody one Waleran de Grismont, lord of Defford, upon the wish of the empress. It appears that he bought his freedom after Lincoln by promising to transfer his support to her, but thus far has failed to fulfil that promise and her patience is running out. So, much as you told me, but the failure to change allegiance seems thin reason for detaining him. Men change sides often enough. No need to look further than our lord William de Beauchamp himself. Strictly speaking, as the king's representative, he should be commending de Grismont for his, er, loyalty.'

'Ah, this is more in the way of keeping both sides sweet, I would imagine, my lord. The Empress Maud is renowned as an unforgiving woman, and the lord sheriff would not flout her command if it did not break the law. I expect she would also like de Grismont rattled a little to find out who else is less than trustworthy just at present. She'll miss that now, of course, but I don't suppose she's a lady to fret on it.' Catchpoll ruminated for a moment. 'Looks like what Master Elias said was true, about de Grismont going to the Jew of Oxford. You certainly would not think him poor to look at him.' Catchpoll frowned. 'But why delay changing sides? He could have done so almost straight away, and if he lay close with someone powerful like Robert of Gloucester he would not have risked being dragged off by the king.'

'I imagine he wanted the lady d'Achelie wedded and bedded first. Hamo d'Achelie was loyal to King Stephen, and he might not have received so warm a welcome from the lady if he had just shown himself inconstant in his loyalty.'

'Ah, there you have it, my lord. A very fair reason, and, if the clerk found out and threatened to tell both lady and king of the planned change of allegiance, neither would respond well. There is your motive for murder.' Catchpoll nodded to himself, content.

Bradecote was ahead of him, though, and was puzzling over practicalities rather than motives.

'This is all very well. Catchpoll, and we know that he really was the killer, but how did he manage to commit the murders? The evidence does not make it clear. How, for instance, did he get into the church, with Sister Edeva in St Eadburga's chapel, without being heard? The west door is in clear view of anyone coming out of the guest hall and the courtyard much frequented; the door to the masons' workshop would be barred from the inside, and even if it was not, then Brother Porter would have seen anyone. He swore none had entered, and we have absolutely no reason to doubt him.'

Catchpoll sniffed, set his face working, and scratched meditatively under his left arm. Bradecote, addressing the same mental problem, merely frowned in concentration. Eventually it was Bradecote who brightened.

'It could be done, and only by de Grismont, if I have it aright. We know he found out about Eudo the Clerk's threats to his lady-love before Vespers, and reassured lady d'Achelie, so it would be safe to assume that he had words with the clerk around the end of Vespers, but could not speak his mind where others might see. Eudo, ever wanting to be in control, and having another meeting already set for the workshop after supper, then suggested the Lady chapel, expecting capitulation rather than violence.'

He paused, awaiting Catchpoll's agreement. It came simply as a nod, and he continued. 'De Grismont hears the masons talking about their unexpected evening out on the town, and sees the chance to prepare his crime. He probably expects only to have to threaten or at worst mistreat Eudo a little, but if the worst comes to the worst, well, using his sword would really cut down the number of suspects, whereas a mallet could have been used by anyone. In addition, he decides he could get into the church without being obvious. He sends his groom out to exercise his horse, remember. I have no doubt that if we asked the groom, he would say he had strict instructions to be back just after supper. Brother Porter sees nothing unusual, especially as the groom has been out some time and is expected to come back. While he is letting him in, and making a little polite conversation, de Grismont lets himself into the workshop and bars the door from the inside.'

Catchpoll smiled. 'Which was how the apprentice comes into it. He was bribed to leave the door open, no doubt fed some story of a tryst, and after the murder the lad works out he might have information we want. He sees Waleran has all the trappings of a rich man and takes the opportunity for a little "threatening" of his own.' The smile twisted. 'He hadn't enough sense to see that a man who commits murder once will find it easier a second time, especially if threatened. Fool of a boy. That mistake cost him his life.'

'Yes, but we are ahead of ourselves, Catchpoll.' Bradecote was trying to be methodical. 'We have a method by which de Grismont enters the church, and picks up the murder weapon, without passing St Eadburga's chapel, so the footsteps Sister Edeva heard were Master Elias's.'

'Indeed, and de Grismont was already in the Lady chapel with the clerk. The lady Courtney cannot have known anything, because she came and went almost certainly before de Grismont arrived. Which gives us a puzzle of sorts. We don't of course know how early in the meeting de Grismont killed Eudo, but it is of no importance. Since he is most unlikely to have called out, there was nothing to hear.' Catchpoll's face performed one of its thinking manoeuvres. 'By now he was dead, because de Grismont had just put the mallet back and must have heard the mason's footsteps approaching. He slips back to the Lady chapel, up the side of the choir stalls and waits, and nothing happens. He could leave the body where it is, and I for one would have done so, but he is a bit of a risk taker and has a very dry humour, thinks himself very witty, so he drags the body on its scapular to the high altar and puts it in the penitential pose, both to distract us and to show Eudo needed to be penitent. He can hear the mason still in the workshop, so disappears down the nave to the porch. He can make sure nobody is in view before slipping out.' The serjeant grinned. 'We didn't consider that, did we?'

Bradecote wondered if the 'we' really meant both of them, but on balance of recent history, thought not.

'He then,' concluded Catchpoll, who had warmed to his theme, 'leaves the porch just before the bell for Compline, biding his time until nobody is in sight and nipping out to head back in through the cloister like a devout member of the community.'

Bradecote was satisfied. It all fitted neatly enough, even if it was a bit convoluted and time dependent. After all, if it had been obvious, they would, he told himself, have seen it all earlier.

'I see why the apprentice needed to be got rid of, Catchpoll, but surely we have a greater problem with that killing than the first one. The north transept is clearly visible from the gatehouse, which is risky, and Brother Porter reported nothing out of the ordinary.'

'Yes, my lord, but the weather is the major accomplice. It was raining so hard, and had been doing so long enough, that those who had gawped when it began had lost interest, and everyone was finding tasks to do inside. I think de Grismont wasn't sure how he was going to get rid of Wulfstan. Perhaps he had arranged another meeting. Anyway, he sees him by chance, running to fetch the pitcher of beer. Coming up behind someone in that downpour would be easy, and a man like him could have broken the lad's neck in a trice.'

'But de Grismont would be wet, very wet.' Bradecote was perplexed.

'And so he was when we saw him.' Catchpoll noted the frown, and could not resist feeling smug. 'He came out to see what was going on, which none of the other guests did, remember. No, he came out because he would not be noticed as he approached, not with a body lying there, and by the time he got to us he would he soaked anyway. Clever move, I have to say.'

'And he took the pitcher back to his chamber, and "discovered" it because, logically, no murderer would keep it. Therefore it must have been planted on an innocent person.' Bradecote shook his head. 'The more we delve, the more we find out how devious de Grismont could be.'

'Aye, but the last killing was not up to his standard. Lady Courtney gave herself away at break of fast and so he had to act swiftly. Luckily for him, he was able to catch up with her outside, on her way to the abbot's lodging, bundle her through the wicket gate, drop Ulf with a good blow and strangle her. I suppose she was too stunned to scream. He then went back and packed for his escape, because we would be running out of suspects.' Catchpoll sucked his teeth. 'He very nearly made it too.'

'But what on earth could lady Courtney have remembered that would implicate de Grismont? We know she entered and left the church before the murder.'

'We only know for certain, my lord, that she lit her candle and left before the body was moved to its position in front of the altar. We are assuming de Grismont had not already entered, but he might, and I only say "might", have already been in the Lady chapel with his victim dead at his feet.'

Bradecote made an indecisive noise. 'But that would not have given her anything to remember, and whatever it was had something to do with being cold in church.'

Both men set themselves to ponder this problem. Eventually a slow and particularly evil grin spread over Serjeant Catchpoll's weathered face. 'I think I may have the answer, my lord. She said she always wore a cloak in church. I wonder if de Grismont wore one that afternoon? I dare swear he wasn't wearing one for Compline. Can you recall, my lord, for I do not?'

Bradecote tried to envisage the scene on that first evening, when he had studied all those present with the eyes of a stranger. He remembered Sister Edeva, so cool and calm; Sister Ursula, pale and shocked; the lady Courtney with the fluttering hands and next to her Isabelle d'Achelie, who had eyes only for de Grismont. These were people he did not know, about whom some of his first impressions had been right and some so wrong. Yes, now he could see the man in his mind. He had looked slightly puzzled, but calm, and he had been the only person Bradecote had recognised at all. What had he worn? Nothing that stood out, just the garb of a well-to-do lord, which was a deception in itself. A cloak, though, no. There had definitely been no cloak.

'He wore no cloak, Catchpoll, of that I am sure.'

'Well then, it would be nice to have it, but since we cannot get proof positive of her suspicion from the lady Courtney, it matters but little.' Catchpoll was about to continue when a thought hit him, and it was as obvious to Bradecote as if he had been struck by something tangible.

'Wait there a moment, my lord, and we could have the last element in the puzzle.' Without saying anything more, Catchpoll strode to the west end of the church and disappeared inside the porch beneath the tower. Bradecote disobeyed his instruction, and walked slowly towards the door, with muffled groans and a grimace. Catchpoll was nowhere to be seen, but the door to the tower was open. Bradecote did not fancy climbing a spiral stair.

Nothing happened for a while, and then Catchpoll re-emerged with something clasped tightly in his right fist and a look of triumph on his face. He held out his prize before Bradecote's nose, and gazed at him in the manner of a hound expecting praise on completion of a command.

'There it is, my lord.'

'It' was a crumpled piece of fine olive cloth, that when shaken out resolved itself into a man's short cloak. It was dusty and marked by several dark stains.

'Blood, for sure, my lord.' Catchpoll's voice was authoritative. 'I reckon he used it when he found he had blood on his hands, or else to wipe the mallet. He hadn't bargained for quite so much blood flowing around. He should have known, though, having seen battle. A little blood goes a fair way, and there was more than a little, aye, and brains too.'

'And where did you find it?'

Catchpoll smiled. 'Once we thought about him leaving through the nave and porch, it was a likely place. There's a stairway up to where they ring the bell for the offices. Up there I found some sacks in a corner. I don't know exactly why they were there, perhaps to have something to stand on when the tower is cold and their feet get chilled. I neither know nor care. Anyway, under the sacks I found this.'

Bradecote inhaled to sigh, and groaned, clutching his chest. For a moment he said nothing, then he pulled a face worthy of Catchpoll and said, 'I am convinced. It will convince de Beauchamp, won't it?'

'Oh, yes, my lord. The lord sheriff will be very content.'

'Then tomorrow we will take de Grismont's mortal remains

258

to Worcester, and I shall go home. Tell the men, Catchpoll.'
Bradecote felt suddenly very weary.

Serjeant Catchpoll could see his superior wanted to be left
alone to 'enjoy' his aches and pains in private. He nodded, and
went off to make whatever preparations were necessary and to
see the guestmaster.

Bradecote eased himself up straight, left the church, and walked
slowly and deliberately towards the guest hall, but changed his
mind when he saw Miles FitzHugh emerge and try to attract
his attention. The last thing he wanted to hear was the squire's
plaudits or excuses. He went instead back into the church, via
the cloister, and headed towards the crossing. He wondered
where they had laid lady Courtney, for the mortuary chapel was
occupied, unless the apprentice had been interred with some
speed. As he passed the south transept he sensed, rather than
heard, someone in St Eadburga's chapel. He felt he knew who it
would be, and for all that he had no wish to disrupt her prayers
or face an impossibly difficult interview with her, he realised it
might be his only chance to apologise.

Sister Edeva did not look up immediately when she heard
the footsteps, but finished her prayer, the Latin sounding
mellifluous and otherworldly to Bradecote's ear. She then
raised her head and half-turned to look at him. There was
a prolonged silence, then, with an easy gesture of her hand,
she invited him to kneel beside her. It was, he thought, an
appropriate position in which to beg forgiveness, but one
which his wound made extremely uncomfortable to adopt.
He winced as he lowered himself, and the nun put out a

hand in case he needed support, though he did not take it.

'I am sorry, my lord, I should have considered your injury. Does it pain you much?'

'I would be lying if I denied it, lady, but not as much as my conscience. I had to speak with you. This morning I behaved unforgivably, and my explanation . . .' He had called her lady again, and it felt right.

She put up the hand to silence him. 'No, my lord, there is no need for explanation; at least not on your part. It was not something that was planned. It just happened.'

'I thought you were going to admit to lady Courtney's murder.' It sounded ridiculous now, as well as insulting, and he looked at the floor, guiltily, not wishing to meet her gaze, but knew he owed it to her to face her. He raised his eyes to hers, in which he saw compassion. 'And suddenly I couldn't bear you to do that. I could see the consequences, and they were too grim. I did not mean to insult you.'

'That I know already. I had not considered myself in the light of prime suspect, but, even if you thought I had killed Eudo you could not, surely, have thought I would kill the boy or lady Courtney?'

He shook his head. 'No, and yet I had convinced myself of it because I feared it.' He closed his eyes. 'I am . . . confused. I have never met anyone . . . a woman . . . like you before, and somehow it was as if there was some intangible thing between us, and . . . I don't understand, but I acknowledge my guilt. Forgive me.'

She turned fully to him then, and had a passer-by seen them it would have seemed as if they were exchanging vows, not confessions.

260

'There should be no need to forgive. It would be proper for me to say "But there was nothing, my lord", and that would be a lie. I felt it too, but I have an advantage. You see, I know, in part, the cause, at least on my side.' She bit her lip, and continued. 'You understand that I left the world, the secular world, before I was sixteen, and I have spent longer within than I had without. I entered to find peace, to be allowed to wallow, yes, wallow, in my grief, and keep Warin's memory like a candle burning in my heart. Yet over the years the memory has blurred, faded. I have counted myself unfaithful because the pain diminished almost to a memory of pain. Can you understand?' Her face looked suddenly pinched, and her eyes unnaturally large.

He nodded, though it was only a partial understanding.

'I had not left the enclave in twenty-one, no, twenty-two, years. Then I was sent on this mission.' She shook her head. 'I truly had no idea how difficult it would be, seeing the old world again. It brought everything back, highlighted what might have been. You can imagine how much worse the shock of seeing Eudo made it. Then he was dead, and I was relieved. Yes, relieved. I even thought God had brought me to this place so that I might know that Warin was avenged. It was a stupid and wicked thought. When you arrived I was at first too much caught up in what had happened to be conscious of it, but you see, even by the end of that first interview I knew.'

'Knew what?' Bradecote was now lost.

'Knew that I ought to keep my distance because you reminded me of him, of Warin, or what I thought Warin would have become. The "something" between us was, for my part, a ghost. I looked at you and made you what you were not, and, for my sins, it made me . . .'

'Approachable, in a distant sort of way. I see.' Bradecote spoke almost to himself. He only half-saw, but it made sense. If she had been truly uninterested, he would not, he hoped, have been tempted by her. 'That was why you seemed, just for a fraction of a moment, so responsive.'

She hung her head. 'Yes,' she whispered, and then looked up again, with tears in her eyes, 'but you are not my Warin. Warin was shrouded half a lifetime ago, and I should have closed the book, not just the chapter. For one "fraction of a moment", as you called it, I permitted myself a living dream, and it was wrong of me. It was an unintentional sin, but sin it was, and I shall pay a heavy penance for it.'

'What will your mother abbess say?'

'Nothing, for this is not a sin I will bring before Chapter.' She smiled, a small lopsided smile. 'A house of nuns is still a house of women, and if you think there is no gossip, however much it should be repressed, you know nothing of the "weaker" sex. I will not confess this before my sisters because it would encourage them to gossip, and be bad for their souls also. But do not think I escape penance, for I know now what I must do.'

The tears were falling now, and she wiped them away with the back of a hand, ashamed by the weakness. 'I pray every day for the man I once loved, and it is a solace, but now I must pray first, on every occasion, for the soul of his brother, his murderer, who is in so much more need of prayers. And I must learn to mean what I pray. It will take me a long time, but I will strive, and when I succeed I will have absolution, and,' her voice faded to a whisper, 'I hope, peace.'

'And what of my guilt, my penance?'

'Your guilt is your penance, my lord. The condemnation of your conscience, your shame, shows you are, at heart, a good man. You have imposed your own penance. You will know the penance is complete when you can look back to these last few days and not feel that shame as a raw wound, as raw as the wound you carry now.'

She reached out her hand and, very gently, touched him where the bandage showed beneath the torn and stained undershirt. It was not a sensuous gesture, rather one of blessing. He held his breath, though he could not have said why, and then the moment was gone, and the Benedictine was no longer Edeva, the woman whose heart had been broken in the vulnerability of youth, but Sister Sacrist, the cool and competent bride of Christ.

'Will you join me in prayer, my lord?' The voice was strong now, calm and confident; it was once again the voice of the woman who had first sat before him in the abbot's parlour. He nodded assent, and they commenced with a prayer for the dead.

When Sister Edeva finished her orisons and departed, Bradecote had no inclination to view de Grismont's last victim. He had prayed for her soul; he would see her body in the morning, and Ulf had been killed in combat rather than murdered. He left the church the way he had come. Abbot William was coming from his lodging, looking rather weary and disconsolate. The murderer had been found, and justice, if not the law, satisfied. Yet his abbey had seen four violent and unnecessary deaths in as many days, and the peace and sanctity of the enclave had been disrupted. It would be some time before the lives of the brothers felt normal again, and that was dependent upon the routine of prayer and everyday tasks. He acknowledged Bradecote with a nod and the slightest of smiles, and would have spoken to him, had not a flurry of activity by the gatehouse distracted his attention. Bradecote's eyes followed his, as a mounted figure, followed by three retainers, rode into the courtyard.

Their leader was a spare, thin-faced man who had the bearing and manner of one used to command. He looked to be a man in late middle age, with grizzled hair receding at the temples. His face bore an unnatural degree of weathering, being tanned and lined, especially round the eyes. Bradecote was conscious of a sinking feeling in the pit of his stomach. Such a face was seen on lords who had taken the Cross and journeyed to Outremer.

The lord exchanged a word with Brother Porter and rode forward to halt a little before Abbot William. Unbidden, one of his men dismounted swiftly and came to his horse's head. The gentleman dismounted, somewhat stiffly, and approached the abbot. He made obeisance courteously, but his words, though softly spoken, were a demand, not a request.

'Good Father Abbot, my name is Courtney, and I am here seeking my wife. I have followed her trail over half the kingdom it seems, and at Tewkesbury they advised me she was coming here. Is she here, or has she already departed?'

There was a stunned, uncomfortable silence.

'Well?'

Abbot William paled and turned in mute appeal to Hugh Bradecote, who felt distinctly uncomfortable. He cleared his throat, but no phrases formed themselves in his brain. How did one tell a man who had not seen his wife in several years that he had arrived no more than eight hours after she had indeed departed, but in a violent and permanent fashion, and that she lay cold upon a bier within the church.

Bradecote cleared his throat again and attempted to appear as official and competent as possible.

'My lord, I am Hugh Bradecote, Acting Undersheriff of Worcestershire. I think it would be best if you were to come with me. I am afraid . . . I regret, that lady Courtney has been the victim of a vicious attack and,' the words came out in an unseemly rush, 'I am afraid she is dead.'

Courtney gazed uncomprehendingly at Bradecote, and then the words sank in. He crossed himself, slowly and deliberately, his brow furrowed. He shut his eyes and withdrew into himself, almost visibly growing smaller.

Nobody moved; no one said anything. In truth, there was nothing that could be said. After what seemed an eternity, Courtney opened his eyes again and looked at the sheriff's man and then Abbot William.

'When did this happen?'

'This very morning, my lord.' Abbot William had recovered his composure, and his voice was calm and even.

'She was discovered this morning, after the guests had broken their fast,' Bradecote added.

'I would like to see her.' Courtney's voice was as calm as the abbot's.

'Naturally, my lord. Come with us.' Abbot William, like Bradecote, was a little surprised by the bereaved man's reaction.

He would have expected outrage, anger, horror even, but not the regretful and almost contemplative way in which Courtney now spoke.

Grief took people differently, thought Bradecote, as the representatives of secular and spiritual authority led the way into the church. Bradecote hung back far enough to see where the abbot was leading. They headed for the mortuary chapel. They must indeed have taken Wulfstan away pretty smartly, thought Bradecote, making way for a more important corpse. Even in death, rank seemed to matter.

He was relieved that there had been time to lay Emma Courtney out decently, with the pale lids closed over those reproachful bulging eyes. Her hands were folded devoutly across her breast, and he thought how odd it was to see them stilled. Ulf's body lay upon the stone floor, crosswise at her feet. Bradecote wondered if Catchpoll had been involved in that. The man was not sentimental, but might see it as the man's right. After all, he had followed her like a hound, and at her feet he was at peace.

Courtney reached out a hand slowly, to touch the folded hands.

'I arrived only just too late.' He shook his head, sadly. 'My poor Emma.'

'Your wife was exceedingly devoted to you, my lord. She was afraid because you had not returned, and was making pilgrimage to shrines to pray for your safety. Such a devout and gentle dame will receive due merit in the world to come. And we will be pleased to inter her earthly body in the nave here, if you do not wish to take her back to your manor.' Abbot William spoke with genuine belief, and Bradecote was impressed. So often the clergy sounded pompous in the aftermath of death. His words certainly seemed to have an impact on Courtney. He looked visibly cheered.

'Indeed. I shall pray for her in every hope that God will judge her generously, and I accept your kind offer. It is a long way back to Sussex, and though it seems chill to me, the days are too warm for great delay.'

Once again Bradecote was startled by his response, but explanation came quickly.

'I was going to tell her of my decision,' continued Courtney, heavily. 'I believed her to be a religious enough woman to accept and even applaud my choice.'

The widower read incomprehension in the faces of Abbot William and Bradecote, and smiled wearily at them. 'I had decided to withdraw from the world upon my return from the Holy Land. Only in the cloister, with a life of contemplation and contrition, will I find peace.'

So that was it, thought Bradecote, indignation rising on behalf of the poor woman who lay upon the bier. She, though temperamentally unsuited to running her lord's manors, had done so for a number of years, desperate for his return to take over the reins and leave her to the simple tasks of the devoted wife. She had traipsed round the country, lighting candles and generally worrying herself to death, for a man who was about to come back only to tell her he was deserting her forever for the sake of his soul. If Courtney genuinely believed she would have been happy at this decision then he knew very little of his spouse. Poor woman, perhaps death was less of a disaster for her.

Courtney was on his knees now, the picture of piety, intoning the same prayer that Bradecote and Sister Edeva had used so short a time before. Abbot William joined him, though Bradecote did no more than kneel. He would have left altogether, had he not thought that Courtney deserved to know what exactly had happened to his wife, and how her killer had been brought to account. When lord and abbot finally rose to their feet, Bradecote took his opportunity, and Abbot William withdrew, his inbuilt monastic clock telling him there was little time before the next office.

Courtney listened without comment to Bradecote's exposition, his face betraying almost no emotion, even when the discovery of his wife's body was described. Bradecote, having at first felt sympathy for the man, spared him no detail, hoping it might jar him into some feeling, but it had no perceptible effect. At the conclusion Courtney pursed his lips, and stared very hard at Bradecote for a moment.

'Could you have discovered de Grismont's guilt before he killed my wife?'

It was an impossible question for Bradecote to answer, for he did not know the answer himself. He had thought about it, briefly, and come to no conclusion. He had certainly not thought of de Grismont as the prime suspect until he had murdered lady Courtney, and then it had been largely because it could be none other. Once the facts were revealed, however, he wondered if he could have seen how likely it all was far earlier. He held it as a consolation that Catchpoll, with all his years of experience, had been no closer to the correct answer. It was that which he put to Courtney, for he could not see how he could be blamed by the sheriff, if complaint was made, if Catchpoll had been equally in the dark. That was not the same, of course, as not blaming himself. He thought, grimly, that the post of undersheriff was one which gave almost unlimited opportunity for self blame. He would be glad to be rid of the job, he told himself. Yet a part of him had found the task both exciting and challenging. The voice of reason within agreed, but noted that excitement and challenge were infinitely better in small quantities.

'My lord, we did not. That is all I can be sure of, but we worked hard upon it, and so I would like to say no.'

He escorted Courtney to the guest hall, where the guestmaster received him. It was there that Catchpoll appeared, making a good attempt at looking the picture of innocent industry.

'I have everything finalised for the morrow, my lord. De Grismont's men are going to return to Defford, where they will see to it that a cart is sent to Worcester if the lord sheriff releases the corpse. I don't know that he will wish to put the body on display, but he may. Do you wish to depart early, my lord?'

'Not particularly, Catchpoll. The weather is cooler, and besides I think I should wait until after the lady Courtney is interred. Father Abbot has said she will be granted a place within the nave, and it would not be polite to absent ourselves, especially,' he stressed the word, 'since her husband will be leading the mourning.'

Only a flicker of the eye betrayed the serjeant. 'That was who it was, was it?'

Bradecote wanted to laugh, but it hurt to do so. 'Come on, Catchpoll, you cannot make a fool of me that way. You would have known who he was from the moment his men went to the stables, even if you didn't hear what passed in the courtyard. Wanted to keep out of the way, eh? Well, you need not have bothered.' He explained what had passed in the chapel. A thought struck him. 'He never mentioned Ulf at all.'

Catchpoll shook his head. 'Not the type to notice serfs, or slaves, and my guess he was her slave.'

'Under the law or of heart, Catchpoll?'

'Both, my lord.'

'And was it you who had him placed as he was?'

'It was my suggestion, my lord. We cannot know how he thought but by his deeds, and I think he was faithful to death for her.' The serjeant pulled a face. 'But for her long-awaited lord to return with news that he was going to take the cowl! Who would have thought that, though. Poor dame. Ah well, if we look on the bright side, it was as well we didn't catch on to de Grismont too quick. She would have hated what he had in store for her, worse than death I reckon.'

'You may well be right, Catchpoll, but I fear that if you went around with that attitude, the "they would not have minded being dead" one, an awful lot of evil opportunists would go free.'

'Fair enough, my lord. it was only a thought.' He grinned. 'It wouldn't do to talk ourselves out of a job completely.' He was silent for a moment, and then continued. 'Will you be eating with the other guests tonight, my lord? I only ask because if you do you can expect lots of questions from master squire, the tactless cub, and probably a few from Mistress Weaver. Master Elias, of course, will be eating with the masons.'

Bradecote had forgotten the master mason in all that had

happened since breakfast, as was clear from the look on his face. Catchpoll refrained from comment.

'How did he take his release? Was he relieved or ready to commit murder for real?' Bradecote felt guilty for forgetting the man.

'He hadn't enjoyed his night, I can say that for sure, but I think relief was higher in his mind than rending either of us limb from limb, and in view of the day's events thereafter, I would expect him to be reasonable. Anyway, we are about to find out, because here he comes.'

Bradecote groaned, and turned, with circumspect slowness, to see the master mason approaching. The man was not smiling, but nor was he red-faced and belligerent.

'Well then, my lord. I am glad to see you little the worse for your endeavours.' Bradecote wondered if he was in any way quite pleased that he had suffered.

'Thank you, Master Elias. And you look little the worse for an uncomfortable night.' Better to broach the matter and get it out of the way, and besides, contrasting his injuries with a night in a cell would help take the sting out of any response Master Elias might have festering within.

The master mason grimaced. 'Aye, I cannot say being held in a cell and contemplating being hanged for a crime I did not commit made for a good night's slumber, my lord, but all is put right now, and it takes a lot to keep Elias of St Edmondsbury out of sorts.' He paused. 'You'll be off, I take it, to Worcester.'

'In the morning, master mason.' Catchpoll replied.

'It'll make it easier to get the men back to normal routine, that and laying poor Wulfstan to rest today. A sad business, all

271

of it, but work must go on. I've suggested to Eddi we might carve a wolf's head for a gargoyle up on the transept. "Wolf stone" for Wulfstan, you see. A sort of memorial for him.'

'Very fitting, Master Elias, very fitting.' Catchpoll kept an admirably straight face, though Bradecote was seized with a coughing fit, which left him hugging his ribs and groaning in pain.

'You'd best get something from the infirmarer, my lord, if you have a cough as well as that wound. Mighty uncomfortable else,' recommended the master mason helpfully, as he turned back to the workshop.

Once he had turned the corner, Catchpoll thumped his superior on the back, in an effort to help him.

'Thank you, Catchpoll,' gasped Bradecote, his eyes watering, 'but thumping quite that hard does not actually make me feel any the better.'

The serjeant's look might just have intimated that it did not matter to him.

'Fair took me by surprise, what he said, my lord,' commented Catchpoll. 'You never think how a craft influences the rest of your outlook on life. Among the masons I'm sure that carving a water spout would be regarded both as touching and clever. Good job his name wasn't Hengest. You'd have to wonder where the water would come out from a stallion.' He guffawed at his own joke.

'Are there things that only law officers find funny?' Bradecote was feeling almost lightheaded now.

'Only folk claiming innocence with guilt writ large upon 'em.' The accompanying smile was more of a sneer.

It brought Hugh Bradecote back to earth with a bump, and he actually swayed.

Catchpoll's eyes narrowed. 'I reckon you are in need of food, my lord. I think I can persuade the cooks to let you have a mite of bread and cheese before the eating hour. You get to your chamber, keep the nosey guests at bay and I'll be along as soon as I can.'

He was in nursemaid mode again, Bradecote decided, but it was too tempting to give in. He stepped slowly into the guest hall, hoping to avoid any encounters. He was at the door of his chamber, thinking he had been most fortunate, when he heard Mistress Weaver's voice behind him.

'Mind you rest careful, my lord. There's no saying even a slight wound can turn nasty if you don't give it peace to rest in. Betony is the best thing for wounds. My mother, God rest her, swore by it, but no doubt Brother Infirmarer has used it already.' She smiled at him in a motherly way, laying a hand on his arm as she passed. 'You did a good thing today, my lord, for whatever the reason for ridding the world of Eudo, there was no cause to harm that poor apprentice, nor my lady neither. I'll say no more than that.' She left him with a valedictory pat, and he was relieved that she had not treated him to either inquisition or proof of her own deductive capabilities.

Catchpoll arrived shortly afterwards, bearing not only bread and cheese, but a bowl of hot broth. He looked vaguely embarrassed.

'When I said as how you was feeling a bit faint, not having eaten, the cooks thought you most deserving and heated up some of this, left over from the lord abbot's table last night. It seems your heroics have put you in high favour, my lord. They even asked if you would like a pigeon patty for supper. I said yes, because if you don't feel like it tonight, we can wrap it up for the journey tomorrow.'

Bradecote took the soup gratefully, though he was not sure how much of an appetite he would have later. Truth to tell, he wanted no more than to eat and then sleep.

'Thank you, Catchpoll. I feel exhausted, so I do not know if I will be at supper, but it was a good idea.'

'Right then, my lord. I'll set Reynald outside your door to see nobody disturbs you.'

Serjeant Catchpoll left, leaving Bradecote to finish his repast alone. When he had finished he removed his boots, with muttered curses at the pain of exertion, and then lay back slowly and carefully upon his cot. He was expecting to rest but not to sleep, for his ribs complained at every breath, but soon that breathing was slow and even. For the first time in several days, the acting undersheriff slept in a deep and dreamless slumber.

The Fifth Day

Chapter Thirteen

The sun was well risen when Bradecote awoke in the morning, and he was conscious of a sensation of well-being which he let wash over him in a pleasurable wave. It lasted until he stretched without thinking, and swiftly regretted it, for his body complained vociferously. His groan was both an expression of pain and yet also the luxurious feeling of having slept well and not having to leap from his bed. Despite his injuries, which necessitated pulling on his boots slowly and with as much wincing as when he had removed them, he arose in a good mood, and with a ravenous appetite. He looked forward to breaking his fast, and was not at all disconcerted by the thought of sitting with the other guests, either besieged by their questions or in an atmosphere of silent constraint.

In fact, it was not his presence but that of Simon Courtney which created awkwardness, and kept the other guests from making mention of the events which lay uppermost in their minds. It made for a peculiarly quiet meal, but Bradecote and Catchpoll derived a large measure of unholy pleasure from the sight of Miles FitzHugh attempting to make conversation without saying anything that would upset the widower, while showing the others present that he was a man of equal standing. The bereaved lord himself ate sparingly and in sepulchral silence, staring into space as though he were alone in the chamber. The Romsey nuns were also silent, but this was their usual manner of taking a meal and they were quite at ease, using only the hand signals of the cloistered to indicate their need for pitcher or bread. Bradecote permitted himself but one glance at Sister Edeva, and was struck by the fact that it was only twenty-four hours since their momentary but shaming contact, and yet it seemed in the distant past. Her face was serene, otherworldly again. The guilt, despite her absolution, flooded back, dropping like a stone into the calm depths of the day's satisfaction and sending unpleasant ripples through it. He did not look in her direction again.

Gaining no response from one end of the table, Miles FitzHugh turned his attention to lady d'Achelie, who was reducing bread to crumbs before her, abstracted and curiously reminiscent of the lady lying in the mortuary chapel awaiting interment. When addressed by name she looked up at FitzHugh, startled, and with incomprehension clear on her beautiful features. Her frown disconcerted him, and the words withered on his lips. Mistress Weaver's lips twitched. That the lordling did not demean himself by speaking to her troubled her not at all. She retained the desire to cuff him round the ears, but this morning gained as much enjoyment from his flailing ineptitude as Serjeant Catchpoll and the acting undersheriff.

When the meal ended she approached the two law officers, and made a polite obeisance. 'I will be leaving this morning, my lord, if you have no objection. I need to get back to my business and my son as soon as it is convenient. The only way to keep things running efficiently is to be on the spot. I allowed two weeks for this journey to the Marches and back, and the extra wait has been . . . difficult. You do not think that there will be any objection to my leaving before my lady Courtney's burial? I would not wish to seem disrespectful, but . . .'

'No, you are quite free to leave, Mistress Weaver, and I wish you all speed with your return to Winchester. I hardly think your presence is expected this morning. You met the lady but a few days since, and you have good reason to depart early.'

Bradecote spoke formally but smiled at her, and a suggestion of pink tinged her dimpled cheek.

'Thank you, my lord. I will be sure to put something by for prayers for the poor lady's soul when I return next year.' She gave a swift bob, like a wagtail, said Catchpoll afterwards, and turned to walk away, competence and confidence in her step.

The funeral service for lady Courtney was all that her husband could have wished, presided over by Abbot William with great gravity and honour towards both the departed and the bereaved. In the cool dimness of the abbey church, the air heavy with the incense from the swinging censers, the abbot gave a eulogy which stressed Emma Courtney's piety, faith and loyalty, and he promised that she would be remembered in the prayers of the house even before Courtney proffered the rents from one of his manors, in perpetuity, for the continued offering of prayers for his wife. When he heard of the offer, Bradecote thought it a sop to the man's conscience.

The ever-faithful Ulf had no eulogy. There had been some discussion among the clerics about where to bury him. They did not want him among the Pershore brethren in the cloister garth, and one voice even suggested he be sent to holy ground in the parish churchyard. Catchpoll ended the matter, and though none but he, the priest and four lay brothers attended, he was given full rites and laid in a grave. When the grander funeral took place, none looked at the earth at the bottom of the grave to wonder why it looked loose. At no point in the eulogy was mention made of the manner of the lady Courtney's death, beyond the word 'untimely', and even that was qualified by the abbot, who stressed that since the Almighty was beyond all time, so were the realms of glory, where years passed in this life would be as a grain of sand upon the shore, and 'time' was irrelevant.

Miles FitzHugh made a great show of looking suitably severe, and succeeded only in appearing risible. The Sisters of Romsey made no attempt to stand out, but their dignity and poise were in marked contrast to the noble youth, and even to lady d'Achelie, who remained distracted for much of the service, and fidgeted with the folds of her gown. She was clearly too involved in contemplating her own future to dwell too much on one whose fate had already been decided. It was also patently clear that she realised that her position, having been the paramour of the murderer, even if the fact was known only to the sheriff's men, made her presence more than slightly difficult.

* * *

After the interment beneath the flagstones of the nave, Hugh Bradecote visited the infirmary for a change of dressings to his wound. Brother Infirmarer also gave him a small pot covered with a waxed cloth, containing a salve of cleavers fresh made by Brother Oswald, to apply to the healing flesh. Bradecote thanked him for his care, then he and Catchpoll prepared for their own departure. It was then that Bradecote raised the matter of 'the other corpse'.

'I assume Ulf lies where most fitting, Catchpoll?'

'Oh yes, my lord.' Catchpoll's smile spread slowly. 'It certainly found favour with the lay brothers who dig the graves, and who have been rather busy these last days.'

'Good. I think the lady would approve, and I doubt her lord would consider the matter at all.'

'Aye, and if he did, well, it is too late now.' Serjeant and acting undersheriff exchanged glances in accord.

They barely noticed FitzHugh ride out, head held high, with his servants following sullenly in his wake. Lady d'Achelie was herself ready to depart, and looked small and delicate among the sturdy stolidity of her men. She averted her eyes from the blanket-covered body that Gyrth had slung across a pony, but made a pretty obeisance to abbot and acting undersheriff, and the wistful smile that accompanied it was purely for the latter's benefit. Catchpoll looked after her as she trotted away on her neat grey palfrey, her faithful retainers gathered protectively about her, and then turned his attention to a rider approaching the gate from the Worcester road.

Bradecote did not watch the lady, becoming suddenly aware that the nuns of Romsey were already mounted and about to leave. One of their men led a mule with the reliquary secured to its back on top of a thick cushioned pad, lest the bone of the blessed saint be uncomfortable on its journey back to Hampshire. Sister Edeva's mount stamped a foot, as if eager to be gone, and shook itself with a shudder that ran rippling down the mane to its withers.

The sheriff's officer walked over and gave the beast an absent-minded pat. He looked up and found the nun regarding him as if recording him for her memory.

'My apologies,' he said ruefully. 'You have borne the brunt of my suspicions. I have insulted your honesty and your calling.'

She looked at him with those sad, grey eyes that he had first seen as granite hard. Was that only a few days ago?

'Then let our apologies be mutual, my lord. I knew that I was not Eudo's killer, and that what I told you was true. I was therefore ahead of you, but chose not to think. I must also confess that I did not give any information freely. I did not want Eudo's killer caught because he did what part of me believed I should have done, but could not. That you believed I had committed the deed was, at first, almost a compliment.' She gave a small, wry smile. 'De Grismont was not an instrument of vengeance . . . "not an avenging angel" as you termed him; he did not know that he killed a murderer. He was just a treacherous, avaricious and lustful man who feared unmasking. The world is full of such.' Her tone was suddenly weary. 'I will be glad to return to the enclave in Romsey, and of a surety will not seek to leave it.'

'You have a strong and quick mind.' Bradecote gave her a wry smile. 'Perhaps you would make a better undersheriff?'

She laughed then; a genuine and melodious sound. 'No, my lord. You are a novice, yes, but I would say that you will do very well if called upon again.'

She reached down her hand to where his rested on the mule's neck, and touched it fleetingly. Her expression was solemn.

'In this one matter I did naught to assist the law, and perhaps not even justice. Eudo was not killed in revenge for Warin; judgement only truly lies with God. You know my penance. And I will hold you also in my prayers, my lord.' She paused. 'Leaving Romsey has taught me a lesson. My grief has fed upon itself for years, trying to recreate someone who no longer exists. God has shown me my error. I can only pray for his soul, not yearn any longer. It has been a painful lesson, but one I had to learn.'

She frowned, but then her brow cleared again, and she continued in a firm tone. 'If, though it must be unlikely, you should ever find yourself near Romsey, you would find a true welcome in our guest house, and any assistance you might require. But I do not think our paths will cross again.'

She held out her hand, openly, in a gesture of benediction, and her eyes met his squarely. 'God be with you, my lord Bradecote.'

'And with you also, lady.' He could not bring himself to call her sister, but perhaps that was a salve to his conscience.

He stepped back and she pulled the mule's head round and rode out of the courtyard, through the abbey gate, with never a backward glance, her back lance-straight. She sat her mule with the manner of a grand dame upon a fine palfrey, with Sister Ursula following a little behind and the Romsey men forming a protective escort in front and rear. The habit would never conceal the nature of the woman beneath, and he wondered how he could have been so wrong in his initial impression of her as cold. The party turned to the right and were lost from view.

Bradecote turned, and was surprised to find Serjeant Catchpoll also gazing out of the gateway. The sheriff's man hawked, and spat into the dust in a gesture of finality.

'Nearly got that one very wrong, didn't we?' he said contemplatively, still staring at the trackway.

For a moment Bradecote wondered whether he was referring to the case, the woman, or both, and noted that there was that use of the plural again, though this time Bradecote felt it was marginally more inclusive.

'We, Serjeant? I thought all the errors were mine,' grimaced Bradecote, suddenly unconcerned about who was 'superior'. After all, this had been a chance pairing. He was just one of William de Beauchamp's vassals, who had done as his lord had commanded. He was not really a sheriff's officer, and would be back in Bradecote by sunset.

Catchpoll smiled, though it was a twisted smile. 'Most of them were, my lord, but you'll know better next time.'

Bradecote gave a bitter laugh, and gasped at the sudden discomfort as his ribs reminded him of their injury. 'I hardly think there will be a next time. I do not think William de Beauchamp will cast aside his regular deputy on the basis of this case.'

'Perhaps he wouldn't, my lord, but that counts for nothing now.' The serjeant sniffed, and affected disinterest. 'While you were bidding farewell to the good Sisters of Romsey, news came from Worcester.'

He paused for effect.

'Well, Catchpoll? I am not sure that I want to hear this, but . . .'

'It seems we are to be shackled together, my lord. Fulk de Crespignac died three days ago, according to the messenger. There's a letter from the lord sheriff,' he drew a folded sheet of vellum from his tunic, 'but it don't take a serjeant of my years' experience to guess who he'll pick for the vacancy.' It could be worse, thought Catchpoll, and the lord Bradecote was no fool.

Serjeant and newly appointed undersheriff stared at one another for a moment. There was silence. Bradecote opened the letter and gave it a cursory glance. The missive confirmed what Catchpoll had said.

'Very well, Serjeant Catchpoll.' Hugh Bradecote tried to sound as though his 'elevation' meant nothing to him, though he was torn between pleasure at having won his overlord's approval, and the realisation that his simple manorial life was to be set aside. 'Let us take our culprit back to our superior, and await his further instructions.'

The pair mounted, and led their men through the gateway, heading for the Worcester road, and Brother Porter closed the gate behind them.

Elias of St Edmondsbury, master mason, looked down upon the departures from his vantage point at the top of the north transept scaffolding. He saw the tall undersheriff on his big steel-grey horse, upright but comfortable in the saddle, the sheriff's serjeant astride a less well-favoured mount beside him, leading the men-at-arms. Only the pony trotting along behind a soldier at the rear and bearing its covered, lifeless burden, gave indication of what had passed within the walls of the enclave in the past days. Master Elias let himself rest back against the stonework, taking an almost spiritual comfort from its sun-warmed solidity. The flesh was, as had been shown so clearly, very fragile, very transient, but these good stones, erected with due care, would last for many centuries to come. One of his masons drew his attention away to a detail, and when Master Elias again looked out over Pershore, the horsemen were gone.

Historical Note

Historical fiction perforce blends the imagined with the factual, overlapping fictional people with a known world. Abbot William and William de Beauchamp, Sheriff of Worcestershire, were real people, but although we know a few facts about them, their physical form and character are lost in the past. I have therefore created both around the core of their true existence.

By the same token, I have created the Pershore Abbey enclave from a combination of the standing building, archaeological evidence and standard Benedictine claustral arrangements. The outlying buildings are those one would expect to find, but their locations are invented, and I make no claim that they stood where I set them. The herbalist's hut has had to be shown a little closer to the other buildings to fit on the page.

Pershore Abbey is a beautiful Grade I listed building, and its south transept, a fine example of twelfth-century Romanesque, would be recognisable to Abbot William. The north transept collapsed in 1686, so you cannot see where my Master Elias had his fine view.